THE SHADOWS
ARE WAITING

H. J. Pithers

Amazon

CONTENTS

Prologue

The children of the shadows will fear not
death; the gods above will save us all.

As we nourish the land with every breath,
the gods above will keep our souls.

Our departed, brothers, will lead us sure,
to blessed shadowrealm or hell,

For trust in them is more than lore, in our
land and hearts they dwell.

CHAPTER 1

I was the one they called Devil's-Breath. I was the one they called Blood-Pourer. I was the one they called Hell-Sent. And I had come for them.

In the darkness when silence should rule, chaos did and chaos was where I thrived.

I raised my sword against a flickering fire in a small iron bracket and laughed. The only thing any of these people could see were my green eyes against this dark night. I swung the sword in two easy strokes through the air and got back to my hunt. A women wailed as she ran across me, being chased by several smaller, wailing children. I almost stopped, I almost wanted to step towards the children, to comfort them. Almost.

"Ah," came a yell from my left, followed quickly by a streaking flame. I dodged easily and sliced my sword low two times. The air bended with the sound, and then his pitiful screams as an overgrown man crumpled to the floor.

This was where I thrived.

I crossed over the little ditch the village used as boundary. It was barely worth it. A boy tried to run at me with a wooden stick. I growled through my black cotton scarf and he was running the other way, stick strewn on the grass.

I strolled towards the huts and barns that made up this wretched village and took a deep, filling breath. I had come for them.

A group of men made their attack from behind a hut, cheers and yells louder than the cries of their children. I stood my ground and smiled, regripping my sword. This would be fun.

Two men at the front broke off from the group, boots slipping on the grass. One step to the left and my sword swung low to high, dripping with blood. I circled back in three steps and I cut through gut. The man stumbled around, coughing then slumped to the ground. I cleaned my sword on his hide coat, noting the quiet around me.

Slowly I stood up, looking at the group of men standing frozen in front of two dead bodies. They couldn't see but I was smiling. My body suddenly throbbed with a weak pulse but I paid no attention to it. Before any of them moved, I jumped over the bodies and was slicing and cutting my sword through anything that got close. And then it was done.

As the wails and sobs of the newly orphaned children faded in the night, I closed my eyes and prayed. I prayed the shadow gods would hear me, that they would know that I did this for them, because of them. I prayed that all the shadows would help me. They heard me, the shadows, I knew that. But the shadow gods... they were so far away.

I crouched against my sword, leaning my head on the hilt. This wasn't the life I had planned for myself but it was the life I had and I was good at it. Good at hunting, at thriving where others feared.

And so I prayed that this would not be the only life I knew but as it was, I prayed that I would be good at it, no, great at it. And I was.

As I walked back across the darkened village, I looked back. I could burn it, just that end house. I could let angry flames brighten the night sky but thought against it. It would be no secret what had happened here, who had been here. No lie would be told of this night, for I had come and they knew that.

I walked to the outskirts of the village and untethered Midnight, my strong, black mare, just in time. One more breath and my legs gave way underneath me. They were strong now, and getting stronger. The pulses. Or I was still weak to them. I leaned on Midnight as they ran through my veins, quick and thick. My forearms started burning up and I held them close to my chest, feeling the pulsing blood. The warmth of the pulses was a dreaded comfort that blackened my mind. I knew I needed them, however much I dreaded them, I needed them. What they did to me though... what they did to me scared me.

Pale golden rays started to lift the night out of the sky. This was my favourite time of day, when the sun rose like a new-born, the evils of the night before long forgotten.

As I sat on Midnight, I sighed. I had to be back and soon. The house would be waking and I would need to be found sleeping. Midnight and I travelled to my home town before the dawn, crossing the town within the remaining shadows. I liked the town, like this anyway. Quiet. I slipped through the front of the house and sneaked into my room.

My limbs throbbed as I laid on my bed, waiting for the pulses to fade. My mind wondered back to the events of the night. The night was when I came alive. But at what cost? I pushed that aside as I rolled over and smiled. I was getting closer.

***

The next morning was grey, there was drizzle in the air but it didn't seem to land, it just hung there, teasing. I was strolling across the town in the early hours of the morning, watching people get to wherever they were going a lot quicker than I was. I made for the large stone common rooms that were the other side of the lord's hall. The stone was thick and an off-white, built long ago and kept the kitchens, healing rooms, school rooms and more. I headed to the kitchens to sneak an apple or two for breakfast, then slipped silently through the little archway that connected the kitchens to the healing rooms.

The smell of lavender was always the first thing I noticed, warm and deep. I walked across the corridor that opened out on to each healing room, as I looked for what I needed to refill Midnight's saddle pack. The first room was empty, so I took my time looking around, reading parchment labels for jars I already knew the contents of, brushing my fingers over crumpled pieces of parchment and feathers. I found the jar I needed, then moved on to the next room, but was hastily pushed out by some of the healers, as fresh herbs were being dried and something was starting to ooze from a small iron kettle.

I heard the laughter before I saw it. In the next room, the

largest one so far, a lesson was happening. The children sat on a large, brown hide rug before Cledwyn, engrossed in whatever shadowstory he was telling them today. I quickly scanned the room for the shelves of dried herbs and edged my way over, trying not to be noticed, but of course, I was. Two of the tiniest children had run over and grabbed both of my legs, making my legs feel like lead as I tried to step. A chuckle escaped me and I hugged both of them to me as Cledwyn coughed loudly and drew himself up tall. He didn't get far, he was a stocky man with bushy red hair and Cledwyn was... well, Cledwyn. Whilst he was valued for knowing more about our ancestors than any other person in the South, he really did like the sound of his own voice. Very much. But the children loved hearing his stories and he told them with unmatched energy. So, naturally, he hated being interrupted.

I quickly reached over to the shelves with my little helpers, placed the herbs in my belt pocket and sat on the rug with the children, listening to Cledwyn, as he continued.

"The shadowmagic that yet remained

Learnt to hide within,

By blood and birth those it stained

Forgot it like a sin." He filled his lungs with a huge breath, drawing all the children to him as he lent on his knees.

"There is a time coming fast

On land as well as sky," he was whispering now, so much that the children and I had to lean in closer to hear him.

"When magic gone will be recast,

A dark will burn the night,

From thunder, they will rise."

***

Thunder it did.

I had not known a thunderstorm like it, or any recently, really. Large drops bounced off the roof of my room. I had was hiding myself away from everyone, mainly my father. The rain drops were few and far between then stopped altogether. Then a distant rumble moved overhead. I peered out my small window, struggling to get a good look at the storm clouds. As the storm moved closer and closer, the sky filled with a grey fog but no more rain fell. Thunder shook the sky and the candlestick holder standing on my bedtable rattled. I laughed, this was amazing.

Another rumble sounded overhead, long and deep until it

cracked into a scream. Then my smile faded. A scream? The shadows.

I left my room and ran out into the town to stand at the stone well, where a crowd had gathered. All were staring with craned necks at the sky. The air was different here, thick. I could barely hear the people around me nattering to each other, barely make out the clothes they were wearing.

Another deep rumble came from behind us, I span round to see the swiftest, faintest crack of blue lightning fade from the clouds. A quick rumble had me spinning back around.

"Gaaw," I yelled, as Cledwyn was staring straight at me, red streaks blowing with the wind. I breathed quickly and took a step back. He kept his gaze on me, squinting.

"This is no ordinary thunderstorm."

Really? I wanted to say, but held me tongue. He looked back to the sky, shouting.

"These rainless storms, these mean something, something bad, or something good. But they are of the shadows' making." I felt him move closer through the storm. "But we haven't seen the shadows in years." Without a look back he walked away. It only took a few steps for him to fade into the fog. I kept looking after him for a while, even after more deep, screaming rumbles sounded.

The shadows. This was their doing. Lightning. I saw it, out of the corner of my eye. The brightest, clearest, most hypnotising blue I had ever seen started up high up in the sky, right above me and was forking down. It was incredible. I had to see it, I had to watch all of it. Thunder still rumbled, almost constantly now and the lightning was cracking and sparking and it seemed to come straight at me. I had to let it, I could feel it, I had to be where the lightning was. I made to step forwards, to follow it when an arm pulled me back into it's strong, but small chest and dragged me away.

"You shouldn't be out here. Just like your mother." I heard him breath.

CHAPTER 2

"The whole village?"

"The whole village. All those poor children, parentless.
What'll they do?"

"Maybe they're better off."

"How can you say that?"

"You know that village, wasn't nice."

"Blood-Pourer, I used to think they were exaggerating."

"How could one person do that?"

The maids were a good supply of gossip, they seemed to know
everything. I overheard them whispering as I left the house.
How could one person do that? I would show them how.

The next few weeks I stayed at home, laid low. I always did
after a hunt, if I was absent too often, my father would ask
questions. And that was not something I wanted. But that
night I would wait no longer. That night I would show them

how.

Before the dusk arrived, I saddled Midnight, checking the pack
I had refilled and we were riding. Her black coat would be
unseen against the coming night. After a few hours, were west
of my father's land, at a rocky village on the coast. The sea
constantly pushed against the land, creating a bay. The village
was all but hidden against the darkness of the night, with a
few firelights flickering near houses. It wouldn't be the only
thing unseen that night.

The ride had left Midnight a little tired, it was a short journey
but I had pushed her. I tethered her to a nearby rock, stroking
her gently. I didn't really need to tie her up, she whinnied at
me as I put the rock village in my sights and started grazing.
These isolated villages kept coarse, harsh people, but that was
why I had come.

For the hunt.

In the low-hanging moonlight, I stalked the border of the
village. I didn't have long. The sun would be rising soon. The
village wasn't much, a semicircle of rock and wood houses
built into the rocks, opening out inland. The rocks were like
the people here, hard and cold. Hard and cold. Hard minds
and cold hearts. That made for a dreary existence. At least *I*
would have an amusing night.

There was just one problem. They would see me coming, even in the night. The village was open for leagues; all visitors would be seen for leagues. So they would have to see me. Let them see me then.

Let them see that I had come.

I strode into the middle of the village, black shirt, black hide and leather trousers and black cloak and hood covering me fully. People had begun to fear the cloak I wore; they knew what it meant. The cloudy sky cleared and my shadow hung in the moonlight.

The hunt began.

It was different from my last hunt. This time my prey chose to hide. A few men had come out into the night, armed with axes and knives, tried to defend their homes. I respected their choice, a little. They were the first to die. The rest I would find. I would let the moonlight see them.

And I did.

I dragged the dead souls out in to the silver rays. The bodies of parents surrounded by their still-living children, clinging to their corpses. I couldn't stand the sobbing, the wailing, the pain in those cries. My eyes were darting around, I had to drown out those cries. I found some oil in the last house and burnt it down. The whole village. It burnt down in a crescent of fire. The fire would let others know who had come. They would see the fire and they would know.

They all needed to know.

They needed to know that no matter who they were or where they were, I would find them. One by one I would hunt them. Those who had turned their backs on our gods.

They needed to know that I, Blood-Pourer, Devil's-Breath, Shadow-Hunter, Village-Burner, Hell-Sent had come for them.

Midnight whinnied softly as I approached her. She too preferred the night. That was where I had found her all those years ago.

"Ah." It happened again. My legs gave way underneath me as I fell to the ground. The warm throb of the pulses coursed through my body. They had come as soon as the first man had fallen, but I had ignored them until now. The adrenaline had kept me busy until now. How I craved them though, craved the power they sent through my blood. I held tightly onto Midnight's mane, trying to listen to her heartbeat. I knew what the pulses did to me, I knew they gave me more than any human should have, if I was even human anymore.

I didn't ride for home that morning but rode four leagues

south-west. I had some duties to take care of. The new light showed me the land that my father protected. All of it. Most of the South was under his protection, apart from the small areas under the three other minor lords. My father wasn't lord outside of his lands but he was the oath-sworn lord to most of the South and his one choice had affected them all. The land showed that. The soil wasn't as fertile, the trees no longer grew green, fields of crops grew dry, the birds rarely sang. It was dying.

The sun rose to its noon height as I entered the fishing village. The light was bright against the wood huts and glistening rocks. The smell of salt was in the air, and fish. Lovely.

I slid off Midnight and walked her to the stables. As I crossed over to the other side of the road, a mother pulled her children away from me as they scuttled by. I sent them a fake smile and looked for the house I needed. Two knocks on the thin wood door and I entered the small home.

"You know who I am, yes?" I asked the top-heavy, slowly-changing colour man.

He primped and preened and without a word, he chucked me out the door. Well, I let him chuck me out. I righted myself, laughing. I was stronger than he was, but I knew men, they did always like to prove themselves. And make a show. Now was no exception.

He waddled out into the middle of the fishing village and provided quite a string of screams and curses. "You slime-ball. You greasy, slippery, pig-turd. If your father thinks 'e can get away with this, I'm gonna show 'im my fist." His voice was just as duck-like as his walk. "Ten years! Ten years I've been selling to 'im! Ten years I've worked for 'im! Fought for 'im! And now 'e sends his good-for-nothing piece of slime to tell me to leave. And go where? Where'm I supposed to go? Where does my *oath-sworn* lord expect me to go?"

By now, my duck-like friend had turned a nasty shade of purple. It was an amusing colour. I stayed quiet for a few more breaths, just to make sure he was done.

"You have not fulfilled your contract for the last three new moons. My lord does not care where you go, only when. Tomorrow at dawn you will leave. You will leave this village and never come back." I remained calm, it seemed to rattle him more. Stupid man.

"You sliming piece of dog-"

"Now, now. Is that really how you talk to your lord's heir?"

The poor man choked on his own words. I saw his tongue try to leave his mouth. I laughed again, this had been too good.

17

He knew the mistake he had made. My father was still his best hope of protection in these trying times.

"You have until dawn to leave. Leave and you live, stay and you die," I said quite simply.

I turned to the stables and mounted Midnight in one swift movement. I drew a dagger from my saddle pack and tossed it at the duck-man. It hit the ground where he stood, straight between his thighs, making him jump back. The handle shook from the impact. Damn, I missed.

I rode for home as soon as I left. I knew he would leave and I didn't care to see it. The journey back I was alone with my thoughts. At least it was a good memory.

The forest felt alive, the trees, the birds, the sounds. My ears could hear everything, smell everything, mossy and earthy. I was happy, so was my father. We were both looking at my mother, just watching her. She was happy. Her light brown, almost golden, hair shone in the sun's rays and she danced as she picked plants and berries from the trees, carefully filling her woven basket. She loved the forest, we all did. We used to go there all the time when I was a child. My mother glided back to us and gave me a handful of berries, and father her favourite flower, before kissing him on the cheek and dancing back through the forest. Father looked down at me and smiled. He didn't say anything but I knew what he meant.

Mother was happy because the land was happy and the land was happy because she was happy. That was everything to father. It was everything to his people. We heard mother's melodic voice as she started singing. I ran after her and father followed. Better days than that were hard to come by. Especially now.

And I was back in the present.

Midnight's breathing, the wind on my face. I stroked my friend as I tried to focus on them, the sensations rather than my thoughts but my mind wouldn't cooperate. It went its own way.

My father had been sending me out to perform his duties for the last three years. I hadn't enjoyed any of them. It was a waste of time. A waste of *my* time. I had more important things to do. I didn't care about these little things, but, then again, I knew I would have to. Even if I wasn't very good at it, I had to do it.

I returned back to my father's lands and my home town, which was in the middle of the land, the next day. The town was as uneventful as ever. People were bustling about, yelling, trading, leading animals around aimlessly. Trying to make the best of what they had. I went through the south gate and headed straight for the stables. I didn't want to get caught up in the crowd. With Midnight safe in the stables, I made for the south bridge to cross to the other side of the town and got ambushed by a flock of jittery chickens and their flappy owners. Uh, why couldn't they move?

Finally, I made it back to the house. I hated market days.

* * *

"For you," a messenger said so quickly I barely had a chance to take the letter from her hand before she ran from my room. The scrap piece of parchment only had three words on it. A time, a place and the signature of my father. I was to see him the next night. Guess that meant he had heard of my dealing in the fishing village. I sat on my bed and crossed my legs. Rather quickly, I thought. Great. That meant there was something to report.

The next night I stood outside the door to his stone work room, the only room in the lord's house completely built of stone, which was opposite the hall. I wasn't nervous, no words my father could say truly affected me anymore. But still, he was my father, his disappointment could affect me, that wasn't something I wanted. I took a deep breath.

Angry voices came from inside. I leant against the wall, slowing my breathing. I knew the voices, like I knew they weren't angry at each other. I managed to take a step back before the door flew open. The strong, aging man stomped passed, a brief glance all he offered me.

"Dai brought me news. As you can see, it was not pleasing." Dai was my father's advisor, closest friend and my mother's brother. My father spoke from behind his thick oak table, in front of the netted windows. His long, grey hair was loose and his dark green eyes were tired. The dark pendant around his neck stood out against his pale shirt. He remained constant and aware, no matter how tired his eyes. He always did. He didn't look at me as I stood in the doorway, shuffling the parchments that were spread across his table under the candlelight. His work was never over, he always told me. Over the years, I had learnt it was more he didn't want it to stop. Eventually he looked up and his eyes found mine.

"As is your company." I pretended I hadn't heard the words that made my blood boil as I stepped into the room.

"Father?"

His stare became too intense, I had to break it and played with my belt brooch.

"When I ask you to do my duties, I send you as a representative of me, myself. I expect you to do them as I would, not as a child who is bored and looks for fun."

"Father, I-"

"Silence. I no longer care for your excuses. You are of age. I should be thinking of your marriage, not of teaching you lessons you did not learn at school. You are my heir," he sighed. "My only heir."

The silence that filled the room caught me off guard. That did not happen often. I found myself staring at my feet.

"Leave."

The disappointment in my father's word was subtle yet it echoed within me. This was not the life I had chosen but it was the life I had. It was a life many could only pray for. Yet I had it and I did not want it.

The market was long since over but it still filled the town. People were still ambling around, packing up carts, herding animals. I hardly noticed them as I passed all the large stone common rooms to my left, over the bridge, dodged the market stalls and headed south. I just wanted to get to the stables. I walked as fast as I could without running. I kept my head down and ignored the polite greetings and nods from people that I passed.

Finally. I entered the wooded stables and leaned against the half door. The smell hit me but was nothing new. I walked down the walkway. Two stable boys come out of a stable and ran at the sight of me. Usually I would have laughed, today, it just made me angry. I stomped down the walkway, jaw clenched. Where was he?

Right at the back of the stables I found him, he was with Midnight. Her shoes needed repairing. I breathed easier.

"What have you been putting this poor horse through?" he said before I could speak. He put his tools down and patted Midnight before turning to me. "I only fitted these shoes half a season ago!"

Haul was the town farrier, the best in the land. He brushed his rough hands on his apron as sweat dripped slowly down his blistered face. He was one of the few people I really trusted, especially since he took such good care of Midnight.

His expression softened when I didn't say anything.

"What did you do?"

"Why is it always what I've done?"

"So it's something your father has done, no?" he asked quickly. I sighed. I didn't like someone telling me I was in the wrong, even if I knew I was.

"No," I said, kicking some hay.

"So, what did you do?" Haul looked at me patiently. I picked up a brush and started to brush down Midnight so I wouldn't have to look at him.

I confessed slowly, keeping my eyes on the black coat of my friend. "I may have banished someone from their home rather than send them to court with my father."

"Gods above," cursed Haul, "when are you going to stop fighting him and accept your place here?"

I turned to face him then. I expected to see frustration on his face, instead I saw only pity. That made it worse. And me angry.

"I have my reasons. I will accept my place here when I am happy with it." I held the brush up to him. "Don't push me, Haul." Those last words weren't spoken by his friend, but from his lord's heir. I wouldn't be spoken to like that.

My attention returned to Midnight, as did his. I heard him breathe deeply, keeping calm. Something I struggled with.

"I've never asked you what you do when you leave, uh," he raised his hands as I went to protest, "and I don't want to. I don't want to know, but it can't be good if it's pushing you so far from your father."

I felt as if those words sent a piercing red iron through me. I was doing this because of my father. All of it. But I couldn't tell Haul that, I wouldn't. It was my burden to bear and mine alone.

"It has to be done."

I put down the brush and took a step back. I respected Haul, I did, but his words had burnt me. He spoke before I could explain.

"Your father is doing the best he can, you know that. He does this for you, for your mother. You know the shadows still look down on us, even now." He took a step closer to me and looked me dead in the eyes, whispering, "don't give them a reason to look at you."

Oh, Haul.

Night hung over the town as I left the stables. I took my time walking back home, it wasn't somewhere I wanted to be right now. I crossed over the south bridge and sat on the small bank. Dangling my feet over the water, I wished it would just wash over me, cleanse me of all my wrongs. I wished the cool water would give me my life back, when all was well and good and I didn't have to do this. Yet it couldn't. It didn't even reach the top of the bank like it used to. So I prayed. I looked up to the cloudy sky and prayed to the shadow gods to guide me. I couldn't stand this strange seed of doubt that began to grow in my mind.

Eventually I made it to the house, north of the town, and headed straight for my wooded room at the back. But something caught my attention.

As I walked passed the long hall I heard them, two maids whispering in the darkness. I hung back to listen.

"Only three of them but they stole everything."

"Bless the gods. How'd they get away with it?"

"Who could've stopped them? They just came in charging."

"Apparently they've been all over the coast. Gwenfrewi said they took all the fish they just got at the market and burnt 'em, right in front of 'em. Took her two weeks to make enough cloth to trade."

"Well, I heard Dilys say that they raided her sister's town and killed all their sheep, no reason. Then burnt the crops as they left."

I'd heard enough. It seemed I had a hunt ahead of me, and these three were my prey.

* * *

The court sat on thick log stumps in between the lord's house, my house, and the hallowed stone well. The air hung grave. I didn't have to be here but since I had been presented officially as the heir to the South over a year ago, my father practically forced me to be here.

The dull court included me, grudgingly, my father, as lord, and his advisors, who earned their seat at court by acts of bravery or selflessness. My father's guard then stood in circle around the court, facing in and out alternatively, safeguarding their lord. They were part of our household, like the maids. They gave their service for reputation and reward, which was usually good, fertile land. Nowadays, that was hard to come by.

I crossed my legs up on the log as my mind wandered to my last hunt. Someone was rattling on and the conversation got more and more boring. A shape flickered black in my eyes and startled me, making me twitch on my log. I froze upright and quickly glanced at the court, thankfully no one caught my eye. Theirs were all fixed on Dai, who sat to my father's left. His black and grey hair was tied back in a small ponytail; his voice was low and serious and I uncrossed my legs.

Rather than let the shadows back in my head, I forced myself to look at the court, trying to find new details in each of them. It was something I had begun to do lately to keep myself amused. Dai's eyes were growing tired, the last few years had not helped. Today, they looked harder, less willing.

Next to him was Steffan, who had tanned skin and a muscular frame which loomed over me, and he always looked like he would burst out of his loose shirt and leather jacket. He put those muscles to use every day, whether it be with the cattle, the farming, cutting wood, riding, helping families move belongings or rebuild houses. He loved the open sky and everything underneath it and felt its decay more than most. Today, the hands on his knees were blistered and ashy. He'd been helping the smiths.

Steffan's best friend was Siorus, who was tasked with production of weapons and training the guard. He was tall, even sitting down. A skin of scars covered his left hand and arm, from when he pulled a child out of a fire some years ago. All along his fingers he wore bronze, copper and iron rings, which he had used to hide the scarring at first, but now he wore them out of habit. And because he found them extremely useful for punching. He rested his chin on his palm and rolled his eyes at me as Cledwyn began to speak.

"Our days are changing," he was saying slowly. Painfully slowly. "Our nights are no longer filled with…"

"You must go, lord," cut in Steffan. "News has been reaching us more often."

"Then we must. Before the next full moon," said my father.

"But what can they possibly expect from you?" asked Dilwyn, waving a hand towards my father.

"It is not what they expect from me, but what I can do for them. Even if my presence is enough to calm them, I must give it to them."

"Of course, but..." replied Dilwyn, who then turned to me with light green eyes. It took me a few breaths to realise Dilwyn was expecting something from me, his eyebrows raised beseechingly.

"My father is right. Whatever we can do to ease the people's suffering, we must do." I was quite impressed with myself as I said that, even with the hint of sarcasm I gave it. I sat up a little straighter but instantly slouched back down when Dilwyn sighed. He was the newest member of the court, and the youngest, bar me. He took his position seriously, as did his father, Dai.

"Well said," Dai stated, who placed both hands on one knee. "An eastern tour must be arranged then. I suggest three days."

Dilwyn nodded quietly and I gave him a sorry kind of smile. He gave me back the same one, I found it amusing to see my smile on his face, but then again, we were cousins. Our smiles weren't the only thing we had both inherited from our grandparents.

A messenger came then, slipping through the guard behind my father. He was a small, nimble man, roughly my father's age. He passed my father a sealed parchment, who opened it as the court was silent, waiting on their lord.

"Thank you, Elis," was all my father said and Elis snuck away as quietly as he had appeared.

Merfyn and Bleddyn sat to my right, relaying news from the messengers they had sent out. They were both warriors through and through, where their lord went, they followed. Although Merfyn a little more reluctantly. While they both respected the fight, Bleddyn respected the blood, Merfyn, the skill. Their families lived in the town, their children were always messing around in lessons in the communal rooms. Lastly was Trahearn, the elder of the court. His skin was dark and wrinkling but he had youth in him still. He wore a thick leather hide no matter the weather and constantly reminded us all that once, the shadows had roamed this earth freely, and soon, they would do so again. Most brushed off his shadowtales as old superstitions, the shadows had stopped walking our earth long ago. I paid them heed. I knew he was right.

"Then it is set. We ride out for the east after the next market."

I stifled a yawn. It's not that I didn't like the court. I did. I liked them all as people, mostly. I just didn't like this, this bored me. Why I had to be here, listening to contracts, repairs, plans of tours. All things to help the people get through these sparse times. Help the annoyed, frustrated, angry people, by trying to make more bread with less grain, by planting more fruit trees with less seed. By building and repairing with wood over stone since the trees were rotting anyway, putting half the stone masons in the South closer to destitution. This wasn't my idea of helping them. My idea was to be out there, killing the weak, sinful souls to appease the distant shadow gods. So that they might make our land fertile once more. So that our gods might come back to us once more.

That was my idea of help.

* * *

The wind was fierce. It blew the fire beyond the edge of the small wood. In both directions. This was not what I needed. Not now. I had stayed at home for two weeks after my father's rebuke and had behaved exactly as he wished me to.

But I would wait no longer.

The stories of a group of nomadic hunters had echoed across the South. They had moved on from stealing and burning to killing and pillaging. That I would not allow.

I was the only hunter around here. So tonight I would hunt them. Tonight I would feel the pulses again. I was hungry for them and I would feel them tonight. But now this.

The wind blew the fire deep through the trees, the smoke danced through the breeze. The dry land hadn't been rained on in weeks. I didn't worry about that, though. Not really. As I sat on Midnight, with the wind threatening to blow my hood off, I pulled on her reins and cursed. It was the large, mostly wooden, village less than half a league from the wood that was nagging at me. And the three nomads were still five leagues north of here. I didn't have time for this.

I charged Midnight towards the village and found the people outside, screaming, wailing and just staring at the oncoming fire and smoke. Really? Some screamed louder as I approached, cloaked in black, dressed like the night, but I ignored them. I didn't care. The thought of these nomads getting further and further away from me grated me. But this damn village was nagging at me more. It was an unusual feeling.

I had to help these people. They were my father's people, as this village was still in his lands. I was doing it all for them, to save them. I would be a fool if I didn't try to save them now. Damn them.

I used Midnight to herd the village folk together and get them to the main road. It would lead them straight to my father's town. Most of them did as they were told. Most of them saw a rider in black on a black horse and followed quickly, wanting to get away. Some of them ran from me. Some stupid men grabbed their families and ran away from me. Toward the smoke. What idiots.

After I had finally managed to get them all on the road, I breathed. They were on the road to my father, he would pity them until they could return. If they ever moved. Ugh. I trotted Midnight up and down the villagers, searching for the elder. Where were they? Midnight galloped by herself and then I saw her. The elder was at the front of the villagers on the road, long staff in one hand and a firelight in the other. I pulled Midnight to a stop in front of her and she stood out of the crowd.

"You have saved us," croaked the elder. She was so short she barely reached Midnight's knees and I shouted down at her.

"Follow this road all the way to the town. Do not leave the road."

She raised her staff and brought it down on the ground hard. "You, Night-Rider, have saved us. We will follow."

I nodded, as did she and a few of the others who had heard us. I watched them start moving and turned Midnight around. Finally. Daylight was approaching fast and I was five leagues south of my target. I kicked Midnight on and my friend rode like wind. I would not reach them by dawn but I would get them by dusk.

All the road my mind was focused, hungry. I stayed lowed in my saddle, keeping Midnight at a fast but steady pace. Soon my strength would increase, my speed, my endurance. I would find these nomads and then I would kill them and the pulses would reward me.

The hard dirt road was quiet. There was a time when it was busy with people travelling to friends and family, to towns and markets with their iron and clothes, fish and stone. Now, it was quiet.

I headed to where the nomads had last been seen, an ancient henge ruin in some forgotten field. They weren't there but their tracks were. Good. I followed the tracks a league and found the filthy scum filling their water skins at a little stream. This would be so much easier in the dark. No matter. As it was light, I would go with the obvious.

I climbed off Midnight, dropped my cloak and walked boldly out to the stream. Right where they were. There were six of them, more than I was expecting. They all looked alike, dirty, bearded and vile. I let them see me, head-to-toe and smiled. This was going to be fun.

Two grinned as they walked towards me. They didn't even try to get their weapons. Well, that changed quickly. I bounded over to them and drew my sword as I span. It sliced through gut and one crumpled like a dried leaf. I felt a throb start in my forearms and switched my sword to my left hand. I carried on the circle and a shadow danced through my mind. It told me to go left and I did. One quick stab and my sword was red. I pulled it free from the now limp body and switched it back to my right. Before I could even see the man, I saw the beard and aimed a back-handed slice at my eye height. It sliced through neck and he fell. Another throb and another shadow flickered. I rested my sword on my shoulder and sat into a hip. Three down, three to go.

I let the remaining 'hunters' arm themselves. Sometimes I liked a challenge, even if it wasn't much.

They circled me in, growling as they moved closer. I hadn't moved, I wanted to test myself this time, see how far I had come. One swung an axe, making the air whip around him. I would stay away from him for a bit. The two on my left were slowly treading towards me, like I wouldn't see them if they didn't make a sound.

"Ha." All three of these bearded men stopped moving and I almost rolled my eyes. Some fight.

In one easy move, I flipped my sword so the blade was facing behind me and darted straight at the one in front of me. He blocked my first swipe but didn't block my stab back and his mouth filled with blood as I pulled my sword out of his chest. I bared a grin at the other two. They growled in response. I dodged and blocked, stabbed and then rolled low, crouching behind the one without the axe. I stabbed up before he could move and barely moved in time before blood sprayed me. He stumbled forwards and a shadow flickered in my mind. *Stab*, it whispered. I froze. My sword was just at his spine but I couldn't move. Did that? Did I just hear a shadow in my mind? A growl from behind me snapped me round and the axe almost caught my shoulder. I blocked high and the ringing from blade on blade resounded through the clearing. I shook myself clear and struck low, scraping hide. Spinning on one foot, I finished my stab and yanked my sword out of the stumbling nomad. He was limp before his body hit the floor. Red stained the bank of the stream and ran into the clear water.

The one who held the axe and who had a beard that was so long it was tucked into his belt, spoke as I stood in front of him.

"No. No me. Life, spare life. I life," he begged. His voice was harsh and gravelly. I could barely understand him, he wasn't from the South. He begged for his pathetic excuse of a life. But he still had an axe in his hand?

My mind dizzied with black, stumbling me back. I was almost about to let him go, actually let him walk. Thankfully I came to my senses. Thoughts of the children he and the others had killed, the men and women he had abused and butchered, towns he had wasted ran across my mind.

They made me see clearly. That and the sudden burst of pain from my right wrist. The damned nomad had sliced a small seax along it.

"Where'd...?" He had an axe and a seax and was giving up? I stared up at him. His eyes were proud before they saw the rage in mine.

He started backing away, to get some ground on me but I was quick and angry. I strode over to him, sliced my sword down on his arm and stamped one foot onto his thumping chest. He grabbed my ankle and tried to throw me off but I wasn't just angry right then, I was strong, stronger than he was.

"Beg to your gods if you want to live. Not to me."

My sword slashed his neck and quickly ran red with his blood. He was gone. Then I prayed. My blood pulsed through me and my cravings were satisfied. I let Midnight drink from the stream, upriver from the blood as I refilled my water skin and cleaned my sword. It was a plain sword, like any sword that the guard have, with a thin hilt and blade the length of a man's arm. I sat away from the stream and looked at my wrist. It was only a small cut, so I cleaned it and wrapped it in some spare cloth from my pack. It shouldn't take too long to heal, not with the help I had.

I took a moment to breath in the day, the sun, the feeling I had after a kill. Damn gods. I grabbed my sword and held I to my head. I was supposed to meet my father on a tour. I was supposed to join him at the eastern villages. I yelled up at the sky. The market had been three days ago. He would not let me off for missing this one, I had missed the last three. "Damn freaking fire," I screamed at no one. I would never make it now. I paced around trying to think. I had to think of something. I walked over to Midnight and stroked her absent-mindedly, picking up my cloak. I had to think of something to placate him. I had to. What was I going to do?

CHAPTER 3

I was a day late. I wasn't so worried about that, though I found myself fidgeting with Midnight's reins. I got off Midnight and walked her to the tall, thick, wood and iron south gate that bordered the town and it was shut. Only one guard stood at each post. Good. That meant my father, and his men, weren't back from the tour yet. I hoped this worked. I left Midnight in the stables and crossed the bridge to the square by the well, the heart of town.

I waited. I played with the pump of the ancient stone well, while I kept waiting. I scuffed my boots in the dusty ground, fiddle with my belt buckle. Anything to distract me from the knot building in my stomach. Then I heard it. The clatter of hooves, the chatter of voices. Here they came. I stood up straight, deep breath.

He arrived a little while later. Along with half the members of his court and his guard. And most of the town who were welcoming back their beloved lord. Brilliant.

If this didn't work I probably wouldn't be able to leave the land, no, the town, for the rest of my life. And the whole town would know why. No more hunting. I couldn't let that happen.

I prayed that this worked. I took a step forward as soon as I saw my father, trying to stand as tall as I could.

"Father, I know I-"

"No. No more." He climbed off his horse, swiftly for a man of his age, and closed the distance between us in one step. His green eyes were cold, blank. His voice was full of emotion, power.

"No more of your excuses. I have heard enough of them."

"But I got-"

"You are not hearing me. I have had enough." By this time, everyone was there, crowding round. Just waiting for the entertainment this would bring to their dull lives. I didn't want anyone to see this, but it was too late for that. My father breathed a sigh, he seemed to age 10 years. I knew then, before he spoke, that my world had changed.

"If this land, our land, these people," he began, gesturing to those around, "mean nothing to you, then go. Go. Leave it all. Go and live your life without your responsibilities, without your birth right. I don't want to see you here anymore." He barely whispered, but to me his words echoed as if he had shouted.

He started to walk passed me, towards the house.

"Father please. I do-"

"No. Go. You are no longer my heir. You are no longer my daughter."

My world went dark.

* * *

I don't know what happened. I was sitting under a tree, rain splashing down, Midnight close by. Then I was squashing mud with my boots, staining my sword with their blood, sending their souls to hell. Along with mine.

Then darkness.

It was like that for I don't know how long. Rage then pain. Fire then darkness.

There were times when I went weeks without seeing another person to nights on end when I would burn the thieves and murderers. Then back to black. Always back to black.

Midnight nuzzled her nose next to me as I sat picking at grass in an empty dell. Rain drizzled down and I let it dampen me. I had nothing. I sank into the darkest depths of myself. Darker than I had ever known. I, who hunted, killed, sank into a darkness beyond that, beyond the shadows, beyond their realm.

I don't know how long I sat there, empty. When I came back to my clothes were sticking to my skin and fingers were wrinkled. I looked up to see where Midnight was and sprang to my feet, arms ready.

A man stood in front of me, his short black hair was wet, clothes soaked through. His eyes were sad. He carried no sword or dagger. I glanced at the chestnut horse and recognised it. As I looked back at my cousin, a sadness overwhelmed me, forcing me back down to the sodden grass.

"Nerys."

Dilwyn sighed heavily and joined me. He put his jacket around my shoulders as he hugged them. I didn't bother telling him that it did nothing. I was already drenched. We sat together for a while, watching the rain stop. Neither of us spoke, we just sat there as the world went by.

He took my hand in his and squeezed it. I squeezed back, looking at our hands.

"Nerys, you can't stay out here, you'll catch a chill. Come back, get warm and dry," he said gently.

I knew he meant well, that he purposely didn't mention my father or my banishment or where 'back' actually was. I tried to see me from his eyes but I couldn't, the stubbornness in me didn't want to.

"I've been trying to find you for ages. Every spare day I've been riding out, looking for traces of you. You're a hard one to find, you know?" He pushed me with his shoulder and I half smiled. "What have you been up to?"

I turned my eyes to his and sighed. It was easier to look at our hands.

"Not much."

"Thought so. Here, I brought some food, in case I found you and you were hungry. And for me, mainly for me." He stood up as he spoke and went to his horse, who had found Midnight and were grazing together. He came back with bread and dried meat wrapped neatly in cloth. We ate in silence and I was glad for it. And the food. I hadn't really bothered to catch anything lately. When I finished he took the cloth from me and folded it with the other one. I watched him do it, the normality was calming. Since my mother had died, Dilwyn was the closest thing I had to her. Though Dai was her brother and treated me well, he took his role as my father's advisor more seriously than he did uncle. I didn't really mind though, Dilwyn was more than enough.

"So, what will you do?" He shuffled away from me so he could face me properly. I knew he was getting to the part where he mentioned my father. I wished he didn't, I really didn't have the energy to argue.

I shrugged my shoulders, not wanting to speak. I swallowed. "Stay out here I guess, see the land."

"Nerys, please. Come back. Neirin has tried to put up a brave face but he misses you. He's making me do all your visits and teach the children in the healing rooms. You know I know nothing about plants."

I smiled as I imagined Dilwyn trying to teach the children the difference between hemlock and yarrow. Oh, I did miss the children.

"You know he's only hard on you because he thinks he has to be," he nudged me as he said it. "Come back, you'll see."

"No, Dil," I said as softly as I could, "I can't. You know I can't. He'd banish me all over again."

"Gods above, you're both so stubborn." He threw his hands up in the air a breath later, and a small chuckle escaped me. "My father was completely shocked when he did it. Tried to get Neirin to send for you for days after but he wouldn't listen."

"I didn't mean for this," I said to Dilwyn and myself, mostly myself. "Please tell Dai that, he doesn't have to fight for me."

"Of course he does, we're family. If anyone can change your father's mind, it's my father."

Dilwyn pulled me into his arms and we stayed there until the dusk fell. I didn't want him to leave. With him here, I almost didn't feel so bad, so empty and alone. Almost.

Neither of us said another word but he knew I wouldn't be going back. He kissed my forehead, mounted his horse and left. I let out a heavy breath. I had accepted my fate.

* * *

I was lifeless, my body was in the land of the living but my soul was with the shadows, with the dead. I didn't know if I would make it back.

All because of my father. No, all because of myself.

Because I was not the daughter he wanted me to be.

Three new moons had passed since I was home. Since I had seen my father. Three new moons.

In which time I had let the pulses guide me. They had made

me stronger, my muscles were leaner, harder. They had made me a faster hunter, swifter. They had made me kill.

The warmth of Midnight's breath roused me. I stroked her mane as I got up and went to my saddle pack. I forced myself to eat some stale, almost mouldy bread that Dilwyn had left me and half a rotten apple. I didn't taste it, only metal in my mouth. My cravings were strong now. They had been more than satisfied and still they were hungry. The pulses wanted more. The shadow gods wanted more. I would give them more.

The next day saw Midnight and I head north, passed the rocky village on the coast I had already wasted. Passed the river that ran south-east throughout the whole of the South, which we called the Ea. There were people up there I could use, people I could hunt.

As I walked beside Midnight, I kept my hand on her neck, feeling her warmth. She saved me all those years ago, and she was saving me now. We travelled through a wooded path along the bank of a shallow river. The wood was completely brown. No grass grew here, the alder buckthorn leaves were on the floor, dead and crunchy. This whole wood was decaying. Just like everything else in this wasted land. And now the people were getting desperate. But that was why I hunted them, those that had given up, turned in on themselves and away from the gods. To stop this. Funny really, it was all just one big circle.

I pulled my sword out of its sheath and let Midnight wander. At the biggest tree, which was a stumpy-looking ash, I took my aim, again and again. I threw it, slashed it, swung it so many times the bark cut away, leaving a hollow in the trunk.

Then a snap. I span around and scanned the trees. No animal could have made that sound; they weren't heavy enough. So where were they?

I kept scanning, shifting my eyes for the source. Crack. Another broken twig. This time I didn't spin around, I didn't search for the source behind me but kept my eyes forward, my ears sharp. Midnight neighed softly behind me. She could sense them too. I silently stepped back to her and re-gripped my sword. Now I was ready.

Just in time. Two boys barely into manhood, with axes high, ran at me from my right. I span quick and sliced at the first one but the second boy's slash, luckily for him, cut deep across my forearm. My sword dropped to the ground. Great. The first boy ran at me again and I stepped into him, jabbing his ribs hard. His blue eyes widened in shock. Instantly I turned straight into the other one, fist ready.

"Caaa," he yelled as I gripped his small neck firmly.

"Why the hell are you doing this?" He had made to swing his axe but I gripped tighter. He dropped it sensibly. Good boy.

"Let 'im go."

I felt a cold sensation at the side of my neck as the blue-eyed boy stood proud.

"After you answer me." My voice sounded uncommonly strong compared to his weak one.

"Let 'im go or I swing."

I tightened my grip ever so slightly on his friend, watching his eyes bulge.

The cold at the back of my neck pressed deeper. Fine. I loosened my grip and watched the poor boy cough some air back into his lungs. The pressure lessened but the axe remained. I slowly turned to the blue-eyed boy. The axe was shaking in his hand now as he tried to puff his chest out.

"What makes two boys attack a peaceful traveller?"

"D-d-don't talk." His eyes scanned to his friend, no longer coughing. "Quickly."

I sighed loudly in response. The other boy had picked up my sword and made for my pack. "Really? Is that necessary?"

"Hard times. We gotta' take what we can. So keep quiet."

"You two really have no idea what you're doing, do you?"

"I said be quiet." He pushed the axe back against my throat. I took a deep breath. As much as this had amused me, which wasn't much, I was now bored. Suddenly I stepped back and thrust both arms up, one at his hand, one at the axe. It was mine before he could blink.

The boy's blue eyes searched around, probably looking for something to grab. I stopped him short. I swung the handle around in my left hand and drew the blade edge up to his throat, so he would know what is was like.

"I asked you a question. And you can put my sword down boy, or I'll spill your blood first." I turned to face the other one, keeping the axe on blue-eyes. He didn't at first, so I raised my eyebrows. "Now." Then he did.

Turning back to blue-eyes, I knew what this was, why they were doing it, still, I had to hear it. I waited for him to speak.

"'Cause we have to."

"Why?"

"We're farmers."

I didn't respond. He faked a cough and I relaxed the pressure on his neck, slightly.

"You from round here?" he asked, voice clearer from the fake cough.

"Yes." I kept my eyes straight on his, not letting anything escape me.

"Well then, you know. We work on a farm with dry land. We can't grow crops or raise cattle. Family's starving, so we got to."

There it was. What I was waiting for. Another reminder of my father's impulsive decision, and my own, sort of. I don't know why I let myself pity them both, after all, I was actually trying to end this, but I did it anyway. I dropped the axe from blue-eyes and went to my pack, which the other boy kindly gave to me. I took out my silver dagger with my left hand, my right felt warm. The dagger was plain, simply decorated and useful for its lightness. Both boys flinched back as I held out to them.

"Take it."

"What?"

"The dagger, take it. Trade it, melt it. It should keep your family fed for a while."

The boys took a moment just staring at me, then their eyes shifted to each other, then me, then the dagger and back to me. Before either of them found the strength to acknowledge their sudden good fortune, I punched the one next to me on the nose, breaking it clean and kicked blue-eyes hard in the ribs. I forced the dagger into blue-eyes' hand as I said, "So you remember this. Not everyone will give a damn about you."

I picked up my pack and sword and went to Midnight who hadn't tried to help once. I stroked her and she flitted her ears at me, I laughed in response. The shadows hadn't been there this time, my mind was still clear. I didn't look back.

Instantly I regretted my decision, of choosing life over death. How foolish of me. It was then that I craved the pulses. I could have had them, felt them. I could have watched their blood drip. But it wouldn't have been right, it would have left a bad taste in my mouth.

As I walked Midnight along the bank, I felt the pain from my arm. The wound actually looked bad, blood had stained my torn shirt. If it didn't close soon, I would lose a lot more. I searched the woods around me. Oak, I needed an oak tree. As soon as I found a large but dreary looking one, I sliced at it, getting into the bark. When I had enough I shoved my sword through my belt and carried the bark back to Midnight. I had to cover the wound so I reached into the saddle pack and pulled out a strip of cloth and small jar of honey. My mother had taught me to always carry honey with me, wherever I went and I was always glad that I did.

It was times like this I missed her most. I sank down on the ground and started pounding the bark with a small piece of rock I found. The sameness of the action let my mind wander and it wandered to my mother.

She would take me to the lively woods and fields near town and have me name all kinds of plants and herbs and trees. Anything that could be used as a remedy to illness or injury. Then we would bring them back to the healing rooms in town and I would watch her prepare remedies and potions and poultices for people. I could watch her all day. Her hands moved so fast and she always seemed to glow. Well, I remember her necklace glowed.

Grey. Rain splashed against the rock. They came out of the rain like bats out of a cave. A glow shone through the falling water and time seemed to slow. They were drawn to the glow. They all were. Then it was gone. As was she.

Once the bark was ground I cupped it onto the largest, dry leaf I could find and mixed in the honey. I pulled back my shirt sleeve. Smearing it onto my arm stung a little then died down, I covered it tight with the cloth. Making a fist was rough, I wouldn't be holding a sword any time soon.

A week later saw Midnight and I travel back south. I almost felt like the nomads I had ended, just roaming the land, looking for the next hunt. I had ended them. Would anyone end me?

The people I killed haunted my soul but that was nothing. That didn't stop me from sleeping. My father disowning me, showing the whole town that he disowned me, that is what kept me up at night. Every night. Not the lives I took or how much I knew I had changed already, but my father... he stopped me from sleeping.

Summer had fully settled in and the land should have been green and bright and full with colours and fruit and crops. It wasn't. It was bright and clear but the grass was patchy with straw. It crunched under my feet rather than softened. The trees had yellow leaves, the ones that had leaves. The crops just managed to feed the people, the stores were barely half. Some summer.

The abandoned fallow I led Midnight through was surrounded by a small stone wall. We got to the far end of the fallow and left it through a small gap in the stones. The wall had been smashed in places, probably for repairs. Pieces of stone lay scattered, unused. I pulled Midnight round to the right of them, so she wouldn't have to step on uneven, sharp stone, when I heard it.

It was a weird sound. Like a large baby being winded. I wrinkled my nose in disgust because it wasn't coming from a baby. I turned back to the wall and saw a grown man sitting against it. I think he was crying. He was large and dirty and looked like an overgrown baby all huddled in on himself. I was in half a mind to leave him there. Then I recognised him. I sighed out loud. Why did I have to recognise him?

It was duck-man, from the fishing village. So this is what he had come to, after I had threatened him with death. I knew why I'd done it and I would do it again. To anyone who spread stories and lies about my father. To anyone who tried to rally people to overthrow him to end these troubled years. What they didn't know was that that would change nothing. Overthrowing my father would change nothing. Yet seeing this man like this…what had I done? Ugh.

I took a deep breath; this was going to be rough. I walked over to him and cleared my throat.

I was right, it was rough. As soon as he noticed me he stood and stamped over to me, fists waving.

"You, YOU." More stamps. "You really are the piece of, of… You." His finger was wagging in my face and I had no patience.

"What? What is It you're trying to say?" I kept my eyes steady on his and raised my eyebrows. "Well?"

"You!" he shouted again before spinning on the spot, walking away and stomping back round to me. I waited where I stood. Just as his mouth opened again, I spoke first.

"No. Right now you listen. I do not, for one breath, feel sorry for what I did to you." He shouted something incoherent at that, his face starting to turn red. "Anyone who tries to besmirch our lord and overthrow him, *anyone*," I raised my voice at that word and waited a breath after, "will be treated the same by me. Every time. He is our lord." I stared at him for a couple more breaths, then took a few steps back, showing him I had finished. He was definitely holding his breath, his face was getting redder, almost purple.

I raised my eyebrows, daring him to speak. His voice started off strong and got steadily quieter and weaker. "I was just doing what anyone else would've. We can't go on like this! This, this." He looked around the fallow, swinging an arm. "This land, it, it ain't our 'ome anymore. It doesn't feel like 'ome anymore." He slowly went back to the wall and slid down it, staring out to the grass.

I left him there, to his thoughts. He was mumbling something and I didn't care to listen so I went to find us something to eat.

By the time I came back, he had got a small, somewhat flat fire going. Poor thing. I had managed to trap two small rabbits which I skinned and prepared in silence. He didn't notice me wince as I skinned them, my right hand was still sore. He just watched me, at least he was no longer cursing. The silence continued as we ate. Even though his chewing was incredibly annoying, he was grateful for the food. In a strange, lonely kind of way, I was grateful for the company. It was weird.

I felt a wave wash over me, a wave of responsibility. Great. I filled my lungs with the ashy air. I guess I was responsible for this man's livelihood, well, my father was. No, that wasn't true. I took a slow drink from my water skin. I had not behaved as he would have, this was my fault. This was on me. Stupid banishment. My stomach seemed to tighten. For the first time since I don't know when, I rubbed my face and apologised.

"I am sorry, for what has happened to you and my part in it," I whispered to the fire.

He stopped eating, back straight. He hadn't heard it. *I* had barely heard me say it but he knew it had meaning. I sensed him turn towards me, holding the rabbit meat in his hands. I said it again. Barely louder than before.

He just sat there, stunned. I meant it, I knew I did, but him not saying anything back was starting to grate me. I placed my hands on my knees and went to walk away.

"You... thank you." I looked into his eyes and they seemed so sad and grey. I sat back down and watched the fire. That moment did something to me. I had never known anything like it. I think I felt renewed, softened. It was like a flame against the shadows.

I stayed with him until dawn. I had agreed to take him to the boundary of my father's land. I even let him ride Midnight, he had never been on such a fine creature.

We journeyed to the boundary in silence. I preferred that.

* * *

We reached the boundary, a large natural ditch built up with stone that ran the whole perimeter of my father's land, by mid-afternoon. I helped my duck-like friend down and turned to leave when he grabbed my arm. His eyes were dull, defeated, yet there was a flicker of intent in them.

"You can come too. Go back. If 'e'll help me, 'e'll help you too."

"No, I can't," I said patiently. He made to turn around but faced me.

"Where'll you go?"

"Where I need to."

"But you're 'is heir, the whole land knows you're 'is heir," he said, as if that meant something.

"They know Neirin's daughter is his heir, not me. I've done nothing to earn that position, other than be born to it." I gave him a small smile, mounted Midnight and breathed.

I'm the heir. I could laugh. I was the heir to a dying land that had no idea why it was dying. No idea that their current lord was the reason their land was in decay. I pitied my father. It had taken years for my anger and bitterness towards him to turn to pity. Years. I had finally come to accept, even understand, his decision. I think.

The land around us looked alive today, with a lazy glow from the sun casting warm rays on the trees and fallows.

"It has to change, 'e said it'd change."

"What did you say?" I asked, turning Midnight towards him.

"'e said it would change, y'know. If I did it, all this would change." He waved his arms to the left and right, clearly thinking about something else. I slid off Midnight and stepped closer, starting to feel a slow-burning anger rise in me.

"Who said it would change? Tell me." I was fighting the urge not to put my hands on his shirt when he shrugged. He just shrugged.

"Some trader. 'e said if I did it, said these things, it'd all change. Back to the way it was. That's what I want."

"Tell me more. Now."

"I don't know anymore, do I? 'e never came back, see." I tried to take a deep breath but it seemed to get stuck in my throat. I wasn't hearing this. Turning around to Midnight calmed me slightly. Stroking her mane and neck calmed me a little more. I looked back to the man who was trying to not tell me that some trader told him to say things that were causing people to rally against my father. I was not going to accept that.

"You have to know more than that!" I wanted to say more but his face turned back into that purple shade it made and he almost started crying again. "Oh, really?" If someone had made him say those things, I would have to find them. They would be my prey. Some trader. Would nothing in this life be simple? *Of course not*, the shadows whispered in my mind. This time, I didn't freeze.

Back on Midnight, the shadows left me to my thoughts and my thoughts were spiralling. The heir. I had never shared my father's responsibility, not day-to-day. I knew one day I would. One day I would have to. I would make sure that day would not be like this.

Travelling along my father's boundary was uncomfortable. I was home yet I wasn't welcome. I wasn't welcome in the place I had grown up; the place I was trying to save. I clenched my jaw so tight I got a headache. My mind was a mess.

I spent most of the day praying to the shadow gods, asking for their guidance, their forgiveness. The rest of the time, I continued to be a mess. I had to keep going, I knew I did but it took every breath of strength I had just to keep riding. To keep myself in the present, to not let the shadows completely take over me. Like they were starting to, like they were starting to do when they got hungry. When my cravings were strongest.

I pushed these thoughts aside as best I could. I was alone now though; no shadows were with me. I wanted it to stay like that, for a while at least.

Continuing south outside the boundary let me see familiar woods, small towns, villages, farmsteads I had visited, thinned meadows and empty pastures. I kept to the thickest woods, moving at night, Midnight was known round here. The next town I came to, I knew well. I had spent much time here in the summer as a child. Half of me wanted to stay, hear news. The other half wanted to run as far from here as I could.

That night I was stupid.

 I stayed in town, sought out my old tutor.

The town was a mix of wood and stone buildings close together. One road spread down the boundary line, the other ran out from the Ea and west, to the rest of the South. I walked Midnight through the town with my cloak around me and my hood up. I would rather be mistaken for an unfriendly traveller than anything else, that's if someone would mistake me. I doubt they would.

I found Caerwen's house and knocked, looking around at the afternoon workers and amblers. I knocked again.

"Heard you the first time," came a voice as the door opened. There she was, my old tutor. Her small eyes looked bright and shifted from me to Midnight, at least the one that could see did. Caerwen's right eye was a dull white and completely blind. She'd, apparently, refused to pay a man after he'd lost a card game and the man took a very heavy punch with a clay cup as payment. Caerwen had been quite the wild one growing up. Without a word she stepped out and stroked Midnight.

She hadn't changed. Tanned, wrinkled skin, energetic, with an odd sense of intelligence and a slight crook in her spine.

Caerwen welcomed me in to her small house like I was the young student she used to teach. She sat me at her humble table and fed me cheese, beans and ale as she spoke about all kinds of silly things, hands wild. She lit a small fire in the hearth and sat in a comfy-looking brown chair. Her voice deepened and she looked at me seriously. Well, half seriously. I took another sip of ale.

"It seems there are still things I must teach you, young one."

"Are there?" I replied lightly. It was no use, her eyes seemed to burn through me, especially the blind one. "I just di-" She held up her hands to silence me. After all these years she could still silence me with ease.

"Listen to me," she brought her hands close to her chest, "you are no longer a bouncing puppy who can act like a child. Then again, you never were really a child." She sighed deeply and I thought her eye might pop out. "Acting like one, a spoilt one at that, uh uh uh," she quieted as I tried to object, "is not how you should behave. As well you know."

I stared down at my now empty wooden cup. Why did *everyone* scold me?

"He hasn't left his land, our lord." She moved her hands across the table and I managed to bring my eyes back to her, for a blink. "Three new moons and he has barely left the town. Sends the guard out with the court instead, I know. Not doing too good, I'd say."

I knew it was ok to look up then. Her tone had changed, it was still serious, but there was something else in it, something a little suggestive.

"Now would be a good time."

And there it was. I could of. I had been starting to feel that way. I missed home and hearing the maids whisper and sparring with Dilwyn and talking to Haul and teaching the children and hearing their laughter. I missed warm oats with honey and the smell of lavender and metal from the healing rooms and smiths. I could have returned home and begged for forgiveness. I could end this self-inflicted exile.

A blackness flickered.

"No. He banished me. It is for him to decide when I return, if I do. Not me."

"Very well," she sighed. Thankfully, Caerwen changed the subject. She drew me in with stories of a night rider. One who came out of the shadows of the night and slayed the wicked. The townspeople called him Devil's-Breath because he was forged from the devil's voice, like metal by a blacksmith. They also called him Blood-Pourer because he poured the blood of the wicked into the land to feed the mouths of the good. It surprised me, to hear people think of me like that. I didn't really think of what the people thought I was doing.

All this she told me with a twinkle in her eye, as the fire dimmed. She knew. I could tell. But she was being the coy old woman she had always been.

Caerwen let me stay in the small front room next to the open fire. The sheltered sleep was a warm comfort. I didn't mind sleeping outside with nature, however a whole season of it had made me long for a warm bed. Midnight was out back in the small shed. As I drifted off to sleep, I almost forgot about my troubles. Almost.

Until new ones piled on.

The town was suddenly awake with screams and shouts of terror. I jumped off the ground and sprinted out of the house, straight into the crowded street. People were running frantically. Children wailed for their mothers. Horses galloped out of sight. Men were chasing their tails, trying to do something useful.

It was strange. Strange to see a town like this, from the other side. Strange not to be the one they were running from. But these were good people.

These were my people.

I sprinted behind Caerwen's house to get Midnight and as soon as I came back to the front the light hit me. One whole row of wood houses had been set alight. The heat was immense but worse than that, much worse than that, people were caught inside. One woman came crawling out, covered in smoke. She choked, crawled some more then breathed her last breath. She had gone to the shadows; she would join our ancestors in their realm.

The rage built within in me like a spark ignited in the dark.

I grabbed a cloak left forgotten on the ground and ran into the nearest house. The cloak was heavy and thick. Good. I covered my face and searched. Empty.

Next house.

I searched all eight houses. I found four people, all clinging to life. One was a boy, little more than eight. Who would leave him behind?

I went back to the street, searching. There stood Midnight, firm and strong against the chaos around her. She truly was a brave creature. I climbed onto her back as Caerwen approached. Her eyes were darting everywhere. I could use her.

"Get everyone out. Get them out of the town. Go to my father."

She nodded and left, rounding up people faster than a woman half her age.

With that taken care of, I searched for the cause of this chaos. I didn't have to search long. From the middle of the town, through the fire came three men, all on huge black stallions. Their faces covered in hoods. I didn't know who they were, but that did not matter. Who they were did not matter. I would end them, and then find out. So I could send their heads back to their families.

They walked their horses to a stop 10 feet in front of me. Midnight neighed expectantly. I would end them.

The surrounding fire was pressing on my mind, urging me to do something but the riders didn't move, they were just watching me, as I was watching them. The silence amid us ran loud against the din. I waited. I waited for them to make their move.

Finally, they did. The three riders circled me in and drew crude blades from their belts. Each reflecting the fire in their small, dark eyes. They circled and circled, keeping me in tight. I kept Midnight still, facing forward. I wanted to watch them, to learn their movements. To learn something that would give them away. And there it was.

They continued to circle, horses neighing and struggling to break free from the dance. Flames still spat angrily around and a few wails resounded through the night. These men really weren't half as scary as they thought they were. And I was growing bored. Maybe I would make the first move. I waited, taking a few deep breaths, re-gripping Midnight's reins, just long enough for him to get into place. I hit my legs against Midnight's flanks hard and she expertly bucked. Her kick hit the horse behind, the one who had a slight limp in its left leg. The horse buckled, the rider fell to the ground, pinned beneath his flailing stallion.

The other two widened the circle. Then came at me, from both sides. They were quick, I laid flat over Midnight and swung my legs round to the right. I was quicker. My feet made contact with the second riders' sternum. He fell backwards off his horse, and hard onto his neck. I heard the dull snap. Two down.

The next rider came at my left, hooves thundering towards me. I swung back onto the saddle, turned Midnight to him and charged. He galloped with his blade out, like a spear. This would be easy, and also hurt. My right arm hadn't completely healed yet and after this, it would be worse. He was a foot away, blade held fast under his arm. Just at the right moment, I grabbed the blade in my left hand and pulled. The sharp metal cut my hand deep but I didn't let go. I changed it to my right and hit the hilt on its masters' head in one breath, making him rebound forward. I dropped the rough blade instantly and barred my teeth against the stinging pain. We both turned and charged again. I pushed Midnight on, she galloped fast and I got beside the rider before he could get ready. I drew back my hand and punched hard. I put all the force I had in to it and it worked. My fist made contact with his face and I felt a satisfying clunk on impact. His jaw was broken. Good.

I turned Midnight around and instantly pulled him from behind to the ground. I forced Midnight to stamp him and heard another clunk, thicker this time. He was no more. Back to the first rider. He was still pinned beneath his lame horse, poor thing. I slid down and gingerly gripped my sword. He started to struggle more as I stood over him. He even grabbed my leg to try and pull himself free. I let him try. He was going to die; I could let him have a small bit of hope.

"Any last wishes?" I could also try to be nice.

"This over... not," he said brokenly.

"It is for you."

"He coming. He coming."

His head left its body quickly. I wasn't going to drag it out.

With that done, I just wanted to sit down, to wait for the pulses and the pain to subside. It took some time, so I strapped up my hand and changed the cloth on the other one. The wound had almost healed, and now, fresh blood was spilling out. Great.

I stayed in the abandoned town for the next few days, clearing it as much as I could. It would be nothing but a wasteland for a while. I found a spot and buried the heads of the three riders, they could be useful.

I looked at the empty, wasted town, full of life only days before. There were scorch patches on the ground, blood of the riders staining the dirt road. The words of the hooded rider had shaken me. If I let them run across my mind, well, I didn't know what would happen. I didn't want the shadows to have something to hold on to. "He coming." Those words ran over and over and over. I had to find out. I had to find out who and I would only find that out in the Midlands.

CHAPTER 4

The ride was dry and long.

On foot, I crossed the Ea, that ran north-west to south-east, cutting the South in half and headed for the nearest village. Midnight could do with a rest; I couldn't deny her that. It was a small village, barely more than a farmstead, but the people were kind. We spent one day and night there, just enough time to replenish my pack, let Midnight sleep and plan the rest of our journey north. I bowed slightly as we left, thanking the people and headed north for the road. 'He coming,' whirled in my mind, pushing me on.

Midnight and I made good pace each day. The seasons passed from summer to autumn, as my friend carried me on. The soft tread of dying grass was replaced with the hard crunch of stones beneath Midnight's shoes. The browning trees started to brighten with colour, but not much. We followed a thin gravel path through two large grass-covered hills. At the top I got off Midnight and took a moment to look down at the land. It was beautiful, even if it was fading away. A warm, dry summer hadn't helped it at all. *I* hadn't helped it. Black shapes flickered through my mind. They were right of course, the black shadows. I had helped. I was helping, just not in any way the people knew, or could see yet. Midnight started to walk around, chomping at any grass she could eat. I brushed her coat a little and stayed on foot.

As we continued north, woods and dells started to change to valleys and hills. I hadn't been this far north in a long time, and I was still in the South. My lungs started to feel tight, the air thin. I shook Midnight's reins loosely, shaking off the tension in my arms. I rolled my shoulders and took a long, clear breath. All the emotions I had hidden for years tried to swim through me, I wouldn't let them. I rolled my shoulders a few more times.

There was a reason I had hidden them, those damned feelings. I prayed out loud over and over to distract me, even looking up at the dull sky as I did. I knelt my knees on crunchy stones as I prayed, whispered to the shadowgods. "Give me the fight I need to live the life ahead."

It was no good. I focused on the crunch of the gravel, how it gave a satisfying, crushed sound with every step, yet my mind wouldn't listen. I looked down at my hands and saw them shaking, I didn't feel them shake, I just saw them. No. I reached over to Midnight and fumbled in my pack for my water skin. A good drink and some deep breaths calmed me for a while but not long enough. I brushed my hands on my legs, trying to stop them shaking. I was anxious. And I couldn't stop thinking about it, the last time I was here. The only other time I had been in the Midlands. My jaw tensed and I could feel my stomach whirl.

***

The next day saw Midnight and I close to the border, there was just one more village to pass through. As I rode on Midnight along the dirt part, we arrived after noon. The wood huts were built in a large circle with a larger hut at the far end. I couldn't make it out. It seemed to have only half a roof. I slid off Midnight and pulled her through the village, trying to find the stables.

"Wooooaaa," I said, turning to see why Midnight had pulled on her bit. "What, what is it?" I asked her, stroking her neck. She stomped her hooves into the dirt.

I had hardly got far when he came out of nowhere and stood firm before me. His long black hair hung thick in plaits, streaked with silver and his grey eyes filled his sockets, giving him an other-worldly presence. Midnight stomped on the spot and stopped altogether when he placed a gentle hand on her neck. I knew who he was without a word. It would be rude to speak first.

The shaman stood in front of me and behind him, villagers stepped out of their huts. His voice was deep and purposeful. I held on to Midnight tighter.

"You. You have come," said the shaman, raising a hand towards me. "I saw you. Here you are." Before I could move, his nose was directly in front of mine. His copper-like skin looked worn and leathery, though he couldn't be past fifty. I could feel his breath on my face, slow and light. It made me uncomfortable though I didn't move. It would be over soon.

"You. You are not in this land. Mmm. No, you are in both. Good. Join us, now you will. Come." I followed the shaman and was ushered into the largest hut as the rest of the villagers crowded to it. Hands grabbed me and I lost hold of Midnight. I span round to her being led off to a fenced area, I hoped she would be safe. These border folk were strange.

No more than 20 people were inside the hut, all looking up. Some villagers tried to crowd in and they were looking up too, chins high. I fidgeted where I was as I looked at the hut itself. There was a raised hearth in the middle of it and all of the walls were covered in white, elegant symbols that joined and spiralled and danced. I stepped to the nearest wall and ran my fingers over the symbols. These were... how could they be? No one knew it anymore, my mother had always told me, gods, even Cledwyn had always said no one knew it anymore. How could this border town know? These were symbols of the Old Language.

I was gently nudged by a villager as they walked passed me. I looked back at the symbols as I walked a little more around the hut, straw flattened under my step. The villagers inside all took their, apparently set, places and sat down, eyes towards the hearth. I quietly sat down at the back, scanning for any sign of what was to come. Then the shaman appeared by the hearth, eyes closed and humming. A deep, reverberating hum that somehow filled me. I knew the words as if they had been sung to me in the cot.

The shaman and a young girl walked around giving people small glass jars full of some icky looking liquid.

"Take," was all he said as he offered one to me. My body tensed, every single fibre of me completely froze, the shaman had placed a warm hand on my forehead as he moved on. My sight was black, eyes buzzing, my breath got stuck in my throat. My mind moved like lightning. I felt squashed, like I was being sucked through a hole far too small for me and my skin was on fire, burning and sharp. The hairs on my arms all stood up, making me shiver. Then there was blinding light. My stomach was whirling. Everything moved so fast. Then my forearms started to scream with fire, right along the two deep scars that ran from my elbows to wrists. They felt raw, boiling and raw I needed to scratch them. I had to scratch it.

Then back. The pressure faded from my head, my arms were cool and calm and I was sitting on the straw. The shaman gave me a knowing smile as he moved on. I placed a hand on my chest, heart racing underneath. What the gods had just happened?

The humming began to fill my ears again and I watched smoke dance from the hearth. The people around me craned their necks to watch it up, so I did too. That's why it looked like there was only half a roof. In the middle of where the roof should have been, was an open circle where the smoke escaped, revealing the bright sun and sky. I breathed in the smoke and was calm, unthinking. The smoke filled my nostrils with lavender. Lavender and honey and blossom. The humming got louder as it was time to drink. I sensed the others around me drink from their jars and downed mine. I wasn't aware of anything else then. Only the sun and the smoke and lavender. The humming seemed to get further and further away. The sky seemed to flip to the other side of the world. I didn't know the sky could be made out of wood.

* * *

I sprang up and wished I hadn't. Thumping came from inside my head as I looked around the empty hut. I shivered suddenly and saw the hearth had long died out. The sky roof was dark with night and a moon that hung low. "Aaahhh," I moaned as I tried to move my feet, they were tingling and heavy. Pushing myself against the floor to stand was a mistake. I closed my eyes and braced against my legs, something was spinning and my body felt different, achy. A deep breath helped my head clear. Crackling wood and voices sent my attention outside the hut. On unsteady legs, I fumbled against the side of the hut to discover the source of the noise.

Outside in the dark, the village looked entirely different. The flickering fire in the well-trodden middle of the village cast shadows against the surrounding huts. I saw a shadow run across a hut and hid back inside. I thought the shadows were real, that they had descended. When a child ran in front of me, I quickly realised they hadn't. I exhaled and shook myself from that momentary fear.

The chattering people were eating, laughing, dancing in the

shadows. To see a village still able to celebrate even though our land was failing was… strange. Although, being a border town, I guess they were a people of two lands, a people of two gods. Maybe the Midlands' old gods still looked over them, while ours only tormented us.

Out in the dark his grey eyes stood out before I saw him. The shaman looked at me as I watched the people. I would let him speak first again.

"You feel better, calm." It wasn't a question but I replied anyway.

"Yes, actually. I do." I hadn't realised that I did until the words came out.

"No, you do."

I kept my gaze forward and felt him follow with his eyes.

"They live freely. No fear. They take what comes. All that comes will pass. It is a cycle; one we surrender to. No fear. You, you have fear." He turned to face me. I tried to avoid his eyes but his stare was so intense. I would have to look at him, I could just feel them burning the side of my face. I turned reluctantly and found his eyes instantly. His deep, burrowing eyes saw straight into mine, as though they were boring holes into my very soul. I shivered and tried to hide it.

"Yes, you have fear. Oh, you have fear."

"I-"

"No. This you don't speak of. This you act on. It is good you act on. There is another fear within you. Act on it to see past. Once you see past, your fear will be greater."

"My fear will be greater?" I put in yet he continued as if I hadn't said a word.

"It will be great but it will not be of your own. No, it will be your fear you fear then. It will be all. Yes."

I was thoroughly bewildered. My mother used to tell me that shamans meant well and were usually right with their half ramblings. I knew to respect the words he had spoken to me, after all, he could have chosen not to. But how did any of that help me now?

He stepped closer to me and I had to lean back. I'd learnt enough about him to realise this was what he did but I didn't like it. I closed my eyes. I didn't know if it was the dancing shapes of the fire I saw against my eye lids or the shadows. Either way, they stayed all the while he spoke.

"Yes. See your fear. See it, then know it. Then pass it. Then you have no fear. Then you have no fear, only water." I felt a firm hand on my shoulder lead me to warmth, to the fire. He whispered a name I think, something so soft and gentle it could have been the wind. I opened my eyes and he was gone. The fire was so bright I had to rub my eyes. What had he said?

I had to take a moment to shake off whatever that was and was steered to a cushion on the floor by some little hands. The oldest child of them shushed the others as they giggled. He stood taller in front of me and smiled. "We will get you the food, if you stay here and sit with us."

"Of course," I said and nodded. In one breath they had run away and more little ones ran with them towards the tables of food. A very little one tried to run back with an overladen plate and almost tripped over her own feet. I pushed myself up to help but she was already running and laughing at me.

"I got here first, you have my food first," she said with a strong tone. She shuffled in on my cushion as other children surrounded me with more and more plates. So many wanting eyes were on me, how could I please all of them? My little friend nestled in closer and gave me a forceful nod.

"Yes, I will eat your food first," I replied, taking the whole plate of nutty bread. I couldn't help but laugh. Mutterings and pleas broke out instantly from my new friends. I was just about to put a chunk of bread in my mouth when one boy almost lost his plate to an angry friend. "I want to try something from every plate, so please, don't be upset," I said as the children quietened. "I am very hungry." I gave them my best hungry smile as I rubbed my belly. Some children actually screamed as they ran to get more plates. This was such a remedy. I could not move for plates and children. My very little friend sat with me the whole time and babbled on and on about the night's celebrating. Women taught children to plait on my hair, then I had to dance with all the children around the fire. Men sang songs with their deep voices and beat on wood drums with sticks. Some children tried to take the sticks from the drummers as they were drumming and the laughter that followed was so carefree and light. It was so weird. I found myself relaxing, actually relaxing, laughing along with them all. Despite all my present troubles, I was laughing.

These border towns were strange indeed.

* * *

The night was riddled with flashes. My sleep was full of broken dreams and blackened visions. All of when I was fifteen. When he had ridden south for the death day of one of my father's court members and his wife.

Men carried the bodies to the graves. Arrows rained down with smoke trails and the two graves burned against the grey sky.

"My words were the truth, you see that now, my child. You see that it won't be stopped. It is only the beginning, although it has already started, it is only the beginning."

His words swam within the darkness, fading as images reappeared.

The whole town was there, mourning their loss. Their son stood watching, a blank expression on his pale face.

"It won't be stopped...See your fear. It is only the beginning. It is happening again. Only the beginning..."

Fire burnt through my eyes. I sprang awake. Heart pounding, sweat dripping, sticking to my face. I tried to slow my breathing, it took a while. I hadn't dreamt of that night since it had happened, nearly six years ago. He was right. It had only taken me two years to see it but the death day had showed me that he was right. Rather, my father's court member and his wife's murder showed me. The way they were killed, brutally, slowly by nomads with no humanity. It showed me the land was no longer good or rich. That it would no longer protect its people as it had. And that I could stop it.

As the dawn broke, I found Midnight at the stables and saddle her, ready to leave. I made to turn to the road.

"Ah." The shaman stood in front of Midnight, like a trunk.

"Forgive me," I said to him, slightly bowing my head. I felt his warm hand under my chin and looked into his eyes.

"No, no, no." Was all I heard before something ran into my leg, swiftly followed by other children clingy to me and Midnight. She neighed softly and the children laughed. I would miss this.

"It's alright, little one, don't be upset." My littlest friend had a very strong grip of my leg and she mumbled to herself.

"You drink, you drink and it shows you past and present, all in between." I'd almost forgot about the shaman with the children around. "You, you will be it." His eyes were intense, staring at me, yet, there was something else there. I made to speak but he span on the spot and stalked back to the hut.

"You stay with us now, please." My little friend had let go of my leg, I was still staring after the shaman. "Please, please, please." I shook myself from my trance and bent down to her. Midnight neighed again, less softly this time.

"I do have to go now," I said as I brushed her almost silver hair behind an ear. "But I am sure we will see each other again, maybe when you are all grown and strong."

"Waaah," was all I heard as an elder sister came to take her away. I looked back on the village, standing next to Midnight.

I would miss this place. Midnight's tail wacked me and I took the hint. Some of the village children ran beside us until we got to the border, their energy a huge comfort.

The border wall ran from one side of the land to the other, coast to coast. It was a thick stone wall which had crumbled to the height of a man's hip. It used to be a wild place, where the gods of two lands met and wanderers would scurry past. Now, the South side anyway, was quiet, forgotten. Although there were a few gates along the wall for traders between the South and the Midlands, where markets and towns that weren't really towns popped up, I decided to cross where we were. I slid off Midnight and gave her a quick slap. She jumped the wall easily. I jumped over it sideways and my feet fell on to new soil.

I was in the Midlands.

***

This was where I would get answers, whether I liked them or not. With the sun bearing down cold rays, Midnight and I followed a small dirt track laden with rocks. I took off my cloak even though my skin was cold. Walking over the rocky terrain made me hot. The Midlands was just as vast as the South, with hills and rock piles and ancient ruins filling up the land. But it was greener. Even in this nearing autumn, it was greener. Their land wasn't decaying. Their gods weren't demanding death in exchange for life. Their gods just were.

I cursed to myself as the reason why came into my head. I decided it was time for a quick rest. We had been walking for half the day and however capable Midnight was, this uneven ground was tricky for her.

I took out a handful of dried fruit and sat as Midnight grazed. Then I saw to my bandages. My right arm was almost healed, although I would have to wait a few weeks for my grip to get back to normal. I peeled off the cloth around my left hand. Luckily, the cut hadn't been as deep as I thought. The skin was still sore but the wound beneath had healed. All that was left was for the top layer to re-join. Now I could practice holding my sword in my left hand.

I cleaned the wound with some water and honey and wrapped a fresh cloth around it. Then we were moving again. I held on to Midnight's leather reins as I gripped, loosed and re-gripped my sword in my bandaged hand. It would take some getting used to.

A small grey valley came in to the horizon and my heart started to quicken. This was it. I was getting closer, to him and my memories.

The valley was deep and we were almost through it, even with all the trees and overgrowth, it was easy to lose your way round here. All these valleys looked the same. The grass path changed to rocks and pebbles and I had to slow Midnight down to make her steps quiet. Before we reached the end, I knew they were there.

Out of the rocks. Dozens of men and women in browns and greys the same colours as their surroundings. Fashioned flint was in each of their hands. Their pale faces were hard, threatening.

An echoey silence hung in the valley. I shifted my eyes around to each of them, staring, waiting. The nearest one to me spoke quickly, gruffly.

"Gives us the horse, or we take it and kill you."

Men.

"Of course you would," I muttered. "I will give you my life and my horse, if any of you can take either from me."

I saw his grey eyes flash to the others. That had made him hesitate. Good. I spoke again, I was in no mood to wait.

"I wish to see Gruffyd."

CHAPTER 5

The nearest one nodded to those around him and slowly, the flint weapons were put away. One women jumped off a jagged rock and grunted at me. She did nothing as I nodded and I followed the men and women out the valley towards their town. As we walked, the wind picked up, a chill ran down my spine.

"Woah," I said to Midnight after she shivered too, making me loosen my grip on her reins. She calmed as I stroked her, keeping up with the Midlanders. We approached a small dell where the air felt thicker. There were two wood buildings to the south, built off the ground and that was it. Around me was a ramshackle of stones covered in grass. Some of the stone piles were tall enough to fit a man in, most were barely up to my shoulders and those were the ones that had entrances. To a visitor, it was a shepherd's hut with rocks, not the largest town in the Midlands.

"We will go down now, you will bring the horse." The man

who thought he could take Midnight from me stood at the first stone enclosure. I held onto Midnight's neck as the rest of these Midlanders closed in on us.

"Sh, sh," I breathed on Midnight, hoping she would feel calm and stepped into a small, domed room, barely capable of housing two people. Luckily, it didn't have to. Jagged stone steps led down to the darkness. I coaxed Midnight with strokes and soft words as I led her backwards down into a different world.

Once we were below, Midnight stomped and neighed until she was the right way round. "Sh, sh," I said as I held onto her neck, trying to be calm even though my jaw was tensing. The light of the fire-torches shed light on this town below ground. It ran out for a few leagues in each direction, stone built into the earth. The winters were harsh here, survived by retreating underground.

I did not know the path I followed. The dark grey stone seemed endless, broken only by the fire-light. I walked behind my guide for what seemed like hours. The corridor we were walking down was wide but low, I reached up and let out a small laugh, I touched the ceiling.

"Come on, it's ok, come on." I had to calm Midnight as she stomped and pulled against me, her neck brushed against the ceiling.

"She must come." My guide turned round, looked at Midnight
and continued to walk on. I stroked my friend along her
neck, rubbed her shoulders. "There we go, you can do this."
I stroked her nose and took a deep breath. So much for
my guide. Slowly, I got Midnight walking and I carried on
down the corridor. Every now and then, there were airways
tunnelled up to the ground above, keeping the people below
alive. I looked right up one and was sure I saw a batch of blue.

Open archways led off to other areas of the town, people
moved round with their day-to-day activities, just like in the
South. I stopped in the middle of three archways and rolled
my shoulders back. I did not know the way to go and the noise
down here, everything was echoing. A group of children
smiled at me as they were hustled down the corridor I just
came from by a very stern looking woman. I watched them
go, wondering what to do. Three women in long, colourful
dresses stared at me as I turned back. They were coming
closer. They must have seen me as what I was then, a stranger.

"You, I believe, are certainly lost." The middle woman had
hair that looked like bronze and copper. She took a step closer
to me and her women gossiped. I stood as tall as I could and
clenched my jaw. Midnight trotted on the spot, she leant into

my hands as I tried to calm her.

"What a fine horse this is," said the woman. "Does she have a name?" I looked at her then and wished I hadn't, she was beautiful.

"You were not behind me, you should be behind me." My guide appeared out of nowhere, grabbed Midnight's bridle and tried to lead her off. "No," I said as I took them off him. "Now, now, you're ok, it's ok." He made to take her bridle again and I glared at him.

"You must come, my lady. Our lord is waiting." He nodded ever so slightly and turned on the spot, this time waiting for me.

"Good girl." I stroked Midnight again and led her on.

"Lady? Ha." I heard the women snigger as I walked on. I preferred the South. Midnight's shoes echoed off the stone as we turned a corner.

"Wha-," I blurted out. My guide stopped abruptly and I stumbled into him.

"Here," he gestured his arm to a large archway. "I take horse to stables."

I patted my friend and nodded. She was getting used to her surroundings now; she should be ok. Even though I wasn't, my only comfort was walking away from me. Something was whirling in my stomach and my jaw clenched harder. I faked a smile, this was why I had come. My guide faded through the archway, leaving me alone in the corridor, listening to the echo of Midnight's hooves grow quieter. I turned to the door on my right and pushed. I guess it was this way.

Through the door a short tunnel led into a large, domed room. Fires two-thirds up the walls brightened the room well. The man I had come to see sat behind a low, thick table.

"Lord," I said, bowing.

His reaction surprised me. In one breath, the lean, grey-haired man had squashed me in a bear hug.

"Nerys," he said, releasing me.

I coughed to clear my throat and just stood there. I had seen him twice before. Once when he had ridden down for the death day and once when I had been here last.

He sat me down on a thick fur rug and ordered food. Nutty bread, warm jam, smoked meat, fresh fruit and mead. Food I had not tasted in some time. As soon as the smells wafted through the room I was hungry. Once I had had my fill, my mind was alert once more.

"Midnight?"

"Will be fed and groomed. Easy, we have the best farriers here too." I gave an empty laugh. I breathed in the thick air. I was where I needed to be. I rolled my shoulders again, and breathed through my nose.

"Do not worry, child. You are both welcome here. The heir and daughter of Neirin will always be safe in these parts, with me around," he winked as he said the last words. It made me smile, as did his mention of my father. He had always spoken well of Gruffyd; I had grown up hearing stories of his distant friend. It was comforting to know Gruffyd spoke well of him in return.

"Thank you, but I am not here for pleasantries. A town on the western boundary of my father's land was attacked. Three men on black stallions. One of them mentioned a man. His last words were 'He's coming.' Have you heard of anyone moving south?"

"Not from my lands."

Great. I was counting on Gruffyd to know, to be able to tell me who, or where or when. Something.

"But there have been whispers."

I leaned in.

"But let us talk of that later. Now, you. I am interested in you now."

I tried not show that I had just bit my own tongue. I could almost hear my teeth grind from the suggestion. I did not want to talk about myself. I raised my hand but he cut me off.

"Uh uh. No my child, you answer my questions, I shall, in turn, answer yours."

His voice was serious but one look in his eyes and I saw a slight humour. As he wished.

"Excellent," he said as I gave a small nod. "Now tell me, how long has it been?"

"Seven years."

"Seven years." He faded off into his own thoughts. I waited for him to continue.

"Neirin, I take, still does not know."

"No. My father doesn't know."

"Nerys, child. I take it you aren't here on his orders, no need to tell me. He has lost so much. Don't lose yourself too."

Those words struck me. I looked into his wrinkled eyes, trying to find out his meaning. He gave nothing away. His face was still, as was he. The lord of the Midlands gave me a small smile and I breathed, as something black almost flashed behind my eyes. He wasn't trying to harm me, only help me.

"You remember that night?"

"Every time my eyes close," I looked into my hands.

"Yes. Those we lose never truly leave us. Oh dear child, what a life you have had already."

"Gruffyd, please," I choked out. My eyes started to fill.

"Nerys, the path you are on is nothing if not hard. You, you are the strongest of us all. You were meant for this. You will see that, soon enough."

I couldn't hold it in any longer. Gruffyd was the only one I could talk to about this, about all of it. He was the only one who would understand, after all, he was the one that started this for me. I had never said any of this out loud, not even to the shadows. I buried my head in my hands as the tears silently fell.

"I can't, I can't keep doing this anymore. I'm, I'm… not *me* anymore."

"Hush. Hush yourself."

I breathed deeply into the back of my ribs to stop the crying. Though tears still fell. Eventually they subsided but my eyes stung with the salt. I half spoke to Gruffyd, half to myself.

"They crave… the shadows, they crave blood, all the time. *I* crave blood. So much blo…" Another deep breath. "Their voices, some are so urgent, so strong, the only way to make them stop is to… and the other ones, I can hear other ones that are, they're lonely." I shook my head, trying to get rid of the sickening feeling that was starting to creep in me. "But they push me on, they all push me to spill blood. As soon as I do the shadows take over me, it all goes hazy, my mind goes black and I'm not me anymore, or I am me with the shadows, or they take over me, uh, I don't even know. They make me stronger and faster and I've started to… see, I guess. Only briefly." I rubbed my eyes and looked at him. "I think they've started to make me see things, where they'll go, what they'll do. The shadows let me see what will happen. I shouldn't be able to see that."

"Hush, child."

Gruffyd reached closer and held my hand. The contact calmed me slightly.

"How else is this affecting you? Nerys, tell me." He sounded gentle but his tone was urgent. His grey-blue eyes were calm although the wrinkles around them were tight. My face must have looked a puffy mess.

"I… nothing in my head." Lie, screamed a shadow mixed with

my own tiny voice. I took a deep breath again and carried on, avoiding that shadowthought. "Just physically. Mainly physically. I can kill quicker than I used to, fight for longer. My wounds don't take so long to heal, see," I offered him my hands. He removed the bandages gently on my hand and arm. He took his time musing over the healed skin.

"The shadows have gifted you well," he finally said, re-wrapping the cloths. I yanked my arms away.

"Nerys, be calm."

"No. I do not think that this is a gift for killing people. There shouldn't be a gift for that." I crossed my arms in front of me. I knew why I hunted, why I killed, although it didn't always sit well with me. I felt Gruffyd's eyes on me and heard his laugh. That just made me frustrated.

"Ha, child. You're sulking is not necessary."

"I'm not sulking."

"Of course. However, you have been following this path long enough to know that you cannot stop. Not now. The shadow gods demand this. You know this is the only way to restore your land. The killing of those who have turned from your gods, these darkened souls is necessary, your sulking is not. You see?"

I had to admit, everything he said was true. Worrying over blood I had already split was pointless. I had done it to save my people, good people, to give them back their rich land. To fulfil the shadow gods' need to make it so. So yes, Gruffyd was right.

I rubbed my face again and nodded.

"Good, now, shall we get back to the point of your visit?" His voice was light and inquisitive as he bounced on his chair and leaned closer to me.

"Yes," I responded through a small laugh. "What have you heard?"

Gruffyd replied with a brightness in his eyes. He spoke of a Night-Rider in the South whose stories have travelled north. The stories told of one who burned villages, killed men. Who left children parentless and homeless, who knows no pain or fatigue.

"These stories have inspired men."

I held my arms tighter to me.

"These men are cruel. Men who do not live among us but in the rocks and hills. Their history is a sad one," he sighed. It could have been a trick of the light, his face lengthened in sadness. "Their lives even more so. They have long since forgone their reason for coming to this land. They no longer live with us, but against us and that is no way to live. They are harsh and bound to no one, not as they were. These are the men the Night-Rider has inspired."

He looked at me and his eyes changed. They were sad. My arms were almost shaking as I kept squeezing my own chest. These men had been a constant threat to the people here. To us Southerners, they were just legends. My father had insisted Caerwen teach me of them, the only tribe to have landed on this island in all its history. We were so far from any other lands, they must have been truly desperate. But here, in the Midlands, they were real and living and a curse. These men were cruel and cold. No women lived among them. Every year they would raid a village and take the boys. The ones that still lived. Another generation of cruel, cold men.

And stories of my actions had inspired them. The three black riders must have been some of them.

Now what had I done?

"They have heard of this Night-Rider and will ride for the South. All the tribes under one leader. They will challenge him."

"Why?"

"Because, Nerys, that is what men do. These men live for

challenge. Their leader will challenge him," he lowered his voice until it was barely audible. "Challenge you."

"Their leader?" I chose to ignore his last words.

"Their leader, he is like no man I have ever seen. He is a beast among ants. He is violent, fearless, stronger than the rocks he was raised in and he is smart, smarter than any of them before him. He..." Gruffyd looked at me almost pityingly. Before I could ask him why, he carried on, sitting a little straighter. "He will not back down from a challenge. Nor has he lost one," Gruffyd warned me with raised eyebrows.

"He will travel with them?"

"Yes, but he will let his men clear the way first."

I made to speak yet the words choked in my throat.

"Shush child. These are still whispers. It will take them at least a season to reach the South, at least. That will be enough time."

He meant that would be enough time to prepare, if I went back to my father. To withdraw the people, fortify the towns, ready the men. But they shouldn't have to prepare.

This was my doing. My responsibility. I took a long draught of ale, more to ease my guilt than anything else, though I think Gruffyd believed I was scared. I would have to warn my father, and somehow, I also had to prepare. I would not be able to take on several tribes of cruel, violent men without... Without what? I had caused this by myself. I would end this by myself.

* * *

I left at dawn. Gruffyd had been concerned at my leaving. The autumn had been cold and winter was fast approaching. It was going to be a cold ride back. Gruffyd convinced me to delay two days but I could delay no more. I had to get back to the South. Fast. Midnight felt renewed beneath me, she would have to be. This ride would take everything from her, and me, for I did not intend to stop. Not much at least.

That night was dense with the dark except from the light of the new moon. The new moon. We had made it back in ten days but I was spent, as was Midnight. We took the whole next day to recover. And the next. My sleep was still broken. Echoes of the shaman's words whispered in my ears.

The wind was bitter. I pulled my cloak tight as Midnight and I rode east to west along the edge of the large, thinning forest just after noon. We were back in the South, on the northern boundary of my father's land. Although the wind masked most of the decay, it was still there, if you looked for it. We moved through the dry trees and I looked for it. No red or orange leaves on the forest floor. No moss on the trees. No woodland creatures still foraging food. No dew on the grass. It wasn't a living forest. Not really.

This was why I was doing it though. This was why I was following this darkened path. The shadow gods had gone too long without being heard and this was how they showed their distance, their anger. By slowly destroying the one thing we prized above all else. The land. Our land.

I got to the western edge of the forest, near the river and was slightly relieved. Now I could prepare. And I did.

I spent the days digging out the natural ditch the boundary sat on. Cutting wood, carving wood, sticking wood posts in to the ground. Sweating cold sweat constantly. But most importantly, sharpening my blades. I did what I could. Praying to the shadow gods became almost constant. I need them to be pleased with my actions and I prayed to the shadows, that they would guide me. I knew my preparations were good. Good enough? Against those men? I cursed the doubt I felt and pushed it aside.

Yes. I was good enough.

Spending the days alone was not good. Doubt seeped through me. Why did I keep doubting myself? I had never doubted myself before, not like this. It made my thoughts a constant blur, and it kept cropping up like a bad infection. I wanted this to start now, so I could end it. And this feeling. I needed the hunt. It would calm me.

I waited. I patrolled the northern boundary. West to east and east to west. Every day and every night. I tried to distract myself by using my left hand with my sword, just endlessly swinging, stabbing and hitting the same tree over and over. Midnight left me to my practice, I kept swinging until my left arm felt strong and capable, just as it should. I waited.

Finally. A week into my cold, drizzly patrol two scouts from the north arrived. Gruffyd's men. They were wrapped up in thick hides and cloaks, making their way to my father with news. The men of the North had started moving, all the tribes were making their way south. They could move swiftly but they were men. They would drink and raid their way south. They would be fast during the day and slow at night. That meant one new moon. More or less. I could wait. I would wait. The calm before the storm.

***

The night was cold, windless. I heard them before I saw them. A week under a new moon of expecting them had put me on edge, not that I was jumpy, just ready for the storm. I heard the trees creak, branches snap. Loud, deep-throated grunts and chants. I loathed them already.

As they got closer to the edge of the boundary forest, I heard five, maybe six, pairs of feet. Stomps on cold ground. Six men, a scouting group. Good, they were doing this for me.

The six men were hidden well against the woods, but not the night. I saw them run their way to the boundary ditch as I waited, out of sight behind one of the shrub covered posts I had raised. One more breath. I whistled Midnight to me. She came sprinting from the east, invisible in the night, straight at the men. They yelled at her shadow for she was too fast for them.

The nearest northerner to me still ran for the boundary. So, I darted for him. My blade was swift and clean, he didn't even have time to look into my eyes. I could feel the tingles in my blood that meant a pulse. Another soul down.

Midnight let out a wild neigh. Before I looked where she was I was sprinting to the sound of her. The sound of her neighs and deep grunts.

"Yaaa." I stabbed my sword down through cloak and hide and flesh. The man crumpled to the floor, he would no longer try to jump onto Midnight. A heavy hand pulled my shoulder round and almost landed a blow to my face. I dodged to my left and swung through his stomach. A dark pool of fluid leaked onto the ground. Midnight galloped off to the west and I followed her at a distance. My legs were throbbing and heavy.

I heard a scream, a heavy thud and Midnight's hooves stamp down through the night. Ha, she was something.

"You, Night-Rider."

Slowly, I turned where I stood to see the last man of the scouting group. He stood a whole head taller than me. I span my sword round in my hand. A quick throb sent a pulse through my blood and I closed my eyes to it.

"Gggrrr."

I opened my eyes and black shapes told me to dodge. I stepped right and ducked. The man came at me with a closed fist. I ducked again and he punched air. In one clean swing my sword sliced through his stomach. He babbled something as he tried to keep his guts in. My sword sliced him again and that was done.

I had one more thing to do that night, then it was back to the patrol. I didn't expect to see any other men. They would wait, wherever they were, until dawn, when their scouts would be expected to return. But they wouldn't return. Oh no. I would show them where their scouts had gone.

***

The sun rose on a new day. The light fresh and promising. I was ready, but not for what came next. Midnight grazed in the ditch and I was eating some stale bread next to the saddle, trying to think of anything I'd missed. Checking for damage made by animals or weather. The men wouldn't pass me because I was complacent. I hoped.

Then a rider came. From the South. From my father.

I stopped eating, I didn't recognise the rider, or the horse. It wasn't any of my father's guard, or court, or oath-bound men or women. I drew my sword from its sheath, making it flash in the cold sun.

Thirty feet away I saw the rider. He looked familiar but I couldn't place it. I gripped the hilt tighter, steadying myself with its' weight, watching him approach.

"Nerys." His voice was rough but calm. He slid off his horse easily, a long bow proud across his chest. Then I saw his face. Gruffyd, he looked like Gruffyd. I relaxed my sword as I placed him, he was one of the scouts who'd ridden down earlier.

"Nerys, I was sent by your father."

"And who has my father sent?"

"Ithel, son of Gruffyd." So, not just a messenger then.

"I wasn't aware Gruffyd had a son," I said shortly, looking Ithel up and down.

"Neither was I, but I have been his son all my life." He said the words calmly, with a slight bow of the head. I looked around at the dry land, trying to make sense of this.

"Why are you down here? Now?"

"I wished to help. It seems you need it."

I almost rolled my eyes, I didn't have time for this.

"What does my father send?"

He straightened up, looming over me even more. "This. Return to his land as one of the people, where he can protect you, or leave these lands with your birth right, but not here. He does not want you here."

"Why?" I asked, taking a step closer. "Am I too close to him, his people, his land?"

"No." Ithel spoke, but I heard my father in his word.

Ithel's expression changed. He exhaled, a mix of impatience and need. He took a few steps forwards and I could almost see scars on his chin and something filled his dark eyes.

"Nerys, these are people who care about you. Who don't want to see you hurt. Return to your father, he will forgive you."

"Forgive me? What have you-?" I broke myself off, hands balled into fists. Nope. I really didn't have time for this. "Thank you for passing on the message. Once you return mine your task is complete. Tell my father this. This is my doing, therefore my responsibility. I will return to him when my duty, *my* duty to *our* people, is fulfilled. Until then, I will not run from my choices, or their outcomes. So I will be here. *On my own.*" I didn't want him getting any ideas.

I stomped over to my saddle and shoved my sword in its sheath.

I heard him breathe, words trying to escape but catching in his throat. He climbed on his horse and left. I suddenly felt completely alone.

The day was long.

The sun had almost set before the woods started to move. I was expecting twenty, maybe thirty men to search for their unreturned scouts. That wasn't what I saw. Instead there came forty, maybe even fifty, thumping, bearded men from the forest in one, ragged clump.

They sounded like thunder. Great. I jumped on Midnight and headed as far west as I could get. Then I hid out of sight before they broke through the trees. Patience.

The first thunderous man to reach the boundary ditch halted to a stop just before it. Others soon joined him. Good. I watched them as they stood and stared. All of them, pale men built like boulders, with boots that looked far too heavy to run in. They stared at wood posts on the north side of the ditch. Nine in total. Nine wood posts with nine heads on top. That is where their scouts had gone. That is where their three riders' heads had gone. I had ridden back to the boundary town the first day Midnight and I had recovered from our ride. I knew it was a good idea to bury those heads.

As more men joined the group, it grew angry. I had added fuel to the fire. A deep breath filled my lungs. I had waited for this hunt long enough.

Slowly I urged Midnight forwards, towards the men that were boulders. I drew my sword, reflecting the dying sun against its blade. I was ready.

"Yaa," I charged Midnight between the men and the ditch. They only took a breath to realise the attack and arm themselves. As we ran through them, they spread out through the clearing, away from the ditch. I didn't want them crossing it yet. I felt all their eyes turn on me, angry eyes that felt sharp as blades. Now my hunt began. In one breath, Midnight galloped and I swung. They fell like flies. Buzzing, irritating flies.

I slashed my sword against a particularly large one and he fell to his knees, grabbing Midnight's knee. She neighed and kicked angrily, ears twitching wildly. I gripped my legs as tight as I could as my friend jolted forcefully underneath me. Before I could fully settle her, another one ran at my right, flint axe held high. He swung, I ducked, just as another came from behind, jumping at Midnight. She was still angry and bucked out quick. He fell.

I took the chance to look at them, the foul beasts. There were too many of them. They were being smart, annoyingly. Only a quarter of them attacked me at once, the rest hanging back to watch, wait. I cursed the damn shadow gods.

I gripped Midnight's sides as I pulled her back to the other side of the ditch. I jumped off her, grabbed a post and yanked it from the ground. Hurriedly I made a light.

"C'mon, c'mon," I was rushing my hands. They were shouting and running and screaming their lungs out. Then the shadows pulsed through me, calming my hands. The men became silence to me. I was focused, black shapes focused me.

As soon as that post was aflame I held it on the lower north side of the ditch. Fire. Glorious fire ran in both directions along the boundary. Light burned brightly against the coming night.

The flames distracted them for a time but then they regrouped to a raging crowd. I sensed all those eyes back on me and the men shoved at each other, trying to find a way to cross the fire. I showed them a way.

I mounted Midnight, walking her backwards. I stroked her soft coat, whispered to her, calmed her. This was going to be unnatural for her, and me. I knew we could do it, she had survived being underground, she would survive this. I rammed her sides hard and she charged into a run. A breath later we were jumping through the ditch of fire, right into the rampant crowd.

The surprise worked. More fell around me but there were still too many. At least the fire would stop them from crossing. For now.

Midnight was doing brilliantly. She kept kicking and stomping as I kept swinging. The men were falling, and although the shadows danced with me, they did not fall fast enough. I got caught between two beasts of men, both broad and heavy. They flanked both sides of Midnight as their fat hands tried to pull me from my saddle. They almost succeeded, when one pinned my arms to me but I wriggled fast and freed my right arm. My grip steadied on my hilt and I rammed the blade into the skull of the beast on my right. Before he stumbled too far I heaved out my sword from the bone and thrust it into the chest of the other one. He crumpled. The stumbling beast came back at me, blood gushing out his skull. He grabbed my leg and I growled at him, slicing my sword down, cutting through his flesh. Blood sprayed fast.

The remaining men, maybe 20, collectively roared. Hairs all over me stood on end. It was the loudest sound I had ever heard, my nerves were being tested. This was it.

I managed to lean out and grab an axe strewn in the grass before the men ran again, freshly charged from their roar. It was chaos. A mass of swords, arms, grunts and strains, shoves and thrusts and spurts of blood. I had no room for attacking. Short strokes, slashes were all I could manage. I wouldn't be able to hold them off for much longer. Not like this. I needed a plan.

I forced Midnight backwards. She hated it, stomping and pulling against me but I had no choice. I slashed and cut at the crowd as we edged back. The night had arrived now, the men were shadows in solid form. I was drawing them to the fire. I would use it to burn them.

Our progress was slow, tiresome, though I did not stop. Each time I spilt blood, I felt the shadows surge within me. They would not stop. The further backwards Midnight got, the more men swarmed around us. I was beyond angry, sweat dripped down my face and my throat was dry with blood.

"Aarr," I sliced down. This needed to end. Now.

I squeezed my legs into Midnight's sides again, urging her to buck harder than she had ever done before. Several men thumped down behind us, quickly clearing a path. Midnight swiftly trotted back, I continued to slash, barely able to keep hold of my sword. Then a wave of heat hit the back of my head. Men charged, surrounding us again. They moved in waves of knives and spears. A few fell into the fire, no thanks to their brothers. At least I could see them now, even if I was backed against the flames.

How long that battle continued I do not know. Burnt grass was all I could smell, and burnt hair. I cringed at the thought of Midnight's tail hair burning. She hadn't so much as breathed since we began. Salt dripped into my eyes, forcing me to blink constantly. My shirt was sticking to my skin, I was losing grip on my sword but I would not stop. I knew that much. Not until they all fell.

Then it flickered. The doubt, that stupid doubt, began to creep into my mind. I didn't know how much longer I could hold out, or Midnight. I prayed. I prayed to those damn shadows.

CHAPTER 6

A thwang passed my ear, the arrow fell its' prey. Another one flew, another man fell. I lost a breath searching for more arrows. I couldn't find where they were coming from. Then a flash of black made me cut down. I couldn't waste this chance. The distraction allowed Midnight and I to get away from the fire. It was small relief.

Arrows kept flying, with burning smoke trails now. I kept slashing, Midnight kept kicking. There had to be twelve men left. They were all still raging, goaded by the heads of their brothers. All still fighting and stomping. Good. I could do this.

Then a roar, a deep, thunderous roar sounded above the din. The men stopped and turned, completely ignoring me. I stopped and turned too, there was no point fighting an enemy who wasn't fighting me. Someone stood there, just visible before the trees. A large, forceful figure wrapped in grey fur. It had to be him. Their leader.

His roar echoed through the clearing. The men left. In one breathe they just ran to the trees, like children being called back by their father. All of a sudden, Midnight and I were alone. The fire blazed behind us.

I jumped down off Midnight, still throbbing with adrenaline and the pulses. What the gods had happened? Why had he called them back? I just stared at the trees, wondering. Did he not want them to fight?

I stood there, scanning for movement, pacing up and down. I would not be caught off-guard. Yet somehow, I think I had been.

My sword hung limp in my hand. The pulses were still coursing through me but I had nothing. My hunt was over before I had finished. I didn't know what to do, I just stood there. Empty on weak legs. Midnight nudged against me. I didn't know what to do.

A horse whinnied behind me and I snapped back to the present. I jumped around to see Ithel, his bow strapped quietly across his chest.

"I-" I didn't even know what to say.

"Later. They won't come back, not for a few days. That was just the first attack, the bored men. They'll be regrouping. You need to rest."

His voice was calming, firm but calm. He told me to get on Midnight and follow him. I did as he said. My head was getting heavy.

The light woke me up. The room was thinly wooded and small. The sun streamed through the only slit window. I got up and laid straight back down. My head span and pain seared across my arms and chest. I put my hand to my chest and realised I had been stripped to my undergarments. Bandages covered me, my wounds had been cleaned well. I didn't even know I had them. I was relieved to see two bandages still covered my forearms.

The door creaked open and Ithel's broad shoulders leaned in. He saw I was up and walked in, carrying bread and ale. I went to stand but the pain rushed to my head again. He crossed the small room swiftly and kneeled by the bed. In this light he did look like Gruffyd, but his face was smoother, less wearied.

A sudden sense of curiosity came through me. I wanted to know why. Why him. I made to speak but he beat me to it.

"Don't try, you'll open your wounds. Lay back down."

He slowly pushed me down until I laid flat. I tried again.

"Gruf-" I coughed. "Gruffyd sent you here?" I croaked out. My

THE SHADOWS ARE WAITING

throat felt like straw.

"Yes," was his response.

"Why did you come to the boundary, tonight?"

He looked at me with an intense stare that would not
have appeared on his father's face. He seemed to consider
something.

"Eat the bread, drink the ale, and I will answer your
questions." Just like his father. I could live with that. I nodded
my approval and he handed me small pieces of bread and
poured the ale in a cold clay cup. I drank it in one. My throat
was soothed and hunger burst within me. The bread was gone
as quickly as the ale. I swallowed my last mouthful hard and
burst into a coughing fit.

"It's fine, fine." Ithel rushed his hand to my back to soothe me.
I tried to pull away but that pulled on my chest. If it had been
anyone else, I would have protested. I had never felt so weak,
even without the shadows.

I didn't like being cared for like this. At all.

Slowly, I sat myself up. It was a struggle. Pain warmed across
me and I clenched my jaw against it, I didn't want to be treated
like a child, not by him.

"Midnight?"

"She's in the stables. Her tail is burnt, as are most of her back legs." He seemed to hesitate. "I've put on some salve, she should recover. She's one impressive horse."

"Yes, she is," I said proudly. Considering what the shadows were doing to me, I half hoped they were doing the same to her too. Making her stronger, tougher. I knew no other horse that would have survived half the things she had.

"What, where are we?" I suddenly asked.

"The hay village, I believe."

"The hay village? No… no."

"You blacked out, it was the closest place for you to rest."

"I can't be here."

"You have to rest, Nerys." Ithel said so calmly.

The hay village was two leagues into my father's lands. I should not be here. I could not be here. Although, I understood why he had brought me here, I did need rest. I didn't like this, I wanted to scream and punch, do something. Damn.

"Fine," came out of my mouth a bit harsher than I intended. I saw him start to turn towards the door so I blurted out, "Why do you carry the bow?"

It worked. He faced me and spoke slowly, as if remembering the reason for the first time.

"It is the most valued thing I own. It is a part of me. It is a constant reminder, for everything I am and everything I need to be. And everything I am not."

I wanted to say something but I had nothing to offer. He stayed and we both sat in silence, lost in thought. Eventually, I had to do something. I pushed myself over the bed, my bare feet hit the cold floor. I struggled to stand up and this time, Ithel helped.

"I need to get out there, back to the boundary."

I took one step as I spoke and my knees fell beneath me. Strong hands caught me and forced me back to the bed. Stupid shadows. Why couldn't they heal me quicker?

"No," he said firmly. "You need to rest. I have men out there." He was back to his firm, yet somewhat caring, self. "You've done enough."

My eyes darted to his face, seeing the last traces of an unreadable expression fade. Anger rumbled within me.

"What? What did you say?"

He repeated those last words, quietly. With none of the tone he had used moments before.

I stared at him, straight in the eyes. He held my gaze for a few breaths then walked out the room. I slumped back on the bed.

He was the son of Gruffyd, did he know? Did Ithel know I was the Night-Rider? How could he? Gruffyd would never tell anyone, especially not this reluctant son of his. I wanted to know but I would wait for that. I could wait for that. What I couldn't wait for was rest. If they would be coming back, I needed to be ready.

I found my clothes and ignored the bursts of pain as I put them on.

Out in the village I found Midnight and no one else. It was empty; the people must have been moved down to my father already. It was eerie being alone in what was usually a busy working village. I didn't mind though, I was used to being alone with Midnight and my thoughts. My resentful, wretched thoughts. For years I had hunted, we had hunted. For years my actions had no earthly consequences. Until now.

Now they did. That is why I had to get out there. This was my doing.

I stroked the recently cared-for coat of Midnight, seeing Ithel's work, before climbing on her. I didn't get far. Hot pain seared through me as I stretched my burn wounds. Pain was just pain. I could push past that, but I knew I shouldn't. The sense in me knew I needed to rest, Midnight turned her head to see me and breathed gently. Fine. Just one more day. Then I should be fully recovered. Guess Ithel would have his way after all.

I left Midnight in the stables and went back to my room. I sat on my bed and prayed. I prayed for strength. The shadow gods had already given me so much, I prayed it would be enough to get me through what was coming.

I watched the light fade to dark, plaiting my hair to pass the time. My jaw was aching, I didn't like to wait. My stomach kept whirling, waiting for adrenaline that never came. Tomorrow I would be back on the boundary. Tomorrow I would make a difference.

I didn't expect him back that night, I didn't even think about him, focused as I was on recovering for tomorrow. Then Ithel came back into the room. He was wearing a sleeveless brown shirt that showed firm, developed muscles, as well as many, various shaped scars along both arms. He was carrying a small wood tray with a cup and more food. The last person who had treated me like this was my mother. She would always bring me what I needed when I needed it, and I never knew I needed it until she came. Now, I needed food and water. My stomach rumbled in response.

Ithel passed me the cup and I accepted it quickly. I gave it back to him as he swapped me the bowl. He put the tray down on the small wood table next to the bed and watched me eat in silence. I put the empty bowl on my lap and breathed deeply, satisfied.

"Thank you."

He took the bowl from me and put it on the tray. Then he sat down next to me on the bed.

"My father told me to watch out for you, so I will."

"What else did Gruffyd say?" I might as well ask, seeing as he had brought it up.

"That you were the key. That I had to keep you safe." He said the words with a blankness that sounded as if he had repeated the order to himself often, and with an emotion that I couldn't place. Though I knew it wasn't towards me.

"Well, you don't need to worry, I can take care of myself." I tried to sound light but found myself getting irritated by his words. My hands were getting twitchy. I knew Gruffyd meant well but I didn't need a personal guard. I could finish this quest by myself.

"I think your burns would suggest otherwise."

I turned to face him fully. The way he had said that, I couldn't work out if he was trying to be funny or not. His face gave nothing away, just like Gruffyd's when he didn't want you knowing his thoughts. No idea. He was the child of a lord, just like me, yet I didn't see... well, I didn't know exactly. He just wasn't like me.

"I am glad of your help Ithel, I am, but there is no need for you to watch over me. I am already well cared for." I stood up slowly and walked to the door. "You can send Gruffyd my thanks, when you return to him."

I expected him to walk out in anger, annoyance at the least. Do something that showed some emotion. What he did annoyed me more. He just sat there, on the bed and said nothing. I did not have time for him.

He stayed all night. At first he didn't say anything, neither did I. Then the night came proper and he started to talk of the Midlands, to pass the time I guess. He spoke of his town, of the stories Gruffyd had told him of Gruffyd and my father as boys. His stories were entertaining and he used his voice well. I found myself laughing and lamenting over them unashamedly, surprising myself. No more than he had surprised me. His deep voice passed me into sleep and stayed with me there.

***

The morning came and I woke up alone. That didn't matter though, I was healed. I undid my bandages and breathed out in relief, my burns had gone. I stretched my arms wide, making sure no pain came. It didn't, thank the shadows. Good. I had rested long enough. It was time to get back to the boundary. I pushed myself out of bed and got dressed. No-one else would fight this fight for me. Not now, now that I had brought these men to our doorsteps. Not now that I had brought these beasts to the people I was supposed to protect.

Back at the stone boundary, my mind began to wander aimlessly. Shadows danced across my eyes, like a night-dream that clung to the day. They forced memories on me, my memories. They made me remember, the shadows made me remember what I wished to forget.

She sat behind the large oak tree for what felt like an eternity. The darkness was eerie. She was cold though she did not move. Part of her couldn't, she was stiff with sitting for hours and she was scared. She had never done this before. What if the worst happened? What if she couldn't kill them? What if she froze? Or if they killed her? She pushed those thoughts as deep into her mind as she could and took several deep breaths.

These men had killed two of her people. Her father's men had tried to find them but hadn't, they had stopped the search. She had found them. She had tracked them. She had tracked them to the eastern edge of her father's lands, to a small wood with a shallow brook. And there she waited for darkness. For them to put out their fire and rest for the night. This was it. She had to do it now. She had to do it.

She moved as quietly as she could to where they were laying, opposite sides of the dead fire and took out the small but sharp dagger from her belt. Just two stabs. Two stabs and this would be over and things would be right. She would be making things right. She said that to herself over and over. Over and over until she was standing in front of one of them. She could hear his breath, a slow in and out. It was much slower than hers. Her heart was racing and pounding in her chest. She panicked that the sound of it might wake him up. That her heart might thump out of her chest and it would be her on the floor. Before that thought took hold she rammed down.

Hard. A small grunt left her as she drove the blade into his chest. She thought she had done it. She thought he was dead, but hardly a breath passed and his eyes were wide and his hands gripped hers, trying to force the blade up. He had heard her, he had woken, just in time.

She screamed as she pushed harder. Shuffling feet told her the other man was awake but she couldn't look. His hands were so tight she thought her bones might break beneath them. His legs kicked wildly, trying to throw her off. She wanted to comply. She wanted to drop the dagger and run as fast as she could away from here. She wanted to be anywhere but here. But that wouldn't solve anything. That wouldn't make things right.

She mustered what little strength she had and put all her body weight into a final push. It went in. The sound was repulsive. She felt the other man grab her shoulder tight and hold something cold to her neck. She didn't need the restraint though. Just watching the life leave those wide eyes froze her where she stood.

Her breathing was still fast, and now it was heavy. She felt something warm pass through her, like a pulse, like her heart was throbbing all over her body. Then she noticed the cold at her neck had gone. Damn. The man pushed her forward and she fell over the body of her first kill. Her heart skipped a beat as she crawled away from it, repulsed even more. The forest floor was cold and dirty and her eyes began to tear. Thump. Suddenly her head rebounded hard on the ground, getting tiny specks of dirt in her eyes. The living man had kicked her to the floor, her mind was racing with panic. She had to do something. There was no way she could get out of this if she stayed on the ground.

She could barely see his figure through the dark but she heard the *crunch of the leaves and soil beneath his boots. And the wheeze in his breath. She flailed her arms around on the ground, searching for something big enough to grab. There. Whatever it was fit into her palm easily and before another thought crossed her mind, she sprang up and smashed it into where she hoped his skull was. Still holding it and without hesitating, she punched as hard as she could into the soft of his stomach and up into his jaw. He moaned from the pain and she knew she had to act fast. Adrenaline coursed through her, giving her the instinct. She took half a breath and kicked out, connecting with something that felt like his shoulder. The adrenaline, or panic, had made her alert. She heard the man stumble back a few paces and decided it was time.*

With everything else she had she ran and jumped. She jumped up and came down on top of him with a punch to the face with the stone.

They both fell to the ground. She didn't hear the wheeze any more, she didn't hear anything. Only her sobs as she kept punching. Her arms kept punching and punching, with less and less strength as her tears kept falling. Eventually, she pushed herself off the dead man and sat huddled on the cold ground. Tears tumbling. She was cold. Alone. The adrenaline left her and she felt that warmth again. It wasn't all over this time, just in one place. Her stomach. She reached a hand down and felt warm liquid. She was bleeding.

Then nothing.

My first hunt had haunted my dreams for years. Had haunted my soul for years too, as the shadows still did. Ithel's men were dotted between the boundary and the clearing. I had seen Ithel but rode straight past him. This was my fight.

Now, as I looked over at the boundary, the shadows were forcing images of the battle I had just had on my mind. The fire and the blood and the anger. I was twitchy. I jumped off Midnight and put both feet on solid ground. My head span. Damn shadows. The burnt grass smell didn't help. I braced my hands on my legs and breathed into the back of my ribs. Before long the shadows cleared, leaving me to make sense of their timing.

Midnight brushed up beside me then carried on doing whatever she was doing. I followed her and she led me back to the clearing. It dissatisfied me, like a bad taste in the mouth. It was the first hunt I hadn't finished in years. I would finish it nonetheless, no matter how long it took.

A horn blasted. A distant sound from the north, from the woods.

"Stand ready!" came Ithel's shout from behind me. I heard his men jump to alert, metal clashing and boots stomping into lines. They would wait here, on the boundary. They would wait for the movement to come to them. That would not do. I would not wait.

I mounted Midnight in one jump and made to the trees in a matter of breaths. I would find them, before they found us.

"Nerys!"

The yell almost stopped me. There was a passion in his voice I had not heard before. But that did not matter. He would be disappointed and that did not matter. Disappointing Ithel, who wasn't even from here, mattered not. All that mattered was that I protect my people. I had to keep them safe.

* * *

The woods were quiet. It was unsettling. I passed through the beeches and pines swiftly, using the path, losing it, finding it again, making my own one. I knew these woods. I knew where I wanted to go. Neirin, my father, hunted here every solstice, as a test from the shadow gods. Not that there was much left to hunt as the years had gone by. The whole court would go too and he had always insisted I go with him, since mother died. I was glad for it now. Moving through the trees I kept my eyes open, alert, any movement distracted me, but there was barely any. The only distraction was the dry, crunchy ground as Midnight moved quietly. I had to find these men. And I would do it from the west.

I led Midnight further west, into the densest part of the woods. After two days of patient hunting, I found what I needed. I slipped off Midnight as we came to a thin patch of beeches. All of this area had been theirs. The broken branches, piles of ash, rotten carcasses showed that. I slipped off Midnight when I saw it. Crouching next to the small, bony carcass of a faun, I had to turn away and cover my mouth. It was mangled, mutilated.

"Take these men as my offer, my shadow gods. Take these men and spare our land, our animals." Slowly, I closed the eyes of the dead faun as I prayed on my knees. These northerners had been here, then moved further north. Further north? The only reason to move north, to move away from the enemy, was for a water source or to join with others. That troubled me.

Another days' ride led me to a small stream. I was relieved I had reached it. My mind had been wondering the whole ride here, making me relive moments I did not want to remember, moments like my mother's death. Over and over.

I had spent so many nights with that day constantly forcing itself on me. I did not want to see it again, not now. Even though it fuelled me. I had to find those men. If they were the ones who had killed her, I would kill them. Simple.

I followed the stream east as it cut the woods in half. As I
continued in, I crossed the stream again and again, obscuring
Midnight's tracks. As I did, I looked at the woods, at the pines
and oaks and ashes. They no longer looked alive, it was as
if they were just there, forgot. There were hardly any birds
tweeting and flying from branch to branch, no rustling from
jumping squirrels or fighting foxes in the undergrowth. I kept
going.

Half a league further I found them, the outskirts of the
northerners' camp. Midnight stopped behind a large oak and
waited for me to slip off her. We sneaked quietly closer, using
the trees to hide us. Barely 10 feet from us were the boys
who looked after the horses, men sharpening blades, women
blacked out on the ground.

None of that surprised me, it's what I'd expect from a moving
mass of men. I gripped Midnight's mane when I saw it. The
not-so-small army that had cleared an entire area of the
woods. Trees were uprooted, fashioned into stools, benches,
pits, spears, shields. My stomach lurched and I gripped
Midnight's hair even tighter, I saw thick battering rams. I
buried my face into my friend's hair, she didn't move. The
northerners hadn't even got to the boundary and they had

already killed so much of our land. No.

I skirted around the edge of their camp, trying to see all I could. What I saw was grey cloak after black cloak after grey cloak. Swords, tents, numerous fires. There were just so many of them. That's probably why they had moved back north. To join with more of their brothers who had arrived. I cursed.

Dusk was approaching. I had watched the camp all this time, learning. Now I had to move. Night was thick in these woods. As it came, I felt my rage grow, my cravings for the pulses surge. Here, right before me, were the men who threatened the safety of my people. I could end them. Right now. I could finish my hunt. I could be satisfied. But if, *if*, I couldn't finish the hunt? If. Or I could ride back? I could ride back and warn Ithel. Warn my father.

I stamped as I cursed the shadow gods. Why did I have to think like my father now, when I was so close? And why did I have to doubt myself? *Again?* The shadow gods wouldn't let me die, not when I was helping them get back to their people. Still, I had the nagging feeling that I should warn someone. Even if killing all these vile men would bring me closer to the end of my path, what was the point in saving my people later, if I couldn't save them now?

I slept for a few hours under a small, withered box. I didn't know whether to be glad that I didn't have to share my sleep with any small animals or not. Then we rode south. Midnight and I were barely visible against the black trees. At this pace, we would be back by tomorrow's dusk. It was always quicker when I knew the way. Then thwang, a blade flew passed me, stabbing a tree as I rode passed. And another. One came from my right and found its home in my shoulder. I gritted my teeth against the hot, sharp pain and kept riding.

They came from behind, from my left and right. I could barely make out the riders, covered in black hoods and hides but I could see the horses. One quick glance and I counted seven. Seven. Seven riders with daggers and blades and other things they were throwing at me. I had nothing. One sword which I would not be parting with. Damn those farm boys.

I urged Midnight on, faster and faster, zig-zagging through the trees. My only hope was to outrun them, to use my knowledge of the forest. I could also try to have a little fun along the way.

I ducked just as something sharp skimmed my ear. The riders were closing in. My heart was beating fast. The adrenaline was pumping, as were my cravings. Midnight had more in her but I would not use that, not yet. She was fast, we were outrunning them but they kept close behind. Branches and leaves skimmed over me, as did sharp, pointy things. One rider sped up, coming at my left. He held out a spear, drew it back and forward, back and forward, building up for its' release. I wasn't about to be speared. He brought back his spear and I tugged out the blade in my shoulder. I threw it straight, it hit him between the eyes. One down.

Before I could indulge in the pulse, or feel any relief, the padding of hooves on the forest floor got louder. Two riders tried to force me to the right. I wasn't going to let that happen. The pulse filled me up, warm and strong. I squeezed my legs and Midnight halted to a stop. I pulled her to the left and we picked up speed, heading south-east. A spear head twanged in a tree just as I passed. They were serious. Well, so was I.

I circled Midnight tight around a tree, drawing my sword. Two quick slashes, two more down. A blast of pain. Another blade landed in my shoulder, near the bone. I pulled it out instantly and threw it back. It missed. No matter, the shadows weren't with me yet.

The remaining riders drew back, using the trees as cover. I grabbed the nearest blade out of a tree and headed straight for them. I heard them come at me before I saw them, horses hooves and quick breathing. They rode in one line, dodging the trees. Now they were making it easy for me, they were all in one place. The middle rider was my target. The blade left my hand and found its' mark.

But as the rider fell, so did I. A sharp prick in the neck caught me off guard. I saw the world turn on its side and go dark.

CHAPTER 7

My feet were heavy, armpits were sore. I tried to open my eyes but the lids wouldn't move, they just flickered. Even with my eyes shut, my head was spinning. I had to go back to the last thing I remembered, the chase, riding towards them, then black. I tried to think more but my mind wouldn't work quick enough.

I fell down on the floor, hitting my chin. Shouts and yells erupted from all around. My eyes opened then. The scene around me was, there was no other word for it, terrifying. Fires flickered against the dark. I had not felt fear in a long time but I felt it then. I was there, in the camp of the northern men. I was in their camp, alone and unarmed. I patted the ground around me, where was it? Damn. Where was my sword?

I felt a boot connect with my face. I fell back to the ground, eyes streaming. I needed to get out of this. I needed to get to my father.

The shouts and taunts continued. Dirt and spit landed all around me. I didn't care. I scanned the crowd, looking for something, anything, I could use.

Then he came, like a fire through the fog. The figure from the woods. Their leader. He stood in front of them, silent and still. The air around him seemed to bend. His eyes found mine and I tried to stare back, forcing my eye lids to open. I would not break eye contact.

He walked forwards, each step slow, purposeful, heavy. He was fearsome. Truly.

As he got closer I saw scars all over his face, some were thin and long. Some small and raised. Then I saw his eyes. One was blue and one was green, a mark of the shadow gods. But why would they mark him? Why would the shadow gods mark a man who wasn't from the South? These Northerners didn't follow our gods, or any gods. He stopped and crouched down so that his face was in front of mine. His hot breath blew on my skin. Shivers ran over me but I would not break eye contact. Suddenly he roared. The same deep, thunderous roar I had heard before. My hands flew up to cover my face. I'd broken eye contact.

The sound of the men's laughter was harsh. I turned back, cursing. Showing weakness, fear, in front of these men would get me nowhere. And that wasn't where I wanted to be.

I pushed myself up to standing, barely reaching their leader's elbow. I stood my slight frame as tall as I could and regained eye contact. We stood like that, staring at each other, for longer than I wanted to count. My palms were clammy. Then suddenly he turned on the spot and went to one of the men at the front.

My sword. I saw it glint against the flames as the leader took it from his man. They had my sword. He drew it from the sheath slowly, deliberately. Taunting me. His eyes flashed at me, then the sword and back to me. I held my breath as he held my sword above his head in two hands and brought it down, strong, on his skull. Instantly, a rage built within me. The blade snapped clean in two. As did part of me.

"No," I screamed and tried to run at him when massive hands pulled me backwards, forcing me to the floor. His laughter resonated through me. I felt hollow. I wanted those pulses to surge through me then. I hungered for the shadows to take over me, to send this beast to his hell. Cold laughter filled the camp as he showed his army the pieces of my broken sword. Pieces of me. I kept my face blank even though I was seething inside. They would not know how much this was hurting me. Not until I ended them.

The jeering crowd went immediately silent as he chucked my shattered sword on the forest floor. He turned to me with a cold face. When he spoke his words were as rough as his voice, yet oddly grand.

"Y'ere scouting us, my men saw. Y'rode well through trees. You know this forest?"

I didn't want to answer him. I only wanted the pulses, their warmth. To know I would send him to the shadows. I didn't want to give him anything. But if I answered him, if I gave him something, the more he would give me.

"I know this forest."

"You know these parts?" Each word he said slowly, musing over the sounds.

"I know these parts."

"You know one we seek, this Night-Rider?" He said the name with evident contempt. Even though I knew it was coming, I was still surprised to hear him say the name. My name.

"I've heard the stories."

"We use you. You bring 'im to us and then we will see. Then we will see 'ow fierce 'e is."

The crowd roared instantly. How I wish I had my sword then.

Talking over the sound was useless. I waited until they calmed down. Which took a while.

"I do not know him. Only the stories. I cannot bring him to you." I emphasised each word clearly. His reaction was quick. He was before me in a blink.

"You bring 'im to me. You will. Or I kill you, you and everyone I see. Everyone. Got it, my little leaf?" His large, coarse hand grabbed my neck, pulling my face to his. His hot breath tickled my skin as he moved his vile mouth over my face. All over it. Bile rose to my mouth. I wanted to end his life quickly, but also very, very slowly.

He pushed me back, laughed and spat on the ground. I had to get out of this.

"I have, I have heard the stories say he always rides a black horse. Blacker than the darkest night." I was fishing but I needed to know where Midnight was. She was my only hope of escape.

"A black 'orse?" He beckoned a man over to him and whispered. I strained to hear him.

"She rode a black 'orse, no?"

"Yes," followed by a grunt.

"You let it get away, yes?"

"Yes," followed by the same grunt. I guess it was their sound for lord, or something.

"We could have used the 'orse, no?"

"Yes." Grunt.

"Yes." He turned away slightly, as if disappointed with the man. Then he spun round and rammed his fist into his man's throat. A breath later he pulled out a tongue. Blood poured to the ground. The man crumpled, lying in his own blood. I'd never seen a man do that before.

My hope was gone.

The colourful eyes found mine, their steely gaze were hard and a little... pleased. A small smile broke across his face as he gave out a grunt and the camp dispersed. Another grunt and four grey cloaks rallied to him. A quick nod and they were off. Then he was staring back at me.

My chest heaved with a breath. He ran a large, rough hand, not the bloody one, through my unkempt hair. My teeth ground together as I kept still. His thick accent was even harder to understand as he lowered his voice.

"My men, mmm," he held my hair up to his nose and sniffed, "will enjoy you." His eyes looked up and down my worn and frayed leather trousers and shirt. "I will enjoy you." That did it.

I spat at his feet. He slapped me across the face so hard, so fast, I recoiled back. I held my stinging cheek as I growled through bared teeth. He I loathed.

The four men came back with wood and nails. Rough ropes tied my hands behind me before I could object and shoved me to the ground. Like I was going to run anyway.

They worked quickly. One look at it and the tiniest shred of hope I had left abandoned me. A cage. Before the sun was up I was dragged and closed inside it. Brilliant.

I sat there, in that cage, knees cramped, stomach growling, watching, waiting. Days passed. Long, annoying days which only made me irritable, frustrated. Why had I got caught? If I was only that much faster. It was foolish, I knew, to torment myself with ifs and buts. But I had got myself here, in this damned cage, I would remember why.

* * *

A grunt woke me up. I was stiff and cold and so not in the mood. Swallowing just made me choke on my own tongue. I felt as dead as the land. They had given me water but I hadn't touched a drop. Not since the first day. Not since I saw what they did in it. The sun light was struggling to get through the trees. And there they were, three of them. Watching me. Grinning. One of them made a gesture to me that, if I was out of this cage, I would rip his head off for. I turned my back to them, seething. Vile beasts.

I watched their camp during the day. Most of these cloaked men just fought with each other. The sound was piercing, although, after the fourth day, I'd got used to it. And not just playful sparring, actual first-to-severely-injure-the-other type of fighting. The amount of blood I saw drip to the forest floor was beyond me. I couldn't understand how one of them had survived to manhood, let alone this many.

I sensed his arrival before I saw him. Mainly because my three jeering guards finally left me in silence. His hands held a cup of water and a plate of charcoaled meat and dry cheese. I was ready to refuse it, to knock it out of his hands when he pulled back.

"You 'ave not eaten. I know this. I prepare this myself, they 'ave not touched it." He pulled the cup and plate closer to him as he spoke, his eyes somewhat clear. Despite myself, I believed him. A small nod from me was all the leader was waiting for. He, rather gently, put them down through the bars.

"You, your name. What is it?"

I was surprised by his question; at the apparent genuineness with which he had asked it. Do I tell him my name, and give him some kind of power over me? But then letting him talk more might help me get some information. I hadn't decided before my tongue spoke for me.

"Nerys."

"Nerys." My name sounded harsh with his accent. He said it a few more times, rolling out the r.

"Yours?"

"Mine, mine is Gwrtheryn. I am leader of all." I knew what it meant, he wasn't far off. To be given a name like that, 'supreme king', I wondered if he was born to it or changed it. So I asked.

"Did your father know you were going to be the leader?"

"Ha, silly girl. No father knows. I took my name. I earn this name. I killed ev'ryone else who wanted it. I am Gwrtheryn." He clenched both his hands and pounded the earth. I kept quiet, thinking I'd asked enough questions for now. He relaxed his hands and watched me eat the last of the meal. He had surprised me. I hadn't heard many of the other Northerners talk but compared to them, it was like speaking to a Southerner. When had he learnt our language?

"You brave one, aren't you? For riding alone," he began. "Brave and stupid. They will not find you. But we find this Night-Rider. You will break." He turned his face to me and spoke gently, caressing each word. He was enjoying this. "I will break you. You will let me." His voice was rough but powerful. I could have believed him, he said the words with such assurance, anyone else would have believed him. But I didn't. Shadows flashed through my mind, making me smile. He wouldn't break me, for in me was the shadows and he couldn't break them.

He continued to speak when I didn't.

"You will break and I win. Yes, I will win. I will find this one who calls himself Night-Rider and I will win. I will crush him," he showed me with his callused hands how he would crush me. "I will crush him in front of many. He is challenge. I like challenge."

I had listened to his speech calmly. I was doing so well, but the urge to put him in his place took over. I made to speak then bit my cheeks at the last moment. He laughed as he watched.

"Ha, your master still holds your tongue. Soon it will be mine. You will answer me."

"Why would you do it?" My voice caught him off guard,

only for a blink. I barely even saw his eyebrows move up his forehead.

"What?"

"Why would you travel all this way to, to what? Fight one man?"

"You. You not understand." In less than a blink he was on the cage, arms around the bars, eyes wide with hunger.

"Survive. We all must survive. Strength. Strength lets us survive. I am strength. This Night-Rider will make me stronger. I will drink from his skull and I will be strength." He breathed deeply, as if filling himself with some memory or power. "I kill him, it will make me stronger."

I leant back to get away from his penetrating gaze. He believed in himself beyond anything I had known. Then something struck me, 'master'. Master? He must think I was a scout, that I was sent here on the word of my master. I could use that.

After a moment of silence, he peeled himself off the cage and stood to his full, imposing height.

"Keep watching. You'll be in that cage a long time. And I will break you. I will break you like a leaf."

I did as he said that day. I sat in my little cage and watched. Watched them prepare. Despite the constant fights, the blood and the brutality of it all, this camp was ready. They were ready for battle. Not just their leader, all of them. Even the skinny boys who looked after the few horses they had. Even they could wield a sword with force. I saw order, structure and, whether I was surprised by it or not, discipline. Even from the different tribes, the ones with painted skin, or the ones with bones strung through their hair, they all seemed to follow Gwrtheryn. It troubled me. I knew we wouldn't be like this. There hadn't been a battle in the South in years. I knew my father's men weren't ready for this.

What I wasn't ready for was the ritual that seemed to start around me. Before the dusk came, the men gathered in the cleared camp. Stomps and thuds and wood shields beat in an intimidating rhythm. Something was happening.

The leader of all the tribes stood his imposing figure firm in the middle of them all, hungry with all their attention. For once, I was glad to be in the cage. Then emerged a group of men, I counted quickly, nine men. My head started to work. Nine men walked behind their leader and each held up something circular. A cold chill ran down my back as I pressed myself against the front of the cage. Curiosity got the better of me.

The sound that came out of their throats shuddered the trees, these men chanted something more beastlike than human. Another group of men moved to their leader, carrying a large mass tied to a pole. A new wave of sound followed them. My breath caught in my lungs as I saw the dead deer. Deer were beautiful creatures whose numbers had been decreasing and these men had slaughtered one for nothing other than ritual sport. My hands gripped my bars tighter and tighter.

I watched, transfixed, as Gwrtheryn slit the deer open and caught the blood and guts in the circular objects. It was then my stomach lurched with realisation, and bile. They were drinking from their brothers. The nine Northern men whose heads I had stuck on poles. Nine. They had skinned their own men and sliced their heads in half, to use as bowls. And now they drunk deer blood and guts from them.

I didn't move as the bowls were passed around, the chanting dying down as those that had drunk waited for the rest to. My hands began to shake from holding my wooden bars so tight. Once all had drunk and more deer had been slit before me, the forest quivered with their cries. With their war cries. I wasn't ashamed when I huddled into a corner of my cage and covered my ears. They were beasts.

As dark approached I felt it breathe within me, the darkness. I sat on the cold forest floor with numb limbs and a scratchy throat. I hadn't dared move since I witnessed the ritual. The men seemed to be more curious about my cage than they had been before. But I had done this. I had got myself in this cage. I would have to get myself out of it. I would have to get back... What about Ithel, and his men? What were they doing? I growled as I shoved that thought aside. Who cared about them right now?

I guess there was small relief that no one had come for me, at least they were clever in that.

The night sky closed in around me. The air grew cold and the trees still. If only I could keep my mind still. Then maybe my soul wouldn't feel as dark as this night.

Fire started coming to life around the camp. I wanted to feel their warmth on my face, to smell the smoke in my lungs. I had been through worse than this, sort of. I had survived. Survival was strength, apparently. Although I didn't feel very strong right now.

As the camp slowed down for the night, I prayed again. To the shadow gods and the shadows. I needed them, as they needed me. I did a lot of praying, to clear my mind and my soul. That the shadow gods would send down my ancestors, would send down the shadows to hide me. So that I might fade into darkness itself. I prayed that my father would search

Midnight's saddle pack and that he would find it, find me. And I prayed that when the time was right, I would end them all.

That night my prayers were answered. One of them at least.

The night was black, dark, bleak.

* * *

The shadows made me do it. As soon as the night had fallen proper, they stirred within me. The cage took a little time to get out of, my northern beasts had fastened it tight. Thankfully, however, they were distracted. A big, ale-induced fight had broken out and my so-called guards were busy rewarding themselves with more ale and tired women. Most of them, the women, slaves, I saw the ropes, were already blacked out from too much ale. I slipped passed easily. The camp was half awake with men sleeping and half drinking. Moving into the night was easy, despite my heavy, aching limbs. I crouched behind a thin beech, checking I wasn't noticed. A small sigh escaped me, I wasn't.

Now I had to get out of the woods. On foot. With no energy.

I travelled as swiftly as I could with a blurry vision, stumbling every few steps. I felt hunger ravish my stomach but food wasn't what I needed. Not then. The shadows led me, the land led me. That was my food, for now. I would not have long before Gwrtheryn noticed I had gone. Or sent men to find me, and they would definitely find me. But I didn't need long, just long enough.

Moving through this wood gave me life, this was what I knew. The moving through the trees, the stealth, the dark. It gave me peace like I hadn't felt in a long time.

The dark night began to fade as the light took over. I stumbled low and almost knocked myself out on a fallen branch. Gwrtheryn would know I had gone now, my time was running out. I pushed myself up and rushed on. It didn't matter if he knew, I was deep in the woods, my woods. I just had to make it another, much faster day, and I would be out, back in my father's lands.

I broke through the clearing just before dusk. My muscles complained with every step and my eyes were barely seeing straight. I thanked the gods for the shadows then, for them invading my mind and forcing me on with every breath. As soon as I left the woods, my muscles ceased.

Those weren't my father's men. All along the boundary I saw strange new men and the occasional woman, with strange weapons. Men and women in thick leather and hides with thin swords and flint daggers and saxes. My eyes widened, they began to move, forming ranks.

Then movement caught my eye. Ithel. He was moving through the new men, towards me. I exhaled deeply, they were his men, Gruffyd's men. He had sent help. My hands went to my stomach as it was whirling, how the gods had they got here? I didn't think for long. Ithel got to the front of his men and stopped. Our gaze met. My stomach loosened all the tension it was holding. He started jogging into the clearing, long bow still over his shoulder.

Suddenly something got me from the side.

Instinctively I made to block, but was too slow. Dilwyn had grabbed my hand and pulled me into a hard hug, despite how I must have looked and smelled. I tensed, surprised by the contact. As he let me go I managed a smile. It was good to see him; he was family after all.

"You shouldn't do that, Nerys. It isn't just your father who worries about you, you know?" he said nudging me.

"I'm glad to see you, Dilwyn," were the hardest words I had ever said.

"It's been a long year and you... er you look skinny, Nerys. You know there is this thing called food."

My cousin's joke went right over my head. "Year?" Damn. Had I really been gone that long? I scanned the people around me, legs starting to weaken. Dilwyn nodded as I still scanned the camp of Southern men lined along the boundary.

"Much has changed," I said aloud as my thoughts ran wild.

"Yes, but first…"

Dilwyn practically pulled me straight over the boundary, my legs resisted at every step but he did not slow. The men I passed stared, I could feel the quiet, the horror. I made my steps as strong as I could, yet I was hungry and thirsty and cold. It took all my strength not to let that show though. Not in front of my father's men. They knew me as his heir, well, those that weren't at the town that day did. I was a somewhat reluctant, wayward heir to them, not something frail and ready-to-collapse.

Dilwyn's shouts for some maids rang through my ears, they appeared from nowhere and obediently sprang to work. It was the quickest wash, change and hair brush I have ever had. I heard them mutter something like 'she's just bones' but my mind was wandering. The maids pushed me out the tent, not indelicately, and straight into Dilwyn's arms. He took my hand and was off again. My teeth started to chatter and I could feel the warmth of Dilwyn's hands against my cold hand.

I let out a deep sigh as he kept walking. I knew what was

coming but I was not prepared for it. All my mind was thinking of was food, I'm sure Dilwyn must have heard my growling stomach but we both just kept walking. Amidst all the people and horses, tents, dogs, fires, there was one thing that caught my eye. A circle of seven men, sat on thick logs. Compared to the bustle and noise of the camp around them, they almost looked serene. I, however, knew they were anything but.

As I approached the court, my heart thumped, remembering the last time I had been at court. Things had definitely changed. I stood up a little straighter as we got closer.

The court rose as I joined it, I felt the gesture sincerely. Court didn't rise until its' sitting was agreed upon. I made an effort to look each member in the eyes before taking a log next to Dilwyn. He was casting me curious looks every few breaths.

I heard fragments of the conversation around me, deep voices. Nothing really sunk in, my eyes were stinging and I just wanted food and sleep. Plus, the camp made me edgy, like the one I had just come from. I made a point of focusing on each of the court as they sat before me, like I used to, to get my attention back to the present.

Cledwyn was speaking, rattling off some story of a previous, unrelated battle and Trahaern was trying to add in but to no avail. Merfyn caught my eye and gave me a sad smile. I returned in kind, not thinking anything by it. He was a fighter who hated fighting. A long-haired dog padded between the logs and sat next to Bleddyn, who didn't even look down as he started stroking it.

Next to his son was Dai, the lines around his eyes were tighter than the last time I had seen him. He didn't look at me.

Next I turned to Steffan, eyes strong and intense. He was looking down at the short, dry grass, listening. Then Siorus, light, warm Siorus. He gave me a genuine smile that put me at ease. A small grin pulled my cheeks.

Dilwyn's voice brought me back to the conversation.

"We can't prepare against an enemy we know nothing about. Your old stories won't help us now. We need to know who they are and why there here."

"Here."

"The *stories* tell us all we need to know. History is our *ally*. The Northern men will not leave their lands when they still have land to roam up there. These are different men," said Cledwyn directly to Dilwyn.

"From where?" Dilwyn questioned strongly.

"You should not disregard our history, boy," came Traeharn's voice.

"They are here, all we need to do now is prepare," offered Bleddyn, "we can answer these questions once they are dead."

"Yes."

"No. We need to know the enemy, only then can we prepare against them," Stefan added, fists clenched.

"Yes, but it's too late for that. They're here, they're right here. Tell them, Nerys."

Damn. I wasn't ready for this, I looked at my knees, trying to keep my jaw from tensing. Dilwyn coughed, I just gave him a small nod in response. He sighed and continued.

"We need to act now. They are here now and we need to be as strong as we can be."

"I agree," said Siorus.

"We need to send out scouts, find their location, motives and fight. That is all," Dilwyn said, arms tense. He'd stopped giving me worrying glances.

The court was getting closer and closer to it; to the reason these men were here. Soon. Soon I would have to talk. My shoulder. I span in my seat to see Ithel behind me, a hand on my shoulder, then I remembered the daggers and felt my shoulder. It wasn't pretty, some skin was flapping off, most of the wound had scabbed over, but I hadn't cleaned it so it was bumpy and brown. Ithel gave me a small nod, as if making a mental note. His face was soft but the lines across it told me otherwise. He was worried. He handed me a bowl of thin but warm stew and I accepted it quickly. My stomach was past growling.

I ate in silence, aware that Ithel was still standing there, watching me and my shoulder. I didn't know whether to be touched or irritated. I smiled at him once I had finished, to let him know I was thankful at least. He didn't meet my eyes, they were fixed behind me, rather, on who was behind me. I looked over my other shoulder to see Dilwyn's eyes locked with Ithel's. Something must have passed between them, whatever it was, it was not good. I looked back round to Ithel and his face was severe. I was about to say something when Dilwyn touched my arm, bringing my attention back to him. I saw his mouth open but nothing came out. Dai had spoken.

"Nerys, it is time."

I guess it was. There was no going back after this. I glanced over my shoulder briefly but he wasn't there. I took a deep breath. The court were passionate, strong, experienced and they had no idea. They had no idea who they were up against or why they were here. Well, I wouldn't tell them that, not yet.

"I have seen them," I started, keeping my voice as steady as possible, "these men. I have been in their camp, spoken to their leader. These are the men of the rocks, the men from the North and they are here, in our woods."

The din around the court had not stopped, but the silence caught in the air of the circle was thick.

"They have left their lands, not for women or boredom, but for sport. They are here for the challenge." Each word was a struggle to say as I half-confessed a truth no one knew, and also because my throat felt like sawdust. "For the glory. They leave their lands for the glory of the challenge."

"What challenge? What challenge do we bring them?" asked Trahearn.

I filled my lungs with air.

"They have heard of the one who has been hunting these parts, the one some call Night-Rider, Village-Burner, Shadow-Hunter. They are here because of him."

"Then he has condemned us all." Trahearn was right. I had. I had condemned them all. The court knew of the one I spoke of. My father had sent them all out at some point over the years to find him. They knew the towns I had wasted, people I had killed, children made orphans. They knew of the pain the South had felt, still felt. But they didn't know why I had to do it, why I had to send those souls to the shadows.

"Yes. He has brought them here. And now we have to fight to send them back. Bleddyn's right, we need to prepare. We need to act," I said, as calmly as I could.

The silence began anew. Doubt began to grow in my mind. Was this right? Was telling them that the Northern men were here for one man, whom they all despised, the best thing to do? Gods above, I didn't know. The doubt kept growing as the silence lingered, I could feel my teeth grinding against each other. What was I doing?

"Then so be it." I was surprised at Dai's voice. He rarely sought violence as a solution. But the calm was over, the peace gone. Now we all had to fight.

Trahearn stood and gave orders, sending each court member off to their given task. I sat on the log a moment longer before Dilwyn took my arm again. He led me swiftly across the camp, again, I knew what was coming. With a quick stop at the mess tent for more food and drink for me, I began to dread the destination.

I cursed aloud. I had been so caught up in myself, I'd

completely forgot to ask.

"Midnight?"

"Fine." I breathed in relief. "She found her way back, Haul's been taking care of her until you returned," answered Dilwyn, a slight twist at his mouth. I relaxed slightly at his side as he still led my arm. Then he stopped me outside a large, circular tent, near the eastern edge of the camp.

"Things may be a bit different now, Nerys. Know that this doesn't change us." He squeezed my arm, gave me a quick nod, inhaled as he looked at the tent and left. I just stood where I was, looking after my cousin. What had happened?

It had been one whole year since I had seen my father. He looked much the same, thinner and greyer, but the same. He stopped looking at his papers as I entered. The lord of the South wore a black shirt that used to fit him well, now it hung from his shoulders. His overcoat swamped his thin inner one. Perhaps I had been foolish, foolish to think my father wouldn't be bothered by my absence, even though he was the one to enforce it. His face went blank, a chill ran down my neck and I felt like a child all over again.

Neither of us spoke. A quietness built up between us, to a point I could no longer stand.

"Father," I said, bowing my head.

I didn't know what he would do, or how he would react. I stood on the spot, not daring to move. For a while, that's where we both stood, exactly where we were. Under my father's gaze, I felt the blood rush to my face. He just didn't do anything. My hands curled into fists, this was a waste of time. He hadn't seen me in a year and still he couldn't, *wouldn't*, talk to me. My sigh was loud. If he didn't want to talk, that was fine. I wouldn't force him. I made to leave, I couldn't endure this anymore.

"Nerys," he whispered. I almost didn't catch it. Slowly I turned back to him and saw him pull out something from his inner coat. He placed it on the small desk in front of him, water filling his eyes. It was a dry, dark flower. The petals were deep brown; the pollen stalks a stark white. It was the rarest flower in the South, it had taken me hours to find. It was also my mother's favourite. It was the flower I had got to placate my father a whole year ago. Only then did I notice my chest was tight with not breathing. My father and lord stepped around the desk, as if to come to me, then stopped. I watched as he glanced back to the flower. His eyes found mine and my anger disappeared. I had to get out of the tent. The air began to stifle and tears threatened to leave my eyes.

Back outside noise hit me from all around. I was back in the world, back to the fight.

* * *

My eyes had to adjust to the newly lit fires. The camp of my father's oath-sworn was alive against the night. Barking dogs, clashing metal, sizzling pots. They were welcome sounds, since it meant they were at least trying to get ready. The smells were welcome too. Smoke filled my senses. Out of all the things I knew, wood smoke, the smell of burning, was one of my favourite things. It made me feel warm and calm and full of new life. But it wouldn't make me feel calm tonight.

Nothing would, except maybe one thing.

Walking back through the camp, my legs were still heavy and I was trying my best to ignore the aches. All through this camp, I saw faces I knew, people from my town, the guard, the farmers, the smiths, some healers. And also others. Men from the surrounding lands had come, men who still followed my father as their oath-sworn lord. Their numbers were large, a relief but still, they weren't enough, not against the beasts they would face.

The makeshift stables lined the western side of the camp. Horses and stable hands went about their business with a quiet urgency. I breathed in and felt instantly better, here felt like the only place that matched how I was feeling. They knew an attack was coming, they just didn't know when.

As soon as I walked into the largest stable, I saw her. Her black coat was smooth and shiny; I knew he would take good care of her better than the rest. He had a soft spot for her too. I ran to Midnight and buried my face in her mane. She whinnied in response and trotted round me excitedly. I felt the same.

"Nerys."

Before I knew what I was doing, I had run over to Haul and hugged him hard. My arms barely reached round him. He kept me there for a while.

"You foolish child," he said as he pushed me back, still holding my shoulders, "you could have got yourself killed. God's above, you had died."

I stared down at my feet, feeling strange. What was I doing to these people?

He hugged me again then turned to Midnight.

"You're lucky you trained Midnight so well. Ha, *I* trained Midnight so well," he corrected. "She's a battle horse through and through." I managed to let out a small chuckle, then picked up a brush and combed Midnight's mane.

"Why must you keep seeking... whatever it is you do?"

I don't know why I was surprised by his question, his tone hadn't changed, or his focus, but something just felt off.

"Haul?" He didn't reply. "You will not know what I do, only that I must do it." I took a step closer to him, to look at his face. His eyes kept darting all over Midnight and his hands, they weren't steady as they usually were. "You told me, a year ago, that you didn't want to know. Why now?" I asked him gently. If something was wrong, I wanted to help.

"Nothing, nothing," he said, but I wasn't convinced. He was one of my truest friends, I knew something was wrong.

"Try again."

He seemed to think for a while, emotions crossing his face before he spoke.

"It isn't easy, when you go off and... do the shadows know what. It's well for you but you leave the rest of us behind." His eyes started to fill with tears. In all the years I had known him, I had never seen him cry, the rare times he did was when he had ash in his eyes.

"Neirin, your father, gave me my life back when my family died. He gave me this job, a home. You're my family now, both of you. I don't want to bury another one."

I squeezed his hand for a while, feeling his pain. I really didn't ever think of the people I left when I hunted. My throat started to tighten so I carried on brushing Midnight, she stood taller with all the attention.

"And then…"

"And?" I stopped brushing my horse and turned to Haul.

"Well," he looked at me with sad eyes. "Your father, he was angry still."

"Haul, tell me." My fingers and toes were slowly starting to tingle.

"Just before we travelled here, not even a week ago. Your father… he-"

"Haul."

"Your father no longer calls you heir. He said those in line, so you or Dilwyn, would have to prove to the court…"

Whatever else Haul was saying I didn't hear. I was no longer heir, the actual heir. I leaned back on Midnight and started brushing her again, though I could barely hold the straw.

Leaving the stables was hard. At some point I snapped out of my trance and had taken my time feeding Midnight. Brushing her mane, her coat, her tail, making a fuss over her. She was safe in there. I was safe in there. Even so, I knew the safety wouldn't last.

Almost as soon as I left the stables, I found Dilwyn. Rather, he found me. He was sitting by a nearby fire, working through wrist manoeuvres with his dagger.

"Seen Midnight?" he asked, walking to me. I didn't know how to do this, he must know. Of course Dilwyn knew, he would have been there. Within a breath, I decided, if he didn't say anything, I wouldn't say anything.

"Yeah, I'm relieved she made it back."

"She's a smart horse, a complete opposite to her rider."

"Ha ha. Is there a message for me?"

"No, no. Just thought I'd check on you."

"Worried I'll run off again?" I joked.

"Well, it is a habit with you." I pushed him playfully and we both laughed. I hadn't realised just how much I had missed since my banishment; how much I had missed my family. We continued to walk quietly for a while, watching the camp.

"It hasn't been easy, Nerys," he began gently. We stopped walking then. "It's getting worse, the crops, the soil. Everything is still decaying. Everything. We just got news that a whole herd of cattle died from bad crops along the south coast. It's still spreading. And Neirin," he sighed, "your father's barely left the town. Not one tour Nerys, not one."

"I don't-"

"You're back. I'm sorry. I'm glad you're ok. Really. We all need you, Nerys." Before I could even offer a reply, Dilwyn kissed me on the forehead and faded into the camp. I really had been foolish. If only I'd got back in time for that tour, I might've prevented all of this. I might've stopped my father from retreating further away from the problem. I might've stopped Dilwyn feeling the pressure of my actions. God's above, what *was* I doing?

I shook my head quickly, to stop those thoughts. I had spent too many seasons blaming my father and myself. I wouldn't start again. I would act, as I had been. Too many thoughts were dancing through my mind. I needed to clear my head. Tomorrow these doubts would only get me killed.

I made my way to the northern part of the camp. It was a slow walk. I managed to grab a few rolls and dried fruits from the mess tent but I had to stop and greet faces, be bowed to, shake hands with men and women who had heard of my... capture. Some ignored me, which I wasn't too fussed about. Though there were some who purposefully turned their backs to me, they were faces I did not know. No matter. When I finally got to the northern edge, annoyingly, I wasn't alone.

It took him a while to notice me, I kept my distance, I didn't feel like talking. Though, as he eventually came over to me, I knew silence wasn't going to be an option. So, I would get it over with.

"They cannot know. No one can know."

"Know what?" Ithel's eyes were calm but his mouth pressed into a line. The longer I looked at him, I saw through the calm and just made it to fear in those dark, deep eyes. Yet it wasn't the fear of a coming battle, this was something else. Whatever it was didn't matter. I had to clear something up first.

"That you came to my aid on the boundary."

"No one can know I came to your aid?" He seemed honestly confused, and he made to move his hand to my shoulder but I swatted it out the way.

"No. No one can know I was there, that I was the one that they seek."

"You are the one they seek? The men of the rocks, the men from the North?"

I didn't bother to hide my exhaled groan. Time to turn this on him.

"Why were you there anyway?" I said, facing his side as he turned to stare out to the boundary.

"To help you."

This was just making me angry.

"Why are you here Ithel? I know Gruffyd sent you, but why are *you* here?"

"Because you are the one we all seek."

"What?"

"You say the men of the North are seeking you. Well, I was too."

He still looked towards the boundary. I had to take a deep breath to calm myself and hold my hands together before I replied.

"What do you mean?"

"You have answers for me. You're probably the only one who can give them to me."

"What are you talking about?" He turned to me then and I waved my arm to cut him off. I could find out later, more important things had to be said. "You are the son of Gruffyd, are you not?"

His mouth thinned before he answered. "Yes."

"You lead in his place?"

"Yes."

"His secrets are your secrets?"

"If he deems them necessary."

"Then you know." I stared him in the eyes. This was the first time since I had known him that I was in control. His eyes were full. Full of something he would not say. Then I would say it for him.

"I am the one they seek, the one they all seek," I said slowly. "If you betray me, I will kill you. That I promise."

* * *

The morning brought good news, more men from the South had joined us. Their numbers were impressive but still, the North men outnumbered us three-to-one, scouts had come back with ashen faces. And they were hungry. That made them impulsive. An impulsive fighter was a dangerous fighter and we were to face a whole camp of dangerous men.

I did not like the day. The waiting, the planning. It was when the shadows were furthest from us, from me. I had shown Merfyn and Bleddyn my previous preparations at the boundary and they took men to improve them, as many hands could do.

As I walked through the camp, I couldn't stop my mind from wondering. I saw the men, and the few women who had followed their men, were going about their routine tasks, scrubbing boots, sharpening blades, stitching hides. There hadn't been a battle in the South for over a decade, not one like this. This was a camp of fighters not used to fighting.

I switched my new sword I had got from the guard's store, from hand-to-hand, for something to do. I craved the fight, the blood. My cravings for the pulses was growing, I was ready for this fight; this camp was not.

Aimlessly I walked, for once, letting my mind wonder as it wished, when Dilwyn, Siorus and Steffan found me. They were all dressed in black and brown hides and leather, with Dilwyn looking like a boy next to our friends. They each had swords and daggers strapped around their hips and forearms. Siorus had his trusted yew bow over his shoulder. At least they were ready, and capable. They would put up a fight when the time came to it. Seeing them made me worried. How was I going to do this? Even with the shadows helping me, how was I going to save my friends, now that I had put them into danger?

Siorus bounded over quickly and hugged my shoulders.

"How you doing today?"

"Fine, thanks."

"Up for a little game?" he asked with a mischievous grin.

"Siorus," warned Steffan.

"What? You're up for it, aren't you Nerys?" Siorus asked, winking at me.

"I think I'm missing something here."

"Siorus wants to keep a tally," Dilwyn explained, rolling his eyes.

"A tally?" Despite what it meant, counting how many we would kill, I couldn't help but laugh at how offhandedly Siorus had said it. "Sure, I'm game."

"Excellent," Siorus said, rubbing his hands together. "Winner gets-"

A roar sounded from the trees. Men all around jumped and started. It took one look for Dilwyn, Siorus, Steffan and I to sprint to the boundary. They were coming.

The men on the boundary drew their swords and shields but nothing was there. No movement came through the trees, though the ground rumbled beneath our feet. The drumming noise drowned out the shouts from our camp.

I yelled for Midnight as I ran back to the stables, leaving my

friends standing on the boundary. My hunt was approaching.
There she was, galloping through the stirring men firmly. I
was relieved to see Haul had put thick hides across her chest
and back. As soon as she was close enough, I grabbed her neck
and jumped. She dipped a little and I mounted her in one
swing of the leg, then we were heading straight back to the
boundary, raising all those we passed.

This was how it started. My fight was coming.

Surprisingly to me, the South men formed ranks quickly.
Then quiet. The silence of our camp was amplified next to the
stamping feet of the North men. It sounded like they were
all there, in the forest, just stamping the ground flat on the
spot. Our silence was that of nerves and anticipation. Then it
turned to awe.

My father had emerged on the boundary, his guard close
behind him, followed by Dilwyn. My stomach twisted. The
lord of the South wore his full grey battle hide that covered
his trunk, arms and thighs. I had not seen it for years. He had
not needed to wear it for a decade. It still made men shudder,
knowledge of its prey woven deep in its skin.

Our lord climbed swiftly onto his horse, in front of the men so
that all could see him. The thundering feet were getting closer
now, I could feel it. The South men stayed silent at the sight of

their lord, at the sound of his commanding voice.

"Brothers, this land has borne us all and it will claim us. This land contains our fathers and this land will feed our children. It is our land. We fight for our land and each other. We will not die today. Fight for each other!"

The men roared, drowning out the sound of the coming army.

My father beckoned me over and I saw Dilwyn move to my father's side as I rode Midnight next to his horse. He commanded all to stand. Those who had already found their horses dismounted, including me and him. The thundering feet were getting close, men were beginning to show their nerves as the ground began to vibrate. My breathing deepened. Soon. But still my father demanded their attention.

I watched my father crouch down, a slight grimace on his face and grab a handful of earth, our land. "Each of you is to hold the earth of our families, our shadows in your own hands." Rustles and murmurs followed as the men did. "We pour our land over each other as a reminder, to all before us and all after us." I stayed as still as possible, feeling the weight of our history being carried on by my father, finally. He sprinkled some of the earth over my head and over Dilwyn's. I kept my jaw tight and stared out at the men. The rumbling was too loud behind me. "The land unites us. It is us. We give our lives to our land and to each other."

The roar sounded again. It was so close. Those who had horses remounted and the men readied themselves towards the trees. I could feel my heart pounding through my ribs.

I climbed back on Midnight and prayed. I prayed I would please them, my gods and ancestors, that they would surge through my mind and blood and feed me. So that I could kill all in my path. There. Birds darted out of the trees as shouts erupted. The first man ran out of the woods and into the clearing. Then the next and the next and the next. They ran out in a chaotic order. Cries erupting from their chests and fires burning in their eyes. They were hungry and wild.

My father raised his sword and his South men roared.

"Nerys, you are to go back."

I span towards my father, clearly not hearing properly.

"Nerys," he repeated, just as calmly. "You are to go back."

"No, I will not." He looked at me then, sword still raised.

"You should not be here now. Go back to the camp."

"No. I am here."

I saw his eyes flicker but that flicker was short-lived and he swung his sword down. Just in time as the Northern men invaded the clearing and saw us waiting for them. This was battle.

It was fierce. The North men poured into the grassy clearing like a never ending wave. Yet still, I expected more. Metal clashed against metal. Limb crushed into limb. Before I could charge Midnight into the fray, I decided to stop. To stop all our men from dying today.

Trying to find him in this mass of chaos was more exhausting than fighting. But I found Ithel, just in time. A man twice his size slung a thick blade at him. Ithel ducked trying to get his sword out of its' sheath. It was stuck, he got caught as the thick blade swung back. I grabbed the first weapon I could reach and stabbed the back of the brute's large neck. He rumpled to the ground.

I pulled Ithel off the floor, ignoring the blood streaming out of his nose. I had to shout to get him to hear.

"Get half the men back. Get them back to the camp. This isn't it. This isn't the fight." I don't know if he understood, but he ran off, shouting as he went. I prayed it would help. But enough of that. I had a pulse. Finally, I would fight.

I turned Midnight to the battle. My mouth snarled into a grin. This was where I thrived.

The sound of it all was intense. The Northern men were manic, slashing and punching and grabbing anything they could. I saw men, my fathers' men, be pulled apart, limb from limb. Ears being bitten off. It was like they had not seen battle in years, that the Northern men had been deprived of it and finally, here it was. None of them were on horses, which gave us some advantage at least. Midnight was a sight. She stomped and kicked with perfect aim and I kept up, striking any beast in my path.

I could not tell how much time passed. We were still here, fighting, with half our number. I hoped it was because Ithel had understood and the men had listened, not because we had lost so many already. But their numbers seemed to have increased. The blue sky turned to grey. The spring air carried a chill. Eventually, the stream of men out the trees thinned. I breathed easier, even though they still outnumbered us. Where was my father?

Two men in grey hides stormed towards me, swords high. I took a deep breath as my eyes closed. There. Shadows. I snapped open my eyes and urged Midnight to the left. I sliced low at the left one before quickly changing hands, stabbed hard at the other. He didn't even have time to raise his sword. Before mine was out of his chest, I turned Midnight, pulled and sliced high. He ran straight into my blade, already red with his own blood. The one from my left came at me again, I leaned over Midnight and swung my sword straight across his neck. He fell to the ground, neck pouring. My body throbbed, not from pain. From the shadows. They had helped me see, see where the men would go. They didn't have a chance.

I turned back round to the chaos. I watched Siorus and Steffan kick a huge man, with hair down to his belt, three times before he dropped to his knees, then Steffan sliced down and the man fell. Merfyn sprinted across my sight, a wild cry escaping his lungs. I could almost laugh. But I couldn't see him. I couldn't see my father. Night was near and we hadn't stopped. The men wouldn't be able to hold much longer. Time to stop this. I urged my friend back to the boundary and she responded effortlessly. I had to see the fight from a distance. I caught Steffan as he ran past me, shouting instructions to him. Time to put the preparations to use.

Men were tiring all around me, barely holding on to their swords. This had to work. As Steffan rounded up some men to the boundary preparations, I went back to the fight. I had to give them time.

I closed my eyes and willed the shadows to me. Again, they showed me the way. Showed me how. I heard the hurried shouts from behind. Good. I slashed my sword as fast as I could at the remaining North men. Waiting, waiting for my father to get back to the boundary. Most of the men heard. Most of them got back. Those that didn't... well, I wasn't thinking about that.

A horde of wild men charged at me, seeing the rest of us retreating. I held Midnight still. I went to the dark place inside myself and waited for the shadows. A new pulse sent them through me. They coursed through my blood, danced behind my eyes. The shadows showed me. In less than a breath, I knew two would charge for my right. One would miss. Another would punch high, catching me from a dodge. Then I was back. Seeing five pairs of hungry eyes, all aiming for me.

I knew what to do.

I jumped off Midnight, I wasn't on her in the shadowvision. Immediately I lunged left and my blade slashed low, taking out the two who would tackle me. Then I doubled back and pushed it high. Blood poured from the one who would miss my right. Before he made it to the ground I turned to the remaining two, they were still facing Midnight. I thrust my sword through the ribs of the nearest beast and ran. I heard bone crunch. One groaned shove and more bone crunched. I had two men impaled on my sword. Lovely. I yanked it out with a curse and ran to Midnight. We had to get back fast.

There was less than fifty or so of them left now. The Northern beasts. They chased after me as I urged Midnight faster. Then they fell. I made it just in time to see them fall into a pit dug in the ground. The men at the back kept rushing forward, pushing those at the front further into the pit.

Then thick pitch covered them. Buckets and buckets of it. The beasts at the back couldn't see and still pushed their brothers in. Fools. The boundary was bright as flaming torches flew from behind me, landing in the black pit. It was alight in an instant, as were the men. Their screams pierced the dusk. It was brutal, it was battle .

The remaining North men were cut down easily. My father's men had found their confidence and fought, renewed. They cheered and whooped. They had done it. I saw him finally. My father walked through his men, clapping them on the back, shaking hands. They all breathed, relieved.

I knew it wasn't over.

I ignored the warm throbbing of my blood, trying to clear my mind.

"Get back to the camp," I ordered, shouting as loud as my tired muscles would let me. My father was in front of me in moments, face stern.

"Nerys, what, you?"

"Father, it is only beginning."

"No. We have won."

He looked at me with concern, like I was a confused puppy. I had to get them back.

"My lord, I implore you. Get them back."

CHAPTER 8

He just looked at me. My father's face was weary and tired but his eyes were as strong as ever.

"It is over, Nerys," he whispered harshly. Men stood all around us, waiting for orders.

"Father, you know battle. You have seen it. This was not it, please." My head was pulsing. I could feel them swimming all over my mind, black shadows. They were encouraging me, urging me to seek more blood. I pushed them as far back as I could. Not now. "That was the start. You know this. Father, please. Save these men now. Get them back."

The clearing was eerily silent. The sky had darkened. I could see the coming moonlight shine in my father's green eyes. They were looking at me, searching for something. I hoped he found something to persuade him because this would be hard enough on my own.

He surprised me. Without a single blink he ordered all his remaining men behind to the camp. Then I breathed easier, relieved.

Back at the camp, the men were unsettled. Half were edgy, angry, frustrated at being called back without a fight. The other half were tired, cold, beat. It wasn't good. Especially as bodies of the dead were being dragged back to the edge of the camp as quickly as they could be moved.

I found a quiet spot and examined Midnight, letting her eat and drink as I did the same. My throbbing head had eased but my worry had increased. Those pulses were stronger, the shadows more insistent. They had already made me heal quicker, and see attacks before they happened, what else were they going to do to me?

I rubbed over my forearms, worrying about what was happening to me but before long Dilwyn found me, a small smile greeting me. Tears were along his brown sleeves, small cuts visible through them, otherwise, he was fine.

"That was... uh...," he shrugged off the rest of the sentence.

"Don't," was all I could say.

He sat down next to me on the dry grass. The ground was hard and cold. That was how I felt, hard and cold. A small breeze passed my face and brought my attention back to my surroundings. This was all their fault, the shadows, the shadow gods. They started this. They were responsible for all of this. For making me do all of this. A deep sigh escaped me.

"Thinking?" Dilwyn's voice broke my thoughts.

I just nodded in response.

"You should stay back now, Nerys. You know your father would want-"

"Would want what, Dil?" I faced my cousin, staring into his green eyes.

"I just meant, you know." He fidgeted with his belt. "If you're to be lo-"

"If? If? So you think-"

Cries ran through the camp. I didn't get a chance to finish, we were both up and racing back to the boundary. I heard Cledwyn and Trahearn yelling out orders but I didn't take note. I had to get there fast. My legs felt feeble beneath me but I ran.

The clearing was bleak, eerie. My father, his guard, the court and Ithel were there, forming ranks in the empty space. We waited and waited. What were we waiting for? There. Just as I was about to vent my frustration, they appeared. Black and grey cloaks, barely visible. They entered the clearing, not like last time. They entered slowly, precisely, filing out into ranks.

I heard the gasps of men around me. We couldn't take another fight, not so soon after the last one.

The first group was just the front of the attack. The men they could spare. The men who were used to tire us, break us down. The sound of footfalls on hard ground ceased as the Northern men stopped appearing from the trees. If the first group outnumbered us, this group was beyond that. How were there so many more of them? Unless more had joined them since I had escaped from them. Gods, this was going to be brutal. I couldn't hunt here, now, with everyone seeing. Not how I wanted, or how the shadows wanted. Damn these Northern beasts.

The roar broke the tension that had built. The breeze sent it our way, a warning to his arrival. The leader of the North men walked in to the clearing, torches suddenly lit, revealing him. He was arrogant. The jeer of his men was deafening. They clearly respected him, or, more likely, feared him. It would make no difference to us. He raised his hand for silence. It fell instantly.

Even from the boundary, I could see his eyes. They were deep and colourful against the firelight. I shuddered to think what my father would make of him, or what he would make of my father. Gwrtheryn was marked by the shadow gods, whether he knew it or not.

The large sword Gwrtheryn raised made him more visible against the dark. I saw him find my father's eyes, realising it was he who led us. Then he saw me. He looked again at my father, noting the resemblance and back at me. A crooked grin made his face ugly. I desperately wanted to feel the pulses then. Their warmth, confidence. I didn't, however. I just felt cold, isolated.

"You are mine, little leaf," came his voice across the clearing. "Daddy's little army will not stop me. You are mine."

He pointed his sword at me as he spoke and I stared back, not wanting to see my father's face. All I wanted was to rip Gwrtheryn's head from his chest and throw it at his beasts. He was a threat to me. To me as the Night-Rider. If he found out, if he revealed me, well, I would definitely rip his head off, slowly. His sword turned to my father.

"I kill all your men. All men. Bring me the Night-Rider and I will spare your women and children. Do not and I kill them too, after my men have fun. They want fun." A huge roar. "Bring him to me." He looked up at the dark sky, sword to the moon. "You have time, not much." He pulled down his sword in three clear strokes. Three hours.

The leader of the North men turned his back to us and walked through the trees. As did his men with an eerie calm. But they had not gone, I knew they had not gone. Things were getting worse. Seriously worse. Now what was I going to do?

My father looked to his court. He was tall but in this light he seemed small, defeated almost. This was my doing.

We stood there, waiting for orders. When they came, they were short, direct.

"Find this Night-Rider. I must talk to him. Now."

The court dispersed, determined. I didn't know what to do. I caught a glance off of Ithel, half-warning, half-pleading. This was not what I had planned. At all.

"Father."

He stood as I walked over to him, face expectant. I could have told him then. I could have told him everything. But then I would have to tell him that I blamed him for all this. That I could not do. So I didn't.

"I know who he is."

"You do? How?"

"When, after...I met him on my travels."

"Very well. Find him. Bring him to me."

"Yes, father."

I still didn't know what to do. I had to figure something out. Fast.

The time passed within one breath. No time at all really. All I had done was pace and panic. Two things I didn't do. What a time to start. I had achieved nothing. And now I was condemning my own people to death. That wasn't going to happen. It was the only way.

All of the South men gathered back on the boundary and the court gathered around my father. Then he ordered me over. I swallowed hard. This was it.

"Nerys, have you found him?" he asked, unable to hide the desperation in his voice.

"I have."

"Where is he?"

I took a deep breath before I answered. All the court's eyes were on me, wanting answers.

"He'll be here."

"Nerys, this is no game. If he does-"

"He will be here," I said firmly. My own father looked at me with uncertain eyes but I did not hold his stare. I walked to

Midnight and faced the clearing. *I would be there.*

***

The sheer amount of men gathered was impressive. Almost 1200 of them. Some of the men not badly injured from the fight before chose to fight again, most couldn't. The guard and trained warriors were strong, the farmers, fishers, masons were loyal and ready. I was doing this for them, their families. Surrounded by them all now gave me strength, or rather, courage. They were why I would do it.

My father stood firm in front of his men, facing the trees, his horse by his side. Even in the moonlight he was commanding, his battle years visible in his stance. He would die with, for, his men. It wouldn't come to that though, not with me here. I stroked Midnight and prayed it wouldn't come to that.

We stood on the boundary, a chill in the night. I saw the silhouette of the trees, the emptiness of the clearing. The wind had stopped, making the clearing quieter still. My eyes had to adjust to the vastness of the dark before me. I was patient, I knew my eyes would and just in time too.

They re-emerged from the trees. The Northern men. Quiet, calm. My heart beat faster. The dancing firelight played with my eyes. Gwrtheryn walked back into the middle of his men, just as quiet and just as calm. Midnight trotted on the spot, I felt the same.

Then Gwrtheryn's deep, rough voice boomed out through the still air.

"The Night-Rider, bring him to me."

There was a breath of hesitation this side of the clearing, I could feel the men tense up. It was time. I inched Midnight forward but a fast arm grabbed me.

"Nerys, what are you-?"

"Hush, father."

I walked Midnight into the empty area of the clearing, Gwrtheryn directly opposite me.

"I am the one you seek," I said quietly, so that only he would hear, but firmly. I was in no mood for games.

"You, you the daughter of a little lord. You are not Night-Rider. I know this. Bring him to me." His words rumbled with the command.

"I have."

His laugh was just as repulsive as before.

"You wish to play games, my little leaf? You have not found him, if you are this Night-Rider. Then let us play. Only, this time I will have you, before you run. Right in front of your father."

I spat on the ground. He laughed. Wonderful.

"You think you are this Night-Rider. Prove it."

Well, I guess I should have expected that. He called a man over, a beast of a man really. His face was scarred and his hair matted and his thick arms threatened to rip open his shirt sleeves.

"If you are this Night-Rider, you will kill him."

His demand was a simple one. Adrenaline pumped through me. Strangely enough, I had never killed like this before, not as a contest.

I climbed off Midnight and sent her back to my father. My opponent was on foot, so I would be on foot. His stare was so intense it was almost blank and his grin was bare except for two teeth. Oh, this was going to be fun.

The beast of a man raised a long sword. It gleamed in the moonlight, ready for its prey. I raised mine. It wasn't as light or familiar as my old sword though it was strong. I needed strong.

He swung straight at me, closing the distance instantly. His swing was forceful and practiced, but not precise. Brute force,

I could work with that.

He swung again. I dodged and ran at him, testing his speed. He was slow. I managed to scrape his cheek but I felt something warm run down mine. I had scratched his cheek as he had scratched mine. No matter. I would soon find his weakness and use it. I didn't want the shadows taking over my mind for this one. I wanted to remember this one.

He grinned smugly, an ugly, greedy grin. Rage built.

I circled him, waiting for him to strike first. He followed the circle, keeping his blade high.

With each step, the shadows were scratching at the side of my mind, I didn't care for waiting. The sooner this was over the better.

I stopped circling. He didn't have time to react as I doubled back and span, using the rotation to swing my sword at his neck. He fell to the ground, head still clinging to his body by a few muscles and tendons. I stepped over him and finished the job. Done. As a new pulse coursed through me, I cleaned my blade, happy I had done that alone. Although, the shadows were still clawing to get into my mind and lead me.

I turned to their leader and smiled at him. He wasn't expecting that.

"He was my best fighter."

"He wasn't much of challenge."

Gwrtheryn screamed to the sky, it was so piercing I stepped back. There was pain in that scream. He threw his thick grey cloak on the ground.

* * *

The cool, smoky air was calming. I would have been happy, content even, if this was another day. But it was not. Torches flickered in the night. Grunts and cheers echoed around me. Horses neighed, boots stomped, nerves stirred. None of that affected me. None of that reached my senses. There was only him and me. And I was ready.

The fires gave a smoky mist to my surroundings. I breathed in the air like it was the only food I ate. It would calm me, calm me before I let the rage out. Before I let the rage out and the shadows in.

"Now you fight me," said Gwrtheryn. "I want the Night-Rider but now I fight you."

I growled in response. My blood was warm with the shadows. I would use their gift now, I would end him and send his soul to them.

Gwrtheryn turned to his men and shouted, loud enough for all to hear.

"Now we fight and I show you how men kill. How I will kill the Night-Rider." His voice lowered so only I could hear him. "Soon, my little dry leaf. I take my time with you. I will break you, Nerys." He almost hissed my name and it made my skin crawl.

He pumped his sword into the night and his men erupted. They were wild. The sound that came from my father's men was silence. It almost made me chuckle. I licked my lips as I loosened the grip on my sword. Something like fear was about to grip me but I shook it away. Now wasn't the time for feelings. It was the time for action.

His sword gleamed against the trembling firelights and I saw it properly. It was unlike any I had seen with a curved tip and nook marks along one side. Oh, and it was sharp, I could see that. A repulsive smirk crossed his fearsome face. I spat on the ground. I would remove that grin, as slowly as possible.

Without another breath he lunged, sword swinging. He swung high and low, making me dodge and duck. If he kept this up, I would be the one who tired, not him. Another lunge had me stepping back to block. He was strong and large, and I was faster. Time to change the game.

I breathed in the smoky air and focused on the shadows. In less than a blink I had ran in on his swing. My sword thrust under his armpit as I met his blade with my other forearm. He shuddered back. The surprise on his face was all I needed. My mouth curled.

His hand moved to his wound, the blood sticking on his hand. I could see it dark against his pale skin. Hungry eyes found mine. I had awoken his rage. Time to awaken mine.

I paced back and closed my eyes. They were ready to come to me. It was risky but I knew they would come to me. I heard a grunt as he ran at me. I didn't move. Not until the last moment, when I felt his breath brush my face.

I stepped to the side, raising my blade. I could feel the shadows; they were with me but they weren't there. They weren't behind my eyes as they usually were, showing me the way. He slashed his blade hard, several times in a row. I parried them but he was so strong, stronger than I could take. Where were they? He slashed again, I dodged the worst of it but got caught on the arm. Where the hell were they? My breathing quickened, not from the adrenaline. I felt the warmth from my blood but ignored it. I had to stay focused.

Our blades crashed again and again. I focused on the sound of metal ringing. I listened to the fast heave of my breath.

Anything to make me ignore the panic creeping in my mind. I felt them, the shadows were with me, I just couldn't find where.

He gnarled as his sword swung at me. It was a ferocious swing. My sword should have flown out of my hand like an arrow. It didn't. My grip held. Maybe...?

Rain. Instantly the heavens opened above and heavy rain fell down. Yes, actual rain. Any other day and I would have danced in this welcome downpour, but not today. The shadow gods were on my side. My vision blurred through the downpour, my focus did not. I knew where the shadows were now. And I would send another soul to them. No, I would send *the* soul to them.

The swords knocked and clanged against each other, reverberating in my grip. Yet I did not let go. I didn't need to. I could feel the shadows now, oh, I could. They were in me, making me strong. Very strong. I took another swing from him then decided to test my new strength. Gwrtheryn drew back his sword for a slash that I got to first. My blade crashed heavily into his, though I hadn't put more force into it than normal. His sword went flying through the night. Very strong. Even through the rain I saw his face darken. I had done it now.

I didn't wait. I dropped my sword and ran at the beast of a leader. I dodged the claw-like hand aimed for my stomach as I sprang up. The running jump sent me high, then I punched down, hard. I felt his nose crack under my fist. I felt the warm blood pour out. I liked seeing his blood pour.

He stumbled back, nearly slipping on the newly wet grass. Before another breath, I ran at him again. He was expecting me; he was expecting me to jump again. I didn't. A quick lunge and I drove a punch to his abdomen. He staggered back several paces, bent over. My fist immediately connected with his jaw, knocking him to the ground. I was gliding on the grass and standing behind him before he recovered.

His yell was monstrous as I jumped on his back. He stood up, grabbing wildly in the air. He managed to get a grip of my leg and pull hard but he couldn't stop me. I had his lifeline, his neck, in my hands.

I squeezed. The shadows were hungry, I was hungry. My grip was getting tighter and tighter. The more he struggled, the more I squeezed. I was in control. I controlled his life. The shadows were racing inside me. Almost there. I pressed tighter and felt his pulse throb. Every fibre of my being told me to let go, to run, but I couldn't. The shadows were telling me to kill. *I* was telling me to kill. I felt a surge of strength through my hands. Just one more squeeze.

Pain. A white hot sensation rolled down my shoulder blade. It consumed every part of me. I let go then. I let go and dropped to the mud.

"Aaahhh."

The damn fickle shadows. My surroundings were a fog. I couldn't focus. It was there, something was in me. I couldn't get to it. Every movement I made sent fresh, searing pain through me.

I had to get it out, whatever it was. Through the dark rain I could make out figures dragging their leader away. Why were they… why were they…?

There was something… some lone strain of thought telling me to get it out. I used what little strength I had left and reached an arm around back.

"Aaaaahhhh," the scream pierced through the darkness like lightning. It was a dagger. A dagger was sticking out of my shoulder blade. My eyes started to stream. I was ready. I would die here. In the rain and the mud. I knew it. That was fine. I could die now.

I welcomed the black, the seeming-less void. It was coming closer and closer. It would take me to them. Then my ears pricked up, I heard something. This wasn't a void. Why wasn't it a void? I wanted the void.

"Nerys, no. Nerys, come on. Don't shut your eyes. Don't you dare shut your eyes."

A hand grabbed me. Why did it grab me? Just let me die. Another primal scream left me. I thought I had been stabbed again yet I saw a flash of metal through my hazy eyes.

"Nerys, come on. Come on, damn it."

They grabbed me, the hands. I was safe in their carry.

"Take... me to... to. Shado... I die... to."

"Nerys no. Come on, just a bit longer. Come on Nerys."

* * *

I awoke with a start, jolting my heart. It pounded through my chest.

It took me a few breaths to realise I was safe. Alive. The night, the battle, the rain came flooding back to me. My whole body felt like lead.

Two maids entered the small, circular tent I found myself in and tended to me. They were kind, gentle. It took me a moment to recognise them. They were my maids, Celyn and Mairwen. My mother had taken them into our household when both their families had been killed by nomads. They had been my maids, my friends, ever since. Although, they only knew me as a wayward heir, but I didn't want them to know. I didn't want them to know me as a killer. They were sweet and generous. I sat up in the small bed as Celyn put a poultice on my back wound.

"This may sting," she said, her big brown eyes set on my face.

"Uh," was my reply.

"How do you feel?" asked Mairwen, laying out my clothes. Her long, dark hair was held tight in a low knot and her voice was clear, almost commanding. Then I saw the night dress I was in. They had changed me. I made to cover my scars but found Mairwen's eyes on me, still waiting for an answer. They had both seen my scars many times before over the years and never asked about them.

"Fine," I lied.

"Lady, we know you're not," replied Mairwen, not even a breath later.

I breathed deeply. I wasn't fine. That battle was different, I was different. I had been ready to die. To give up and go to the shadows. Had I really been so selfish? Did I really want it to just end? The shadows had felt insistent, too insistent. It was like they were no longer just helping me but rather, they were using me. Like I was a vessel for them to act in. That was a scary thought.

"Lady? Nerys?"

"What?"

"Mairwen was saying, you need to get up now. We know you're tired but they came back, those men."

"What? Who?"

"Last night," Celyn said as she placed a calming hand on me. Her blonde hair was falling out of her plait. "They're not here." I had jumped at the words 'came back'. Celyn continued when she was sure I wouldn't run.

"They came back, a few of those men, screaming and shouting they were. They said all sorts of things."

"They said," cut in Mairwen, always the direct one of them, "it wasn't over. They would be back at noon to end us all, they did." She moved to the bed and sat on it, fear and passion in her blue eyes. "They were wild, truly. Wild. Please don't go out there again, Nerys."

I was surprised by her appeal and my name. Her deep blue eyes were filling, which I would never expect from her. Celyn maybe, not Mairwen.

"I have to Mairwen, Celyn. I have to. Thank you, thank you both. You have always been kind to me." I slowly pushed myself out of the bed and into the middle of the tent. "Now, help me dress."

A small part of me winced at how readily they obeyed. I quickly ignored it. I also ignored the throb that was toying with my shoulder blade. I felt the poultice covering it. I recognised Celyn's handiwork.

"It's a mixture of ground ivy, nettle-"

"Yarrow and honey," I finished. I could smell the paste from over my shoulder. "It's good work Celyn. Enaid would have been proud." I saw a quick smile reach her cheeks at my mother's name. She had taught us three the art of healing together when we were younger.

My maids helped me into my trousers and cropped bodice. My back was stiff and I couldn't twist into it myself. Then I felt their hands stop still. I turned to see why. He had entered.

None of us moved.

CHAPTER 9

I felt his eyes trace my body. I might be healing quickly but
for some reason the shadows didn't heal my scars and I
was usually glad they didn't. Right now, under my father's
scrutinising, pitying stare, I wish they did.

"Leave us." My maids obeyed. I felt the loss of their warmth
instantly. I turned my face away from his. I knew the scars he
was seeing, knew their stories, I didn't need to see his face as
he saw them for the first time.

"Nerys." There, in one word, he had his arms around me,
embracing me, and all there was was a father and a daughter.
Together. I nestled my head on his shoulder. I couldn't
remember the last time I had hugged him, but his smell, I
could remember that. A mixture of oak, wax, and baked apple.
It had always been his favourite food. The memories came
pouring back. How had this happened? How had we grown so
far apart?

I couldn't believe that I was hugging my father. A small laugh left me and my father echoed it. We both relaxed and moved apart. His face barely recognisable. It was still weary and lined and aged with worry, yet somehow, he was twenty years younger. A smile grew across his face, his eyes were bright and he looked like my father again. How I remembered him with my mother.

"Father, forgive me." The words tumbled out as I snapped into a low bow.

A hand under my chin moved my head up, my eyes, however, remained on the ground. Then I felt his warm hands trace the two large scars I had on each forearm, the two scars that had changed me.

"It is I who should be asking that of you. You chose to fight for all of us. Not knowing you would li-. I should never have banished you. Will you forgive me, Nerys? My daughter, my heir."

"Of course, father," I said as I found his eyes. I could not take this in. I beamed at him and squeezed both this hands. I had my father back. Not my lord, my *father*. We both stood together, silent. I let him trace a few of my scars with a hand. His touch was hesitant, caring.

"My heir. I shall inform the court again." I nodded slowly,

there was so much I wanted to ask him. "Why did you do it?" His voice was soft, gentle but my guard was up before I could stop it.

"Don't ask me that. It's done."

He took a step back and looked at me again. Not just at the scars but all of me.

"Something has changed within you. I see that now." His voice was still gentle but the softness of it had gone. He was finally seeing what years of distancing himself from his only child had done to me. I let go of his hands and turned away

"Something changed when my mother died. That was a lifetime ago to me. And *now* you see me." That was harsh, I knew it yet no part of me tried to stop it.

"You're disappointed," he sighed. "I see now; I have not been your father as much as I was."

"No," was all I could say.

"I have not given you the kindness your mother would have done." He squeezed my hand a little and I didn't stop him. His words choked. "I tried. I did. I couldn't let... I could not let it happen. I tried, Nerys, to make you strong, to not let this world harm you. To not let anything harm you." He sighed deeply as though expelling all the air in his lungs. "It seems I have failed. I have made you too strong."

"No. No father. I am not strong enough."

It had changed. As suddenly as it had come, my happiness had gone. I pulled my hand out of his and purposefully looked him in the eyes. I needed to say this as much as he needed to hear it.

"There were so many times when I missed you. When I just wanted to talk to you or for you to hold me. To put the world to rights as you used to. But those times have gone. You are my father and you'll always be my father. Yet I cannot stand where you do. I cannot sit through papers and contracts and ignore the shadows gods while our people suffer."

"Why, Nerys? Why must you do this? Why can't you let it be?"

"Because of you," my voice had risen. I took a breath and said it again quietly. "Because of you, father. I will make this right, if you will not. This is my place and this is where I will remain." A quiet filled the tent. It hung all around me, almost ripping my heart out of my chest. We both stood where we were, barely breathing. Until the quiet fell.

"Do what you must." It was less than a whisper. Yet as soon as he had left the tent, it moved me to tears. They poured down the sides of my cheeks until all I tasted was salt. And they kept falling. When I thought I could cry no longer, I did. My chest felt hollow and at the same time heavy. I didn't know how I would bare it. This would be a scar no one would see.

* * *

It was an hour before noon. The camp was busy working, but the men were silent. Nerves were a strange thing. Midnight was waiting outside my tent, I assumed Haul had led her over. Her warm body was the best comfort to me as we headed to the boundary. Walking through the camp was different this time. Men still ignored me, but their shy eyes kept glancing at me as I passed.

Just before I got to the boundary and court, I was grabbed by a strong hand and pulled behind the nearest tent. I didn't have a breath to object before Ithel started, still holding my arm.

"You saw them, yet you don't seem concerned. All the other men are shocked and scared." His dark eyes were intensely locked on mine. This was the first time we had spoken since I threatened to kill him, apart from the battle, and I had no idea what he was talking about. "The men of the rocks are the purest form of evil I have encountered, yet you alone, don't seem concerned by them."

"Is there a question in there or are you just trying to pry into more things that don't *concern* you?" I asked hotly, pulling my arm from his grip. I had stung him. His brows furrowed slightly before he regained his usual, slightly soft, composure.

"You, the South, you have not faced such men before. You do not believe in such men anymore. Now you have. My *question*," he continued after a pause, "is how are you not affected?"

The actual emotion in his voice clung in the air. I knew then that the men we call Northern men hadn't just ruined my family but his as well. Still, I was in no mood to worry about his life story and share tears. I had already lost too many this day.

"You're asking me why I am not surprised by the evil I encounter in these men? Yes?" I waited until he nodded. Pulling up my shirt sleeves, I stepped close to him and held up my arms. Those scars were proof of what I had done, still did. Even if there were only two people who knew what they meant. "This. This is why. Because I have faced far more in myself." Instantly, I pushed down my sleeves and marched to the court. I would make myself think no more of that conversation.

The court spent little time going through the battle plans again. My shoulder was stiff, my range limited. Every now and then I would twist the wrong way or move my arm too quickly and a sudden burst of pain would punish me. That wouldn't last long though, after another kill, a new pulse would come and I would heal even quicker. Now I just had to wait.

As noon came we were ready. Half the men were at the boundary, ranks formed, weapons ready. The other half, thankfully, were a league back, waiting. Although it diminished our numbers considerably, it meant we would at least have fresh men ready when we needed them.

The sun shone high over a cloudless sky. Perfect visibility for all. Great. And then they came. I jumped on Midnight at the front of the ranks. I was ready, blades, daggers, sharpened stones clung to my leather trousers and jacket wherever they could. A few birds scattered from the trees, the tall, browning trees shook in defiance. But nothing stopped them. The North men were here. Again.

They burst into the clearing like a blackened wave. They had only one intention, to kill us all. My father roused his men and they responded with a loyal charge. The two sides met and the battle began. Again.

I ignored the pain from my shoulder as I sliced down and then, thank the shadows, a beast fell at my sword. How good it was to feel that pulse then, to have the shadows fill me now.

From Midnight I was easily cutting down all the men that were in my path. Fear would not rest, so I would not rest. But I didn't need to. I was hungry and thriving. I barely breathed between each kill, so desperate for the next one. I could feel each pulse surge through me, making me faster, stronger. I wanted only the pulses, and the blood that came with them.

I hardly noticed the battle around me. My father's men were strong and fighting like they had never lost a battle before but it wasn't enough. The North men thrived in battle, as did I. The grass stained red around me but I did not see. All I saw were the shadows, what they wanted me to see. And I cut down each beast that I saw. There was no us or them. It was just them.

"Nerys, no!"

The shock of my name brought me back to the battle, to me. My heart thumped to my stomach. I nearly slipped off Midnight as I looked down my sword. There, at the end of it, cowering, neck teasing with blood, wasn't one of the Northern men. He wasn't one of the beasts. No, he was one of the South, my father's men. I chucked my sword suddenly, recognising him as one of the farmers from town, *my* town. He sprinted away as soon as his courage allowed him.

I... what had I nearly done? Even worse was the expression on Ithel's face as he watched me. He looked at me with disgust then he was back in the fight.

What was I doing?

I tried to re-join the battle, moving, slicing after I had picked up my sword but it wasn't the same. I couldn't let that happen again. I would not let the shadows take over me like that again, to the point that I didn't even see light and dark, only blood. Even as I thought that, a small flicker in my mind said I would.

I scanned the clearing, trying to distract myself from my own thoughts. The fight was bad. And then it got worse. However many men we killed, just as many seemed to storm through the trees, fresh and thirsty for blood. Even with our men waiting, we would have no chance. Damn. I had to do something. Something else.

I rushed through the battle, Midnight stomping on bodies as we searched. I couldn't see Dilwyn anywhere, his short black hair not visible in this sea of metal, wood and hides. I had to find him. I did another round, nothing. Where was the damn boy?

I charged Midnight through a clump of grey cloaks and found

Dai in the middle of them, one arm limp at his side, the other swinging wildly. He gave me a quick nod before running back into the fray. My eyes followed him and saw him make his way to the guard, their shiny, polished shields the only of their kind on the battle field. Good. That meant my father was still alive, but where was Dilwyn?

"Get out of here, Nerys!"

I looked down to see Ithel, bow across his chest, sword loose in his hand. His eyes darted the fight, looking for oncoming threats.

"No," I replied defiantly. I was repulsed by myself for what I had nearly done, even more so that he had seen it. And been the one to stop me.

"You're helping no-one. Get back." His eyes found mine, unflinching. I hated this, I hated the small voice of doubt in my head that agreed with him. I couldn't waste time on that, just as I couldn't waste any more time trying to find Dilwyn. Regardless of how much I trusted Ithel, at that moment, he was all I had. I didn't care if he trusted me, I knew he would do the right thing. He seemed the type to.

With Ithel gone my mind was back on the battle, the hunt. I had to end this, all of this. I was getting close. I could feel it. A few more pulses, a few more souls, and I could end this.

He shouted for an age. I barely realised what was happening. All around the North men ran back to their leader as he shouted like no human could. Men were still trying to fight but the North men ignored it. They bolted behind Gwrtheryn and as one, charged. As sudden as the shout, they were on us. We were stampeded. My reflexes saved me then, as I stared in disbelief.

My father's men fell. There was little they could do. A few of the men rallied around their lord as they fought harder than ever. They fought like animals backed against a wall with no way out. That was what they were. I fought my way towards them, towards my father. Life seemed to slow. I watched Gwrtheryn, his large, dominant figure stalk towards the lord of the South with an intense gaze. He raised his sword. There was nothing he could do. My father was being hammered by two men and their crude axes.

I couldn't get there fast enough. I shouted and slashed and ran and pointed to get to him. The beasts kept pounding him. I sprang over lifeless bodies, never getting any closer. I was watching a shadowvision, like something I had seen from the shaman's draught. Everything was so slow. Every detail was so vivid yet I couldn't hear anything.

Then I saw another figure move towards my father. He wasn't trying to kill him though. He ran passed him and straight to Gwrtheryn, who didn't even blink as he knocked him away like a fly. Dai fell to the ground, unmoving. Still I tried to reach him. Still I ran and slashed and yelled.

He didn't see it coming. He didn't see the leader of the North men deliver a blow so hard he crumpled to the earth instantly, never knowing who had struck him.

My stomach came up to my throat. Life sped up as though it had never stopped. I got to him then. I got to my father but there was nothing I could do. His green eyes faded as the last thing they saw were mine.

"Ith... Ithel," he breathed his last. I picked him up in my arms but he was lifeless.

"No, no." I fumbled with the body in my arms, willing it back to life.

I felt Gwrtheryn's laugh as he passed me. A piercing, malicious laugh that sent shivers down the back of my neck. I sprang up and raced after him. He did this.

Rage. Blood. Revenge.

A steel-like grip yanked me back and I saw my father's body flat on the ground.

My world was black.

The sounds of the battle faded. The passing of time ceased altogether. My hunt was over. How long I stayed there, the cold body of my dead father in my hands, I do not know. The heat from the sun blazed down but I was cold.

There was nothing left.

Arms grabbed me and ripped me from my father. I struggled. I was weak and they were strong. I struggled. The arms carried me away, letting me struggle. They felt like the arms that had carried my before. I knew they were safe. I stopped fighting then, they would take me. I was glad I didn't have to think. I couldn't think. There was only the dark.

CHAPTER 10

I was back in the hay village. I could tell from the wooded hut I was in. The air was stale and the room musky. I laid on the bed, just being. I breathed in deeply, filling my lungs. They still worked at least. My mind began to think, to remember. I shoved those thoughts aside quickly and focused all my attention on my breath. In and out. In and out. I closed my eyes, still just being.

"Fear… your fear you fear. Act on it…"

Words began to fade across my senses. Words from the shaman. I saw his face behind my eyes and sprang up in the bed. He was not here. He was not here. My lungs calmed, head throbbing. I didn't want to think. About anything. I didn't want to remember anything.

In and out.

Good. I tested my fingers, moving them each, then my toes. Hesitantly, I slid myself out the bed, noticing I was still clothed in my shirt, leather jacket and trousers. Someone had removed my belt, which I was grateful for. My feet were bare, they softened in the dirt ground as I put my weight on them. Once I was satisfied they could carry me, I stepped into the boots that were waiting for me.

My stomach growled. That was the next thing to do. I left the hut and immediately found my friend outside, eating the hay. Just the sight of her made me smile. I leaned against Midnight, enjoying her warmth. I stroked her black coat and ran my hands down her legs, checking... checking for what? I stopped and turned to her head, hugging it to my chest. She nudged into me. I was happy, just to be here, in this moment with my truest friend.

My stomach growled again. Right. I looked around me, hay and dirt were the ground, the few huts near the one I just came out of were all made of wood with a flat roof. There were others clumped together to the south of the village, made of wattle-and-daub. They were the storage huts for the straw and hay. A few carts were by them, as well as an empty pen. It was a humble village, but those who lived here worked hard. A simple life, how I envied it.

I searched close by Midnight for food, I didn't want to be far from her. I found nothing other than straw and hay. Not for me. As I walked a bit further, my ears pricked up. I wasn't alone.

There was a hissing sound, like boiling water over a fire.
That would have food, right? I walked towards the sound
and almost buckled to the ground as my knees gave way. I
wasn't alone. Men. Dozens and dozens and dozens of men.
Over a hundred. They were here. I jumped back behind
an abandoned cart as I took it in. I watched them moving,
cleaning weapons, poking fires, stirring pots. Stirring pots... I
could almost taste the warm smell of stew. No.

I leaned closer as I continued to watch... and learn. I knew
that sword... and that face. I had seen him before. That voice,
he was a farmer. Then I saw a man walk to a fire and put his
hand on another man's shoulder. They spoke and he left. His
short black hair disturbed something in me. Something like a
memory. I glanced back over my shoulder and saw Midnight,
who was watching me. Ok, she was there, she was real. I
looked back at the men, then maybe they were too.

I slowly walked towards them, the sound of their camp
gradually getting louder. Then I was there, at the edge of their
camp. Nothing. I tensed just in case but nothing happened.
No man ran at me with a sword, or shouted a warning for
another to. So far so good.

A woman rushed passed me with a bucket of water, stopped

briefly when she noticed me, then hurried on passed, water lapping up the sides. Still, it wasn't an attack. I looked at the nearest fire and saw a man jump from his seat as he looked at me. His face was stunned as his jaw opened. His blue eyes seemed to freeze in shock. I thought I knew that face, his name... his name definitely began with an 'A'. Then he ran off into a part of the camp I couldn't see.

My feet were rooted to the ground. Should I run away from him or to him?

I decided to just stay where I was, it was easier. I continued to watch the men, more of them noticed me but none reacted as much as the man who ran away. I looked down at my clothes. Sure, there was some dried blood on them, patches of dirt, and a few rips on my sleeves but I didn't think I looked too bad. Then again, I could be wrong.

"You're awake. Nerys. You're alright."

I looked up to see a man with short black hair standing opposite me, his eyes watching me anxiously.

"Dil... Dilwyn?"

"Yes?"

"Dilwyn."

Another breath and his arms wrapped me tight to his chest

and I took a long, filling breath. He peeled away and I found his eyes. Everything came back to me in one sweep and I could feel the black linger in every nook, every crack, every part of my mind.

"Nerys," he said gently, "how d'you feel?"

"Fine," I said. His eyebrows raised. "I am. Everything still moves." He nodded slowly, accepting that at the least, and didn't push the subject any further. Silently he led me to the nearest fire. I let myself be led as I looked back for Midnight. She was still there. A quick whistle and she started walking my way. I looked round to Dilwyn as he busied himself by the fire. I was relieved to see him, my whole gut felt looser. Though there was a weight within me, like a continually falling stone, that didn't want to see him. He was family, blood. The thought made that stone heavier.

Dilwyn sat next to me while I ate and drank, he drank with me as we both sat in silence. The silence that came after battle. I noticed his eyes shifting away to the same place a few times, but I didn't bother to look. I focused on the food in front of me. Once I was finished, and just being was no longer acceptable, I followed Dilwyn a way to edge of the village. There the court were, sitting in their traditional circle, except on the straw floor, not logs. I made my mind clear, relaxing the tension in my brow as we approached. I turned back again and was glad to see Midnight following, and receiving a few strokes along the way.

Each court member rose as we neared, those of them that were left. I looked at them, at each solemn face and stopped the sudden wave of emotion that flowed through me, making my nostrils flare and my mouth thin. They were no longer my father's court. They were mine.

Trahearn wasn't there, he had fallen. Bleddyn, my father's leader of the guard, was bruised, most of his left cheek was a thick purple. Just the sight of it made me wince. Cledwyn wasn't there. Merfyn looked weary, his right arm was in a cloth sling. Steffan looked at me through a black eye and a cut poked up from his shirt. Before I saw Siorus he wrapped me in a hug and squeezed tight. Without a word he let go and stepped back next to Steffan. I was touched but didn't look at him. I looked round for another face, he wasn't there.

"Dai?"

Silence.

I turned to Dilwyn, his face was blank. No, not Dai too. We shared a blink and then we were together, comforting the other for the loss of their father, our fathers. As we separated

I turned to face the court. I had done this before, ignored the emotions that were in me. Pushed them as far into the cracks of my mind as they could go. I could do it again. I hoped.

"Fill me in," was all I said as I sat on the grass, the court copying.

There was a slight pause before Steffan spoke, his voice steady, matter-of-fact.

"It has been four days since we faced them." I pretended not to notice the sudden bout of shock that ran through me as I realised I had been useless for four days. "Our scouts have seen them move west, which can only be for the river. They must need supplies. Even with their numbers decreased, they will need to find food to keep their army strong. The dead have been moved," he added quietly, "and Neirin prepared," he said quieter still.

"We made it back here without resistance," came Bleddyn's strong voice, "they left soon after..." he trailed off and I found myself staring at his brown beard. "Our number has fallen; we now are roughly 800. And those 800 are weak and tired. They still number at least 1500, probably more. We need reinforcements if we are to have any chance. It was a good battle but it will not be their last."

"Our chance has gone," stated Dilwyn abruptly. "They know we are fallen and that we have no advantage. Not surprise or high ground or numbers." He got up and started pacing behind his place. There was no hope in his eyes, only necessity. I guess the necessity now was we all stay alive. My head began to throb again.

"If they are to use the Ea, they will reach the town in five days, maybe less," reasoned Merfyn. I saw him take hold of the pendant around his neck. A small orb of jet. It was a gift from his wife, a reminder of the shadow gods, whom he still prayed to. A reminder of what they could do for the land. "We cannot get there in that time, not on foot or horse. We cannot move back there in time."

He was right. If the North men reached the Ea, they could cross half the land in a day, and it would also lead them straight to the heart of the town, my town. Then we would truly have nothing.

"What do you suggest?" I asked. It was all I could do to stop worrying that I was out of my depth. I could do this, alone. I could hunt, I could kill, I could eat. But for an entire army? To have to think about their routes, camps, food, morale, speed. I never had to think about that before.

"We cannot let them get to the town. Everything falls if they do," said Merfyn. I nodded. That much was simple.

I waited for the rest of the court to continue but no other answer came. I felt expectant eyes watching me. Waiting. Waiting for what?

It took a while for me to realise that they were waiting for the command, my command. This wasn't right. I couldn't do this. I was a hunter, not a leader. I couldn't.

I wanted to run. To hide in the darkness that was always just at the back of my mind. This wasn't my place; this was my father's. My place was out there, killing dark souls and appeasing the shadow gods. Out where no one could see me. Not here, in front of people. Not talking of war and strategy and the immediate survival of our people.

They were all looking to me, the court, the best fighters in the land, trusted advisors, friends. They were looking to me. Fine. I could run when this was over. I could hide in the shadows then. I took a deep, steady breath. Rolled my shoulders back and tried not to think of what had happened, only what must. This was my land now; these were my people now. They were mine to protect now. After all, I had started this. I had brought these men to our doorsteps, I would have to end it.

"We need to stop this madness. They are too many. We have to retreat." DIlwyn faced the court as he still stood. "It is the only way."

No-one responded to Dilwyn. I looked at my cousin and saw hard eyes, he must be hurting so much. I clasped my hands together and gave him a small smile. My voice was stifled with emotion, so I made it as strong and clear as I could. This would be my first command.

"Send men down to the town, the fastest riders. Evacuate the people and secure the town. Keep scouts on the Northern men but at a distance. The rest of us will remain here a day and then head south. They will not take our town."

I stood up and left, not daring to show any of them how weak I felt. A few paces and Midnight stood, waiting for me. I wrapped my arms around her neck and let her walk me out of the camp, back to my hut. Each step seemed to drain more energy from me. I barely made it to my hut before I had to double over and watch my breakfast come up, a pile of mush on the floor. Great. I was a mess.

I went back into my hut and prayed in the serene quiet. I tried to keep my head clear, to keep everything painful, everything that was ripping slowly, steadily at my heart and head, at bay. Then I walked back into the cool, early summer air. I spent some time examining the earth around the hay village, the plants, the trees, the dead and the dying. I dreaded this fight now. Now that I would be the one responsible for finding food for all the men, for providing weapons and leathers for them. For making as many men come back to their families as possible. Was I really so blind to the pressures my father had? Yes. I was. All I saw of him was the one decision he had made. The one that changed all our lives. I never really saw what he did after that.

And now he was gone as well.

As I kicked the dry earth with my boots, I let my mind ease slightly, I let those ever-near thoughts creep in. I had nothing. I used to fight for him, to make it better. I still remember everything I felt when I lost my mother, it was all still so vivid, from the mind of a child. I used to fight for her too, for the memory of her. But now, even with people around me, I felt only loneliness and darkness.

I ached for them, my parents. I missed them both so much now that I had neither. How would I do this without them? What would I do without them, if not fail? I wrapped my arms tight against my own chest, keeping it together. I don't know how long I stood there, thoughts dizzying my mind. My limbs had grown stiff and my stomach rumbled.

Then something urged me and I obeyed.

It was then, listening to that shadow's voice, that changed me. It wanted blood. I wanted the blood of Gwrtheryn. Together, we would both get blood. I went back to the camp.

Walking through the camp was easy with Midnight, she was big and strong and people got out of her way. Most of the men quietened as I passed, some came and gave me their hands to hold. I appreciated the gesture. Some ignored me and others weren't afraid to spit on the floor. Their dislike of a woman leading them to war, though none of them knew my father had restored me as heir. It didn't matter. What they thought of me didn't matter, I had sent more men to their deaths than they had pigs to slaughter. If they had spat at me this morning, I would have broken with doubt. Now, now I would make them respect me. I would give them blood.

That shadow's voice still echoed through me and I still obeyed. I would give them all blood.

* * *

"You're distracted. Focus, Nerys. Don't make me hit you again."

I growled playfully as I lunged at Dilwyn. He dodged easily but stepped back just as I came from the left and jabbed him in the jaw.

"Uh," he spat, "any harder and I'd have lost a tooth."

"You said to focus."

"Oh, now I'm focused," he quipped. He paced back before charging at me, sword high. I waited a breath before running in. As he made to lower his sword, I rolled down to the ground and up. I smiled as I saw my cousin flat on the ground, his legs taken out from underneath.

"Was that," he breathed, "really necessary?" I watched him hoist himself with his sword, making a hold in the mud, then grabbed his other hand to help.

"You wanted to spar, this is how I spar."

He mumbled something which I'm pretty sure wasn't pleasant but I laughed. Dilwyn and I used to practice all the time when we were growing up. It was good to do it with him again, even though neither of us had breached the subject of heir. I knew I would have to but when?

"Best of three?" I asked lightly, as he placed himself opposite me again, his medium frame side on.

"Sure."

As Dilwyn and I clashed blades, dodged punches and avoided being pushed in the mud, movement caught my eye. As well as a flash of black that I pushed aside quickly. Dilwyn noticed and turned his head.

"Does he ever leave you alone?"

"Apparently not," I replied, aware of the slight lie I had just told. Ithel was watching us, but I hadn't actually seen him since... since the battle. That didn't mean he hadn't been watching me though, I hadn't been as alert as I could have been recently. Anger, embarrassment, pride all pushed their way through me when I saw him. I didn't know what to feel. Or think.

"Ah, what was that?"

Dilwyn had got in a blow to my forearm.

"Come on."

I smiled at Dilwyn as I returned the blow, the spar absorbing me again. This is what I did know, fighting. I focused on that.

Back in my hut, I took the chance to enjoy the last few moments of solitude I was bound to get before we moved south at dawn. Celyn and Mairwen had already packed up my clothes and weapons, not like there was a lot of them. So I sat on my bed and prayed. My mind was a mess, rushing all over the place, so I prayed it would clear. That I would focus on each task, and each task only.

I looked at the small table next to the bed. At what was on

it. I didn't know what my maids meant by leaving it there.
If it was even them who left it. My father's necklace was on
the table when I awoke, I chose to ignore it when I left. And
instead of ignoring it now, I picked up the small stone pendant
on black cotton and placed it around my neck. It was cold.

When I had chosen to follow this path, all I had felt was a
dull throb after each kill. I'd soon realised the pulses were the
shadows, taking their soul, sparing me mine. Now the pulses
were the least I felt.

"Lord."

I snapped my eyes to the open door. Lord? I was not lord. Not
yet.

"Forgive me, Nerys, it seems we must talk."

As my old tutor walked into the room, I felt a part of me
slip away. Would I ever be left alone? I stood myself up and
greeted her. It was good to see Caerwen, a familiar face. I
hadn't even known she was here. A small twitch at her mouth
showed me her easy smile and I relaxed slightly. She was a
simple, honest woman, I needed that now.

"Caerwen, it's a pleasure to see you, and a relief." She took
a step back and straightened herself, as best she could, and
looked me up and down. I started to feel like her student

again.

"It's only been a year since, but that year has twisted you, scarred you. What a leader you will make." I let her odd riddle-type-thing fade in the air. I had no idea what she meant.

Caerwen took in the room before turning back to me. She bowed slightly, then took my hand.

"My condolences, young one, so soon after your return."

"Yes." She released my hand and I fought to keep my eyes clear. I could do this.

"Now, to why I am disturbing you," she motioned to the door. "Come in."

"No," I said as my supposed stalker walked in. "What is he doing here?" I turned my eyes at Caerwen, eyebrows high.

"I told you she wouldn't-" A hand silenced Ithel and me before I could voice my protests.

"If you let people help you, my student, I wouldn't have to keep teaching you." I clenched my jaw. "Now, this northern friend of ours could help you, if you will listen."

"He has nothing-"

"Tut, what did I just say?" Her eye was enough to quiet me,

and her white one was strangely focused. There was no twitch on her face now. Ithel took a tentative step into the room, his broad figure taking up the door frame.

"I have been talking to Caerwen," he started, a softer voice than usual, "and we could help. My men and I. Not just with the battle but with planning it." He took another step forward, confident this time. "We know these men; our fathers have been fighting them for decades. They go for the glory. It's how they survive. They will always go for the biggest fight, the one that will give them the biggest fight. They do not care for the men they kill, nor the towns. They do, however want women and, land and easy access to both." He stepped forwards one more time, lowering his eyes. "The South can give them what they seek, as it has been... weakening these last years."

I took a deep breath. He was right, which I disliked. Knowing more about the Northern men, their behaviour, tactics, would only help us. I would be a fool not to listen. Though there was something about him, something that hid beneath his manners and abilities that I couldn't figure out. Something about what he'd said earlier, about me being the one he sought. I didn't trust Ithel, I knew that then. Could I trust his word without trusting him?

I faced Ithel directly, making sure I could see his dark eyes.

"I will consider what you have said. It has given me much to think of."

He bowed slightly then left. I sat back on the bed, aware Caerwen's focus was on me.

"Say it," I said a little too harshly.

"That was a very vague yet satisfying answer. It would have rivalled any answer Neirin would say." She looked up and sighed. "He is proud of you, even though you are wild," she chuckled lightly. "Oh, but the shadows aren't what they once were. We can't always feel them as we used to." She relaxed her spine so that she hung slightly to the left and inched her face close to mine. "We must use our allies. Allies in times of war, can be more useful than friends, or numbers." And with that enigmatic piece of advice, she left.

I was alone again, finally.

Now I had more to think about, or not think about, other than giving in to the looming darkness. I went back to the pendant, holding it against my throat. I can't remember a time when my father didn't wear it. The little red-stripped black stone was always around his neck, a gift from his father. The sardonyx was a friendly weight, almost a comfort.

The night was windless. I still had a few more hours till dawn and I couldn't sleep. There was only one thing for it. I moved across the hay village in the shadows, at the time when they used to roam the earth. I took their place now, since they did not roam it any more. The dark night sky felt thick, the moon barely visible. The wind was biting.

I was going to Midnight, and Haul. I hadn't seen him since the last time we spoke. He should still be up; with all the horses he would have to check before we moved. I hoped he would be.

The small stable was nowhere near big enough to keep all the men's horses, so groups of horses grazed outside on the hay and grass. Haul and the other farriers and apprentices took in the horses they were working on. A quick scan told me Midnight wasn't outside. Even though the night matched her coat, I could spot her half a league away. My boots crunched on the straw as I approached the stable, a light still flickering through the slightly ajar door. I stroked the horses that I passed, they whinnied softly.

As I got close to the door, I heard voices. I assumed it was Haul and another farrier, but it wasn't. I knew that voice. I didn't trust that voice.

"Tell me, now," demanded Ithel, with none of the softness I knew.

"I, I don't think…"

My breath caught in my throat.

"You don't want to know what will happen if you don't. Help yourself."

"There's nothing."

"Listen, help your people. Tell me. Haul. Now."

"N-no. No," uttered Haul firmly.

My stomach whirled. I wanted to rush in and spill blood, Ithel's blood. That lone shadow urged me to do it. It would be over so quickly. I was ready, I could do it. I kept myself pressed to the wood. I grabbed my belt and went to- Damn, where was my sword? The rest of the shadows yanked something across my mind, something like stop. I leaned against the weathered wood and listened, breathing quietly.

"You have one more chance, Haul. After that, you won't be the only one I ask."

"There is, there is nothing."

"You are saving no-one. You will not be free. And you will definitely not be safe."

I heard heavy footsteps approach. My heart quickened as I ducked into the shadows. I watched Ithel's silhouette leave the stable in to the night. What the hell was he doing? Faint sobs from inside made me falter. I slid to the cold ground, head in my hands. Haul, strong, bold, reliable Haul, was crying. My friend was *crying* after being threatened by a man who was apparently here to help.

Haul. Not Haul. Another silhouette left the stables, slumped and shaking. I wanted so badly to help him, to comfort him somehow but I couldn't move. My whole body was as heavy as iron. So was my heart. Could I not protect anyone that I loved?

* * *

The entire town was out in the midday sun. The birds sang, the trees whispered and the people listened. All their eyes were on the stone well, the well that had been there since the shadows first roamed. The eyes collectively shifted to the woman who stood behind it as she took a cupped hand full of water and let it drip on the grass.

"We come together today to honour death, as we know, only death can give life and from life comes death. We thank the shadow gods for this life and we also thank each other. For it is us, friends, brothers, sisters, who have given ourselves to this earth as the earth gives itself to us."

The people stood, transfixed. Hope, expectance, understanding on each of their faces. Even the children were listening, watching the woman with warm blonde hair as she continued to speak.

There were people behind her. A group of men stood to the left, neither in the crowd nor in front of it. They had swords strapped to their belts and wore thick boots, as if they were always on their feet. Another two men stood directly behind her. They had a look, both slightly different but the same. It was a solemn look, an understanding look. One had short black hair, with a kind yet weathered face. He looked upon the woman with a soft expression. The other stood firm. His green eyes were proud, knowing.

The woman turned round to the two men and nodded. They walked forwards and bent down, grasping the earth in their hands. They joined their hands with the earth in all together and the woman took a small handful. She crumbled the earth over her head as she prayed. Blue cracks and sparks of light emitted from her hands and earth.

"Shadows hear us, ancestors hear us. We bless the cycle of life and the cycle of death. Today we honour the passing of death." She faced the crowd, closed her eyes and the people followed. No one saw as she held out her hands, palms to the people. She moved them from person to person, letting the shadows flow through her to them. She repeated the words with her eyes closed. The two men

still held the earth in their hands.

A flash of blue against the pale sky shone down. Bright and strong. Black and white shades danced around the blue light and above the people's heads. It hit the woman mid-sentence, right on her chest. Then it was gone. Absorbed into the silver necklace around her neck. The chain was delicate, with intricate carvings. The pendant was an orb with four clasps in each corner. The orb was glowing blue, blue with the lightning. It was a gift from the shadow gods. It was the necklace of the vessel.

CHAPTER 11

We were on the move. The dawn had come with a crisp, late spring wind. The men were eager to get south to the town, as was I. Though it wasn't for the town, it was for something I would pass on the way.

The court led the men and horses, I kept near the back. A few of my father's guard took it upon themselves to guard me. I let them, I was in no mood to argue. My eyelids kept trying to close on me, the shadows insisted on forcing memory after memory, after memory on me last night. It had made my head pound, as it still did now. Strangely though, I liked the pain. It gave me something to focus on, rather than falling further into the lonely darkness.

Scouts had returned during the night. The Northern men were on the Ea, they would be quick, travelling on water through the land. I didn't want to think about what they would do on their way. There was always that shadow, lone in the darkness, who knew what to do to them. Who showed me what we would do to them. I would do it, and more, when I met them next. I would give in to that darkness then. A small smile spread my lips but I immediately smoothed it to neutral when I heard my name.

It was Dilwyn who had called me. He brought his horse to the same pace as Midnight as he filed in next to me.

"Nerys, are you ok? I couldn't find you last night."

"Did you try?" I asked, not really wanting to talk.

"'course. I just wanted to see how you were. You know, after what we…" he shrugged off the last of the sentence. I turned my head to him and was caught by his eyes. Apparently I wasn't the only one who couldn't sleep last night.

"I saw them, last night," I said, almost to the wind. Dilwyn's brow furrowed. "My parents, and Dai. I saw them at that death day right after…" Right after your mother died, was what I was going to say. Even now, five years later, Dilwyn still had a hard time dealing with his mother's death. I carried on.

"The whole town was there, and more from the land. I remember what it was like, celebrating death like that. Like it was just another step in life. A blessing. It's not like that anymore." I took a deep breath and stroked Midnight's neck, keeping my eyes forward. "It should be. It will be. It will be like that again, Dilwyn. Death will be just another part of life again, as it was then."

"You know it can't be, Nerys. Not now. You know this," his voice was firm, hiding a string of passion.

"It will be again, Dilwyn, trust me."

"No, Nerys. Why are you…? Why would you even bring this up?" His grip tightened on his reins. His voice was angry. *He* was angry. "You know better than most that it cannot be. The necklace is gone. The shadow gods abandoned us. They left us to wither and die. Just look around, Nerys, the trees are dead. The grass is dead. Soon the men… *our* men, will be dead and you want to talk about the past like it's some shadowtale to pass the time. Come on, Nerys." He huffed as he shook his head.

This was not what I wanted. I had to get Dilwyn to see, to trust me. If he didn't, no one would. He had to know, just in case something happened…

I pulled Midnight tighter to the left, blocking Dilwyn from going forward. He groaned in annoyance but stopped.

"It is near, Dilwyn. It is close." I must have sounded mad but there was no way I was telling him everything. I couldn't tell him anything, not about the path I had followed nor the shadows nor how I was trying make the shadow gods return. "It will be like that again, soon. I can feel the end. I know it is coming. Trust me, Dilwyn, please. The end is coming."

I pulled Midnight to the right and galloped ahead. That was enough talking for the day.

* * *

We made good time travelling south. The court had set up camp 13 leagues north-east of the town. The men went about their tasks a little easier, those from my father's lands were glad to be nearer to their homes. They put up tents, moved the horses, repaired saddles. The cooks somehow prepared food to keep the entire camp fed and the maids saw to the court. We were close now. So close.

I avoided the court. I avoided the feeling that kept swimming in my head and stomach. I felt like I had a stone slowly dropping down and down within me, pulling me down with it. So I ignored it. I pushed all those... feelings aside and welcomed the shadows. I didn't need to kill to feel them now. Or just feel that one. That shadow was always with me, always just waiting at the edge of my mind. I liked it. I let it stay there. Soon. Soon I would use it. In the meantime, I did what I could to behave as I should, in the present. It was all I could do to not feel... Nope. I wasn't thinking about that.

I walked Midnight to one of the stable boys. I hadn't seen Haul since... I didn't know what I would say when I saw him, but I needed to. I needed to see him.

"You're wanted, Nerys, by the court." So much for avoiding them.

I turned to see Siorus waiting for me, his blue eyes light and kind. Haul would have to wait.

"Very well."

Siorus played with his plaited hair as we walked to the east of the encampment. I wasn't up for talking, Siorus didn't seem to notice that as he prattled on.

"D'you remember? I haven't played that game since I was young. Well, younger. We should play it again. Of course, I'll win again. I always won, oh, my team, I mean, ha. I remember that," he chuckled to himself, barely noticing the people he walked into. "You remember don't you, the one with the ball and the five people in the box. Actually no, don't remember it, I don't want you to brush up on the rules. Then I can definitely beat you, my team rather, oh sorry, sorry. Ha, where do all these people come from?"

I breathed my apologies to the men and women he bumped into, which was a few since he had decided to walk backwards.

"Would you watch," I told him, gesturing forwards.

"Oh, oh," he said, turning back round. "But we're still playing and I'm still going to beat you." He winked playfully and I laughed. Siorus was one of the few men I knew who never held anger in his heart. He was also one of the clumsiest, even though his accuracy with a bow was unmatched.

"We can do this, Nerys." It was my turn to be clumsy and walk into him, as he stopped abruptly and spoke low. "Know that." He walked ahead to his place at the circle and left me, stunned.

The court was its usual solemn self. I did my best to be concerned and engaged in their discussions, about the scouts, the river, our strategy, food, succession. My ears pricked up at that, as did a new wave of suppressed grief, so I shoved it back down and feigned interest. It was hard since shadows kept looming against my eyes.

Succession. They said it again. My succession. When was I actually to become the ruling lord of the South though? I was the heir and still I hadn't told them that. No-one knew. My father had declared me as his heir three years ago. The same time I had truly become the Night-Rider. I had decided then that completing this path was more important than being the heir, the next lord. I had done the minimum my father had asked of me. Just what I needed to allow me to keep hunting at night. Now though, now what would I choose?

A blackness tickled through my mind. I kept my features motionless as the shadow chose for me. I would follow where it led.

The rest of the day passed uneventfully. The court left me alone, which I was grateful for. I tried to find Haul a few times but he was never around when I looked. I stopped myself from thinking he was avoiding me; he was busy after all. I glimpsed Ithel once across the camp. He gave a warm, yet tentative smile, which I gave a small nod to in response. My stomach twisted as I did. I still hadn't decided what to do about him, whether I should do anything. So for now, I continued as normal. I would speak to Haul first.

I went to my tent for the night. I had to breathe. Celyn and Mairwen kept me company for a while. Both of them seemed ready to catch me should I break but I pretended not to notice. I was about to ask them to bring me some food when Siorus walked in, two hot bowls of stew in his hands. My maids left and Siorus handed me a bowl, sitting down on a stool. I chose the bed, tucking my legs underneath me. Steffan arrived soon after, a bowl in his hand and holding the handles of three wood cups in the other. I wanted to be quiet, alone. Alone with the shadow but a part of me, a very small part, warmed at their company. It was probably just the stew.

I let Siorus and Steffan talk as I ate. The sound of their voices was fine, Siorus's chomping was grating on me. He shoved the stew in his mouth between words, not wasting breath for either activity. I watched them both, noticing just how different they were. Siorus was the one cracking jokes, Steffan adding to them. Steffan was still light and kind, but only after he was serious. I liked them both, growing up with them and Dilwyn had been full of play fights and horse races and spear throws, everything a child could want. Until all our lives had changed.

The conversation slowed as we all finished our food. I felt their eyes on me before I looked up. While their faces were serious, their eyes were light.

"So, what d'you think Nerys?" I raised my eyebrows.

"More like *who* does she think it is," Steffan added, facing his friend.

"Ha, more like who does she *know* it is," Siorus countered. Steffan gave an approving nod before they looked back to me. I waved my hands at Siorus, who let out an exasperated sigh.

"No. Don't play coy with us. Look at her," he said to Steffan, who shook his head mockingly.

Siorus leaned in. "We know you've been lying to us, my friend. Now everybody knows it." He leant back, eyebrows high.

Breathe, I told myself. In and out. They couldn't know. There was no way. In and out. Even if they didn't, there was no way they were finding out from me.

"What?"

"You're going to drag this out, aren't you?" asked Steffan, putting his bowl down. He almost winked at me, making me suddenly very nervous that Steffan might actually know. The way he winked at me, he knew something.

"I-"

"Now, now. There's no need for that. Just tell us who it is," squealed Siorus, practically falling off his stool.

"I don't."

"Uh," he breathed, lifting his bowl up to bring it down. "The Night-Rider, Nerys, Blood-Pourer, Shadow-Hunter. You basically shouted to everyone that you definitely know who he is when you fought for him. Tell us, please."

I breathed easier, slightly. We used to, Dilwyn, Siorus, Steffan and me, come up with ridiculous and far-fetched theories about who he was, the Night-Rider. Something so impossible we would laugh for hours. It used to make me laugh, even proud sometimes, hearing the theories they came up with. Never knowing that the person who actually did all those things was sitting opposite them. Now though, I didn't want to laugh. I was ashamed at feeling proud. Especially since it was because of me that my father had died. That so many of the men had died.

I kept my face as clear as I could and shrugged my shoulders. "Your guess is as good as mine."

Siorus flung his hands up, forgetting he was still holding his bowl. It rattled on the floor as he scooped to pick it up. "After all we've been through," he said, shaking his head, a smile in his eyes.

"It isn't the same." I looked down to the bowl in my hands, aware that I had just shifted the conversation. Steffan's even voice made me lift my head.

"It will never be the same. Nomads killed my parents. The Night-Rider killed the nomads. And I-..." His pale blue eyes darkened. "You will tell me, Nerys, in time." He stood tall, collecting the bowls. With a furrowed brow, he spoke again. "Though, for now, as our friend, as our lord, we are with you."

They left then. They left me, as everyone did, and I felt lonely. Steffan had never... I hugged my knees to my chest for a moment, feeling pity for myself. A blackness told me that was true, that I would always be alone until I spilt his blood. Well, I would do that. I would see every drop of Gwrtheryn's blood on the ground. The black faded though. Pushed out by memories of my mother and father. Of Dilwyn and me chasing about the town, wood sticks in hand. Of the celebrations of death days and life days, the solstices, the shadows, the stars and the moon. Everything that was good.

It was time. Whether the shadows were ready or not. I was. It was time.

* * *

My mind was surprisingly clear as I rode Midnight through the cold night. Despite it being almost summer, winter hadn't released its' grip on spring. The trees and plants had yet to burst into colour.

I had written a letter to Haul. He was there, in the stables, when I went to get Midnight.

"Nerys, I am-" I shushed him with a hand. I couldn't bare to hear him say it.

"I need you to have this, Haul." I gave him the letter and turned to leave.

"You are so like them both," he whispered. I kept walking

towards Midnight, she was waiting for me. I caught sight of my cousin as he made for the stables and nodded, mounting Midnight. I figured sleep had alluded him again.

And then I was there. Just being here calmed me, my breathing, my mind, my soul. I had pushed Midnight to ride as a shadow, she hadn't wavered once.

It was dark and eerie and this was where the shadows had first walked our land.

A little stream rushed over a few rocks and pebbles as the water curved round into an almost circle, leaving a small island untouched. The stream ran from the river to a small pond which was the life source of a few families nearby. It was a sanctuary, hidden between the ancient stone boulders that had slowly collapsed in on themselves over time.

Not that anyone came here anymore. It used to be a silent place, for prayer and guidance, as the shadows and the shadow gods had brought the stones here from a faraway land. The shadows used to dwell in the stones, it was where the necklace of the vessel had been forged. A curved indent, fractured and weathered now, can still be seen on the largest rock. The place where the lightning had struck, offering the pendant to the first vessel. Ironic really, that my father chose to bury it here, stopping our communication with our ancestors and our gods completely.

I let Midnight wander and graze as I took off my belt, cloak and jacket. I took out a dagger from my belt and held it high. The water was cool as I stepped into the stream, it coming up to my shins. I waded towards the island and bent into the water, bringing down the dagger. I dug down and down, where the island's earth met the streambed. Then a muffled thud. I chucked my dagger back and dug with my hands. They were slightly numbed from the digging and the water but I didn't stop until the chest was free.

It was nothing special, just a thick oak chest, but it contained the life force of my people.

I set the chest on the grass and stepped out of the stream. Midnight was curious as she sniffed the chest and whinnied. I stroked her softly, preparing myself. This was it. After everything I had done, every man and woman I had killed, every child made an orphan, every person I had lied to, I was finally here. I knew I was right. The pulses had been getting stronger, the shadows had been closer to me. It had to be time.

I sat in front of the chest and folded in my legs. My fingers were slowly warming up, my arms were slightly shaking. The last time I was here... well, this place had changed my life several times. I just stared at it. I couldn't touch it. The necklace, at all. I had learnt that the hard way. It had been such a struggle as a child, holding my mother, hugging her. She had always been so careful. One wrong touch was all it would take. Well, I had touched it once, brushed it accidently. I was aware enough in those few moments before I lost consciousness to know things were seriously bad. I had awoken two days later, feverish, shivering, constantly nauseas.

"They spared you," my mother had said, "the shadows spared you." Tears streamed down her pale face. I had no recollection of what had happened. Others had not been so lucky.

So I knew, no matter what, not to touch the necklace. Ever. It belonged to the vessel. Only the vessel could touch it. And I was not the vessel. Yet.

CHAPTER 12

The morning brought bad news. Scouts had returned just after dawn. The North men were moving down the Ea quicker than expected, much quicker. They had taken swift boats from the local villages. If they kept up this pace, they would be at the town in two days, maybe three. More if they raided. I cursed the wish of them raiding so that we would have more time, since that would mean them ransacking more of my people along the way.

The court sat in the middle of our encampment. We were still 13 leagues north-east of the town, waiting to move. A quiet haze hung in the early morning air. My stomach growled in protest as I walked over to the last log and sat. I didn't get much sleep last night, and even less food. It was too early for me to be talking, seeing as the sun had only just risen. Hunting, killing, yes. Talking, no. I barely noticed the dozen members of the guard who gathered around the logs, protecting me, or us, I still hadn't told anyone.

"Drystan and his men are still following the Northerners,"
begun Bleddyn. I eyed him suspiciously, he was responsible
for the guard, so he was the one who made them follow
me around. His grey hound curled up on his feet as he
continued. "Our men have the town, but 30 of them will do
little against these blood-thirsty beasts." He rubbed his hound
affectionately then clenched his fists. "At a decent pace, we
can be there in a day, giving no time to prepare, to rest or
actually do anything."

Prepare. There were still villages nearby, this side of the river,
that hadn't been cleared. That didn't have protection. We
couldn't help them and fortify the town and put half the men
on reserve at the same time. I swore under my breath. What
choice did we have?

"So we get to the town but leave those who can't get to safety
to get raided, killed, or worse?" I countered, my voice breaking
slightly from its hoarseness, and also from the building guilt.

"We can't do everything, Nerys, we need more men." Bleddyn
stroked his hound as he spoke, it looked as though it gave
him the same comfort that stroking Midnight gave me. The
comfort needed to make a hard decision.

"We must save the town. Protecting that protects the entire
land, " claimed Merfyn.

"Merfyn's right, it has to be done, Nerys," Dilwyn replied, looking at me as if I were some child to pacify. "I suggest we move to the town. We can send messengers to all the people on our way to get to safety. The town must stay."

"Here."

"I know," I said through gritted teeth, "but what is the point in saving the town if we can't help *our* people, who may not get to safety?"

"Your concern is admirable, Nerys, truly." Merfyn's eyes were soft as he spoke, though I could feel my jaw clenching.

"To win this war we must think long-term." Long-term? Ha. Bleddyn stared at me, no softness in his eyes, they just looked full of pain. How many more people would I let die for me?

"I understand that. What I don't understand is how we can sit here and do nothing while there are people who cannot defend themselves." Each word I said slow and clipped. "I cannot sit here and let them suffer, not when we have the ability to help them."

"Try to see, Nerys, the town must come first. They can't take it. If we let them take it, there won't be any people left to save." Siorus's words pierced me. I locked my eyes on his, keeping mine steady, strong. He blinked his to the floor and I almost would have felt ashamed had I not had a flicker of black across my mind. I didn't even try to stop the blackness then. Didn't even try to stop that lone shadow as it invited more shadows into my mind. I had the necklace, the shadows were close, closer than they had ever been these last eight years. And I was ready.

"Fine. Don't help these people. But they will die and their deaths will be because of you." I made a point of staring at each court member in the eyes. They would see me; they would see the blackness in my eyes.

"Please, Nerys, it is hard to make these decisions but I-" I silenced Dilwyn with a hand.

"Do not say it. I know more than you do about making hard decisions, cousin." I spat the words with a disdain that shocked even me, though it was necessary. "This *hard* decision has been made by you all. What next?" I asked, eyebrows high on my forehead.

There was a moment of silence before Bleddyn stopped stroking his hound.

"We send more men down to the town," he said, ignoring my outburst, "enough to keep it until we can all reach it." More silence.

"And of the Northern men?"

Siorus avoided my gaze as he replied. "Keep Drystan's scouts on them. Learn more about them." Learn more about them...

"It is a good plan, Nerys. It is the only-" Another hand silenced Merfyn, he dutifully stopped but I could see the fight he was having with himself. I sighed a breath. My head was heavy.

"Please, Ner-"

"*Enough.*" I had risen from my log, hands balled into fists. A year ago, I would not have done this. A year ago, the court would not have looked at me as they did now. With shock and maybe fear. Steffan rose, Steffan, who had kept patiently quiet up till now rose and squared himself to me. I respected him for that.

"Calm yourself, Nerys. If it is soon..."

"I said enough!" Those black shadows were a part of me now, swimming through my blood. "Stop calling me, Nerys." My jaw ached.

"But-"

"Each time you say Nerys all I can hear is Neirin!" I seethed, turning my back on the court. My chest pounded, my lungs tight. I couldn't contain it, the rage and the guilt and the pain. I wanted to scream, cry and kill all at once. The shadows urged

257

me to spill blood, to kill everything and anything, regardless
if their soul was dark or not. I wanted to act. My whole body
tensed with the adrenaline. I wanted to follow them but a
stupid small voice stopped me. It was soft and kind and made
me remember warmth. It made me think of stew.

"Nerys, heir of Neirin, we are all with you," whispered Steffan.

I slowed my breathing. I took back control of my mind, forcing
the shadows back. It was hard but they gradually relented.
Soon, I said to them. A little while longer and I would be with
you, I said. I eventually turned back to Siorus and Steffan, to
Merfyn, Bleddyn and Dilwyn, not meeting any of their eyes.

"Who shall we send?" I asked, changing the subject.

"The quickest?"

"No, the most experienced."

"No," I said. "Ithel. We send Ithel and his twenty men." A few
curious looks had me explaining. "They know the North men,
have fought them before. They can help our men at the town
prepare before we arrive."

The court nodded their approval. And that would get him
away from Haul.

"I'll tell him," offered Dilwyn.

"No," the darkness was almost faded from my mind now, "I will." I gave the court a small nod before I said "Do what you must." It took me a few breaths before I realised they were the same words my father had said to me. He must have felt how I did now. That the inevitable was coming.

I would tell Ithel and I would enjoy getting him away from my men. First, however, I needed food, and a hunt. I grabbed some bread and half an apple from the mess tent, forcing myself not to think of how little food had been prepared in there for the hundreds and hundreds of hungry men waiting. I checked my tent, took out Midnight from the stables and was off.

The woods barely a league away were quiet. No stray, wandering men. I had to settle for small game instead. After a while I caught the skinniest of skinny hares to take back to camp, the cooks would be happy with the extra food, not that it would stretch far. I got my blood, it wasn't the blood I wanted but it would satisfy me for a while. It would not satisfy the shadows but their blood would come. So for now, I was pleased. Mostly.

As soon as I reached the edge of the encampment, Dilwyn found me. He had a mischievous gleam in his eyes as he took hold of Midnight's bridle.

"Ithel, N-Nerys." I enjoyed the slight hesitation as he said my name and chose to ignore it. I was calm. "He must be told."

I got down from Midnight and handed her to the stable boy who had run over and gave the hare to a young girl from the stables. Yes, Ithel must be told.

Dilwyn walked with me to Ithel's tent. My father had insisted the son of his great friend have a large circular tent, worthy of an heir.

"I know you want to do this your way, you always do, just be a bit nice, ok?"

"Mmm."

"And Nerys, I know you think you have to do this, but I could do it for you, you know?"

"Mmm."

"And you should not give him a chance to negotiate. Tell him straight and get out of there."

"Sure," I said, barely listening to my cousin anymore. We were almost at Ithel's tent, we got stuck behind two men pulling a cart of shields and that gave Dilwyn the time to rattle on more.

"I don't know why he has been trying to see you and watch you all the time, sometimes I would just watch him watch you. He really is weird. I don't like him being around you so much.

"I have barely seen him, Dilwyn."

"I'm just saying," he raised his hands and shrugged. My cousin had started to annoy me, I brushed it aside for now. I was calm.

I walked into Ithel's tent, Dilwyn behind me, with no announcement. Several of his men sat at the wood table on one side. They all went abruptly silent when they saw me, that made me smile. Ithel stood alone. He pulled his head out of a wash basin and reached for a cloth. It was then he heard the silence. He span his eyes to his men, then me, comprehension hitting him. My smile widened but I dropped it quickly. I let him dry his face before I spoke. Some water rolled down his neck and on to his lean, bare chest. I would have appreciated it had I cared.

"Ithel, I have a task for you and your men," I waved a hand in their direction, "I would ask you to follow it immediately."

"Of course, Nerys." A twist in my stomach made me flinch. The way he said my name, it was too... familiar. He was definitely going.

"I need you to ride to the town without delay, I believe you know the way, and secure it."

"As soon as we are packed but," he took a step closer, "I have twenty men, two are badly hurt."

"Who will add to the thirty already there. Fifty will hold it firm until we join you." He nodded his acceptance. Whatever reply he made to give he bit his tongue to. He put on a loose shirt and walked over to his men, who were doing a wonderful job of stifling their words.

"And when we get there, what then?"

"I would like you to teach the men what you know of these Northerners."

"The men of the rocks?"

"You call them that, yes. And Ithel, it is *my* town," it was my turn to take a step closer to him. I barely reached his shoulder so made a point to stare up into his deep, dark eyes. "It is my town and my people. I will not allow anyone to put fear into them. Into their hearts, their eyes or their minds." I held his gaze a moment longer, until I saw that tiny hint of uncertainty. "Hold my town."

"I will," he breathed. I turned and walked away but it heard it. I heard his faint whisper "Nerys."

As soon as I was out of the tent, Dilwyn was at my side. His step sprang like a puppy as he waited for me to speak.

"Say it, before you wet yourself."

He nudged me with his elbow. "That was," he loosed a breath, "impressive. You…" I allowed myself a small laugh as Dilwyn puffed out his cheeks. I hadn't seen him do that since we were children. "Well, you weren't kind Nerys. Every word was civil, polite even, but gods above you weren't kind."

"It had to be said."

"Did it?"

We had walked to my tent. I felt a tug from the shadows to go in. To be alone. There was something in there, something like their kin, that they wanted to feel. Something still in the chest it had been buried in.

"Kind of," I relented.

Dilwyn flashed a wicked grin that made his face unfamiliar to me. "I never liked him."

"Why though?" I asked with genuine interest.

"Because of the way he follows you around. Were you not listening to me?" He flicked his hands out and sighed. "I had to turn him away from court this morning, he said he wanted to check on you. The creep. Don't see why we needed him anyway." I shook my head at my cousin and chuckled. I felt that stone lift within me ever so slightly.

"It doesn't matter if you like him or not, he is our ally."

"You don't like him either."

"Tch, *trust* him. I don't fully trust him, there's a difference. Besides, his father is our greatest friend, so the son is our ally." I said my words slowly, mocking Dilwyn to understand.

"Well, whatever happens, I guess I can understand that."

"Dilwyn," I warned.

"Nerys, when we are, well, when I am lord and you are lady, we will only need to trust each other."

"Dil, what are you saying?"

"Oh, I don't know. This whole lord thing." He looked at me with sad eyes. "It's just... they should be here, you know?"

"I know." I hugged my cousin and he hugged back, my annoyance with him washed away. We stepped away and I gave his hand a squeeze. "I will do the best I can Dil. I would like to know I can count on you to be beside me, as Dai was to my father." I looked at our hands as I spoke, feeling a lot more honest that I had been in a long time. There was a tug in my something, pulling me away.

"Yes, Nerys. We have each other, we'll always have each other."

"Thank you." I looked into his eyes and saw that he meant

it. We were all each other had left of blood. No parents, grandparents, siblings. We were it, each other's family. Each other and our memories. "How are you coping?"

He took a breath to clear his eyes. "I'd say as well as you." I laughed at that. "We can grieve when this is over. For now, they... just aren't here. We are." I nodded. "We can do this, Nerys, make things better, as they were." I tilted my head to the side, forehead tight. "Together we will make things better."

"Dil, I-"

Without another breath he kissed my forehead and walked away. I would have called after him, to ask what he meant but the tug pulled again.

In my tent, I bent down under my bed. I lifted the dirt lid and found the chest right where I had left it. I pulled it out of the dirt hole I had dug and rested it on my bed. There, inside, was the necklace of the vessel. It lay on a soft cotton cloth. Cold. Untouched. I could feel my scars start to tingle, light and prickly along the skin of my forearms. A curious part of me wanted to touch it. This would all be over if I did. If I just reached down, picked it up, I could become the vessel. I should be, if my lineage was anything to go by. I took a filling breath, closed the chest and put it back in the ground. Soon, the shadows whispered. Soon.

* * *

The scream that pierced through the night thudded my ears and heart. I sat bolt upright in my small bed and was out of it, heart pounding. I yanked on boots and ran outside. Fires glimmered. Bewildered men gathered. Horses neighed.

I ran, searching for the cause of the scream. I ran across the camp and stumbled into Midnight. Her eyes were wide, ears twitching frantically. I had never seen her like this. She stomped the ground and jittered about. She was never one to be frightened. I grabbed her mane and stroked her, spoke to her. Gently I calmed her down. I kept a firm hand in her mane as I let her lead me.

There. I followed Midnight back to the stables. I noticed a tired-looking Siorus ushering men back to their beds as Steffan ordered the guard to set up a perimeter. Most men went back. Some stayed, whispering with the cooks and maids. I left Midnight outside as I entered the wood building. There was a chill in the air. It brought a feeling of dread. This could not-

The straw beneath my boots felt harder than usual. The air thicker. This could not be.

Blood splattered the straw, the timbers. I took a deep, unrewarding, breath. I willed the shadows to me, the only thing I could do that didn't make me feel like hurling. This could not be.

Three bodies. Three bodies lay on the straw. Their faces were pale, scared, distressed. They were stabbed and sliced, slashed all over. It looked cruel, almost childlike. There was no restraint. They would haunt me. These faces would haunt my dreams, day and night. I felt men around me, voices talking. That was all silence. The world stopped as I bent down. I held his cold, rough hands in mine. One tear fell down my cheek. That was all I let escape me. Haul.

My mind was as black and thick as the night when I left the stables. I didn't need the shadows to tell me what to do. I already knew. I grabbed Midnight and sprinted for my tent. My thoughts were surprisingly calm. I had yielded to the shadows in an instant. But I was still in control enough not to lash out yet. Not to end everyone that I saw, yet.

I could hear my blood pumping through my ears. I was at my bed. Opening the dirt lid. Pulling out the chest. The shadows flashed and flickered. I had my hands on it and already knew. I opened it anyway.

It was gone. The necklace of the vessel was gone.

CHAPTER 13

We didn't rest.

I pushed Midnight on faster and faster. She obeyed. All I
had to do was think and she obeyed. It was then I knew the
shadows were with her too. She was no longer just a trained
war horse. She was a shadowhorse.

The Northern men were last seen half a day's ride north of us.
The back of their army. I would be there. The night began to
fade as my mind cleared. Midnight's strength was lasting. I
still felt rage, there would be blood.

The dawn approached and I didn't care for it but we stopped.
Only because they were there. Occupying a small village east
of the Ea were the Northern men. Well, some of them. The
rest would be spread along the river. But that did not matter.
The men that were here would die.

I slid off Midnight and left her behind in a large, mostly bare,
grove. This was my fight. Then, that's when I lost control. Or
gave it up. I couldn't really tell. That's when the shadows took

over me completely. The ring of my sword as I pulled it from its' sheath was all I heard. I let out a snarl.

They didn't stand a chance. I was swift and silent. I was death to them. I was fear. Nothing could touch me, the shadows made sure of that. My sword sliced through bodies as if they were water. I was water, fluid, strong, silent save for the ripples. Nothing could touch me and nothing could stop me. Blood of my enemies splattered me, my clothes and face, yet I did not stop. Nothing did.

And then it was done. Bodies littered the earth. Red stained everything. Weapons were strewn all over. It was done. The fight was done. My chest pounded as it constricted. It was an effort to breathe, the shadows had control of my lungs. They still soared through me and I let them. My fingers had swollen, I thought they might burst. I could no longer hold my sword, it slipped to the ground. I barely recognised the pulses beating through me, what with the adrenaline teasing through my blood as well.

I stood there, waiting. Waiting for my breathing to slow and the pulses to stop. Waiting for the shadows to calm down. I would need to leave quickly. Before the rest of the North men found this slaughter. I didn't move though. I didn't want to go back. Not when I was here. Not when the shadows had control of me. All I saw when they were with me was blood. And the power to get it. Without them, I was alone. Without them, I would just have pain and anger and tears. And now betrayal. I didn't want that. I didn't want to go back.

I picked up my sword and walked back to Midnight.

We had stopped once on the way back, to wash and eat and rest. I was sore and tired but my mind wasn't. It was alert, aware. We arrived after noon, the shadows making us swift. The camp was buzzing with movement and a nervous energy that only a kill in your own camp could bring. As the men packed up to move, I made my way cautiously to my tent. I half expected Dilwyn to pounce on me immediately but he didn't, thankfully. I grabbed some fodder along the way and tied Midnight to my tent as she ate, she would not be going back to the stables.

"What the actual hell?"

I snapped around and was instantly grabbed by Siorus who yelled out "Got her." Before I could say a word, Steffan had appeared and grabbed my other arm and I was marched off. I knew where to and that didn't improve my mood.

Steffan pushed me down onto a small log and stood next to me, arms crossed, weight on the balls of his feet. Siorus took a log on the other side and stared at me, daring me to move. Neither of them said a word. I almost didn't want to break the silence; they were doing an excellent job of being angry. I did, however.

"What was that for?" I kind of already knew.

"What was that for? What was that for?!" Siorus's voice threatened to break and he shrugged his shoulders in dismay. "This, this is because we found three of our men slain in our camp last night and a court member *and our lord* missing. You can't do this, Nerys." He sighed heavily. "You can't just run off for yourself and leave us." I saw the pain in his eyes and quickly breathed an apology.

"Wait. Who else is missing?"

"Dilwyn." Steffan offered nothing more so I looked back to Siorus, his hair unkempt in its loose plait. He didn't get to explain.

Bleddyn and Merfyn strode over and stood tense. Firm, dominant but tense.

"You've heard?" asked Bleddyn. He looked ready to pounce on anyone who so much as looked at him wrong. I nodded my reply.

"When did he go missing? Who saw him last?" I asked my

court.

"We can't be sure, the last he was seen was eating with Aeddan. Aeddan doesn't know where he went after." Merfyn replied steadily, a hand tight on his sword hilt. Aeddan was one of the guard, the lord's guard, and Dilwyn's friend. If he didn't know where Dilwyn was, no one would.

"Surely someone must have seen him?"

"Not if he was hidden," Steffan suggested, face neutral, eyes clear.

"Hidden from what?" I asked.

"We don't know who did this. If it was an attack by the Northerners or one of our own. Either way, they could have hidden Dilwyn in a cloak. Made him look like a bundle of laundry."

"Your ideas are very ready, Steffan," Bleddyn stated as I turned to him. Bleddyn's words had sounded accusative.

"It is our job to think as such, as well you know, Nerys," came Merfyn's response, looking me in the eyes. I nodded my acknowledgment.

I closed my eyes as the weight of the situation began to sink in. Haul was dead. Slain. Dilwyn was missing. They were the last of my family, the last. Blood. Vengeance. I would get them both.

"Was anyone seen at the stables last night?" I enquired to keep myself from sinking further.

"Only the other stable hands and farriers."

I put my head in my hands briefly. It had started to spin.

"We must learn. We must learn if he was taken or, or-"

"Or if he went willingly." Steffan's voice was steady, practical. I stole a glance at his face, it was the same. I couldn't believe that of Dilwyn. That he would run. I didn't believe that of him. Still, my head nodded. The court dispersed, each to their duties.

I sat on that log for a while longer, not noticing the guards still around me and the men passing by. I prayed and prayed that Dilwyn was safe. That I would find him. But who would take him? Who would kill two stable hands, a farrier and take a court member?

Back in my tent I took out the chest from under the bed. I had not told the court of it, of the necklace. I had not told them that the lost necklace of the vessel was not lost, I had it, only for it to be lost again. Still I would not. Not until it was mine. I made an oath then, on that chest that had contained the most valuable possession of my people. I made an oath that I would not cry again. Because I would not lose again. I would do whatever it took, but I would not cry again.

* * *

Before the day was out news had come of the Northern men. Welcome news. They were returning north, up the Ea. Steffan found me in my tent, praying.

"Excuse me, Nerys."

"Yes," I replied, coming back from the darkness.

"What are your wishes? If the men are retreating we can stay here or we can head to the town, as planned." I took a moment before answering. Most of the tents were already packed, the carts loaded, horses ready. My mind was still overwhelmed with it all, the planning, the thinking, the slow pace of moving an army. Of fighting as a defence rather than an attack. DIlwyn would be able to help me, if he was here.

"We continue as planned. To the town." Steffan nodded his acknowledgment and turned to leave. "Steffan," I called. Another breath. He turned round to me, a soft expression on his hard face.

"I, I am sorry, about how I behaved at court yesterday. Things have been changing so fast wi-" I stopped myself from saying *changing so fast within me*. Thankfully he didn't seem to notice.

"It is understandable. Times like these change us all." He gave me a gentle smile that brightened his face, it was a pleasure to see.

"What did you mean, the other day?" I asked and quickly looked at my belt, fascinated by the buckle.

"It can wait. There will be a time for that." His voice was so calm, I was almost envious. "Nerys?"

"Yes?"

He took a steadying breath. I had never known Steffan need to summon courage. "Nothing. It can wait."

Once he was gone I went back to my prayers. Nothing could save me anymore. Not even this damned path I was on. I felt like a blackened soul, like the ones I killed. If there was even a soul left in me. Words, images jumbled my thoughts. *See your fear. Then know it. Then pass it.* Those words swam over and over. Why were they in my head? Where had they come from? Another string of words pushed to the surface - I was nothing. I *was* nothing. I felt nothing, not really. Only the shadows. When they were with me I felt alive, hungry. I had a purpose. Without them, I just went through the motions, pushing aside the tightness, the rope that was wrapping itself around my chest and throat. I missed my father. I missed him and he wasn't here. He just wasn't here right now, that's what I said to myself.

The shadows took me to sleep that night, for I surely would not have.

The next day, the ride south took less time than I expected. The men were in better spirits, knowing the North men were further away from them and their families. Again, I stayed at the back. My hazy thoughts shifted to Dilwyn, the last time we moved south. He had been so sure, so adamant that things would not be as they were. I gripped Midnight's reins tighter until the leather dug into my skin. At least I felt that.

We rounded a small valley, once lush and overflowing with the whispering of grasses. Now it was dry, the grass short and rough. My heart skipped a beat nonetheless. There, a league away, was my home. I had not seen it for a long time. A small stone wall ran the entire perimeter, with timber frames marking the outside farmland. The middle was lined with double timber walls, twice the height of a man. The two gates were reinforced with stone and precious iron, taking five men each to open. My head cleared and my heart lifted. That stone within me lifted.

I was home.

I let the court arrange the men, keeping half on defence on the northern perimeter, outside the walls. The last time I had stepped through this town, was the day I was banished from it. Nothing had changed, apart from it being empty of its' inhabitants. At least there was that, the people were in the southern towns, safe.

I walked through it, an overwhelming familiarity making me feel more human than I had done in seasons. I politely acknowledged the men already here. There was one face that popped into my head then. One face I needed to see. And his was the only one I could not find. Where was the coward?

I passed the stone communal buildings that housed the healing rooms, kitchens, baths, school rooms, town hall. I purposefully ignored Aeddan, who had taken it upon himself to be my shadow, and the other guards who were several paces behind me. Seeing as I was now the only heir around. They wouldn't bother me.

I strode east, over the south bridge to the market stalls. Not there. Along the wall to the south gate. No sight of him. I sighed my annoyance, avoiding the coming blackness that coupled my anger. The coward.

I walked back to the bridge, taking each step slow. I wanted to be in control for this, not the shadows. This was my revenge, not theirs. Then I saw him out the corner of my eye. He was at the stone well, greeting my men who were stationed inside the town. Reason went out my mind. I would do this now. My legs picked up pace as I stalked over to Ithel. I felt my guard rush to match my pace.

As soon as I was close enough, I grabbed Ithel's arm and pulled him away from the men, to the east of my house. Out of earshot, I had enough reason left for that.

"Start talking."

"Ner-, Nerys, let go of me." His voice got stronger as he spoke, as he realised I wasn't playing around. I sensed Aeddan, whose frame was slight and quick, and my guard set up a line between me and Ithel and the rest of the men, all their hands on the hilts of their swords. I didn't care. They were doing their job, I was doing mine and right now, mine was vengeance.

I held Ithel's arm a breath longer before I let go. He rubbed it in his other hand. His lowered eyebrows would have convinced me, if I was foolish enough to believe them.

"Well?"

"Well what, Nerys?" He took a step closer as he looked over to my guard and the distant men. All who were doing their best to not look interested. "What is going on?"

"You had better start talking before I gut you and burn your insides."

"Nerys, breathe. Tell me what happened." Ithel raised his hands to take my shoulders but I shook them off. The way he said my name again, it was too... much. He was the one who had scared my friend to the point of tears, he would not touch me. Haul. He had threatened him. Now I would do the same.

"Don't," I said, shaking my head. I stepped towards him, looking up into his eyes. Something flickered so quickly behind them I almost didn't see it. But that didn't matter. Only Haul mattered now. "I heard you. I heard you threaten Haul. I heard what you said to him, what you did to him."

I was right in front of him now, so close I could feel his breath down on my face. I acknowledged the fact that he didn't move, that he stood his ground. Good. At least he wasn't a coward now.

"I told you before *outlander*. I will not allow anyone to put fear into my people." I felt the surge of the shadows in me then but kept them aside. I knew I could hold them off, but I didn't know for how long. I saw Ithel's eyes widen as he stepped back, he had seen what I had felt. He had seen the shadows through my eyes.

"No I didn't. You don't under-"

"Save it." My hands curled into fists. "He's dead now. Dead. And so will you be if you don't start talking." I stepped forward to match the one he had taken back. He raised a hand to stop me and I walked right into it.

"Lord," warned Aeddan, half firm, half hesitant. I raised a fist to him while my eyes stayed locked on Ithel's.

"He's what? Nerys, I'm so sorry, I am. He was a good man."

I balled my fists tighter, fighting to stay in control. Fighting the shadows to not fuel my rage. Before I would avenge Haul, I needed first to learn.

"Don't you dare."

"But I didn't kill him," he lowered his hand. My dagger slid out of its sheath effortlessly.

"Oh, I know." My words came out smooth as I tilted my head.

"Nerys. I did not kill Haul. I wasn't there. You know I wasn't there." Simple. Clear. I did not care.

"Of course you didn't. You only meant to scare him, to get him to talk. You didn't mean for it to get out of control." I had started circling him, eyeing my prey.

"Lord, Nerys," warned Aeddan again. This time I turned to him and snarled. His face flinched with alarm. His loose blonde hair stopped swinging as the look on my face had stopped him walking towards me. He recovered quickly and stood where he was.

"That doesn't stop you from sending someone else. Getting them to kill for you. To make good on your word. Who else were you going to ask Ithel? Who else of my people were you going to terrify? Tell me, now, and maybe I won't burn your guts."

However much the situation sickened me, I was starting to enjoy myself. And draw a crowd. Even though my guard held them back, more men had poured into the town and were curious, and the cooks did love to gossip.

"I don't know," came Ithel's feeble attempt at innocence.

"Stop with the steady avoidance, please. I just want to gut you already."

"Nerys. Stop."

"Now."

Bleddyn and Merfyn's voices were clear and demanding and the last ones I wanted to hear right now. I did not want them to see me like this. But that didn't make me stop. This was for Haul. I flicked my dagger around in my hand, it's weight familiar.

"You see Ithel, my court don't want me to kill you. I would hate to disappoint them. Why don't we move this along?"

What he did next caught me off guard. He lunged towards me, grabbed my wrist and pulled the dagger point to his chest. Then he whispered low.

"If you really want to kill me, do it. Now. I did not kill Haul." I heard his steady breath, felt his warm hand hold my wrist strong. We stood there unmoving. Right then, I didn't know what to do. What to believe. I felt a surge of shadows in my chest push all the way up to my eyes. His flickered again, a quick flash of blue. It sent a shiver running through me, almost like it pushed the shadows back down. I dropped the dagger on the ground. I believed him. His eyes did not leave mine, nor did his hand.

"I think I know who did."

* * *

It was a warm summers day. The market was busy and the town was almost bursting with people. Dilwyn was behind me, giggling, pushing me forwards as we crept on hands and knees to the bakers' stall. I stopped abruptly and Dilwyn rammed into me, still giggling. I turned round and shushed him quickly. Several boots walked passed me and I started crawling again. Slowly, slowly. I was almost to the stall and I could smell all the warm bread and cakes floating on the cool breeze. DIlwyn's giggling was really starting to irritate me but I would stay focused. "On the count of three," I said to him but before I could even say one, my cousin had screamed 'three', grabbed a tray and sprinted back to our cart at the other side of the market. I wasted no time and ran behind him.

Back under the overfull cart of hay was Siorus, Steffan and Dilwyn all laughing and playfully punching each other as I snuck in. Siorus and Steffan were far too big to be sitting comfortably but I fit under the cart easily.

"You took your time," Dilwyn had the cheek to say. He took a pie from the tray and I could smell it was warm and sweet. I grabbed it out of his hand as I said "You were the one who was giggling the whole way there."

He stuck his tongue out at me and I stuck mine back at his, except mine was full of crumbs of pie as I had just taken a bite.

Steffan was laughing but came to a stop as he ate. Siorus was spitting crumbs everywhere as he was still laughing as he was eating.

"The look on both your faces," more laughter and crumbs. "The baker will not be happy with you."

Steffan stuffed pies into his pockets hurriedly and tapped Siorus quickly.

Siorus ignored him. "I really didn't think you could do it, either of you," he was still chuckling to himself.

"Well, I knew I could. I could have done it all by myself," said my suddenly brave cousin.

"Really?" I turned to him. "You could have got all the way to the stall all by yourself, no giggling?" I mocked his giggling fit and he started fidgeting and puffing his cheeks out.

"Yeah, course. I could have-"

I had no time to hear what he could have done. In less than a breath, the baker's face was under the cart, jeering at us, trying to grab for the tray and Dilwyn and I scuttled out and headed for the south gate, out of the town. Siorus and Steffan were nowhere to be seen, leaving us to run for our lives.

Once we were out the gate and free, Dilwyn and I caught our breaths and laughed some more. Siorus goaded us into taking from the market stalls at least once every new moon. Kept us on our toes he said.

I felt Dilwyn stiffen next to me and I looked up to see why. We were on the outskirts of the town, where the farmers worked the land *for grain. And right there, not 10 feet away from us were both our mothers. I always liked watching mother when she was with people, she just used to glow and move so serenely. She was waving her hand to the sky and back down to the earth and I could just make out a faint blur of blue following her hand on the air as she moved it.*

I felt Dilwyn push me to the side and we ran around to the east of the town wall, unnoticed.

"Let's play lord and vessel," Dilwyn said excitedly, as we climbed over a small ditch. Before I could agree, he said, "I'll be the lord and you be the vessel."

"No, I'll be the lord and you'll be the vessel."

"What? No. I want to be the lord," he said a little sulkily. I knew he was lying, he always liked being the vessel really.

"No, I'm the lord and you're the vessel, we have to practice," I said. I didn't see his face but I knew he was smiling.

***

I turned and gave a quick nod to my court, all of them standing between the guard and the rest of the men, and walked over to my stone and wood house. In the large, mostly wooden hall I waited for them. The floor of the hall was dense earth covered in thick, rough hides. The walls a mix of chalk and wood. It was cold but comfortable. Thick oak tables and wooden chairs of all shapes and sizes were pushed back against the walls, they hadn't been used in some time. Just breathing in the old, almost stale, air brought a dozen memories to mind. The maids had a few candles lit around the hall. I crossed my arms as the court entered, Ithel the last one.

"We are here to listen to Ithel and to hear his words." Bleddyn said to the court but keeping his eyes straight on me. I gave him a quick smile.

"So, you have taught our men some of your tactics?" Trust Merfyn to tactfully change the subject, I was thankful though. It gave me a moment to calm down, even if I didn't really want to.

"Yes. They learned quickly. We have fashioned more spears from all the spare wood and have barrels of oil-soaked cloths prepared." Ithel's voice was a little terse but respectful enough.

"Good, that will help," Merfyn replied.

I saw Siorus look at me with a warning glare which could also be an amused glare and softened my jaw. My court were ready to listen to Ithel, I should at least try to with an open-mind. For a little while.

"Ithel," Steffan gestured his hand as an invitation for him to start. The six of us stood in the middle of the hall, the faint sounds of fires and chatter and work from outside easing in through the open door.

"I don't know what you know so I'll say it all." Although he was talking to all the court, Ithel kept his focus on me. I barely moved my head and he continued. "It started just after Neirin died." My jaw tightened. "He would be constantly around the stables, not doing anything. Just waiting."

"Who would?" questioned Siorus. Ithel held up a hand, dissuading more interruptions.

"At first, I thought he was just waiting for his horse, simple enough, yet he was always there. If he wasn't doing something else, he was at the stables. So I started keeping an eye on him."

As Ithel spoke, I tried to think back to that time. Who could he mean?

"What he was doing, where he was going, strange thing was, he rarely left his tent. I know, I checked a few times, he didn't like that." The slight humour that coated his voice made me chuckle. I didn't know he could be anything but serious. Immediately I shook my head and forced myself to concentrate. "I even found him watching over you, Nerys, a few times, when you were unconscious." A puzzled look from me made him explain.

"Right after the battle, when you were out for four days. That's when I started talking to Haul… when I started asking him if he had noticed anyone around the stables more." He was dragging this out, I started shifting my weight from one foot to the other, fiddling with my belt. The rest of the court all stood still. Bleddyn's hand was on his hilt, Merfyn clasped his hands in front of him. Siorus had both hands on his hips, looking up to the roof and Steffan crossed his arms, legs wide.

"I'm getting to it," Ithel said softly, noticing my twitching fingers. "Haul replied yes. I asked why, he never said. He seemed beyond loyal. So I started watching you more, making sure he didn't get to you. I knew he would, eventually. I could sense it in his eyes. The desire. Then when I came to you," he said this with his dark eyes softly at me, "with Caerwen that night, that's when it changed. That's when he changed completely. I only went in after to Haul to help him. To make him tell me so I could help him. Still, he wouldn't speak. Now though, I don't think it was out of loyalty, or fear, to Dilwyn, only loyalty to you Nerys." My hands became clammy. Dilwyn? What did Dilwyn have to do with this?

"So, you're saying… what are you saying?" Siorus asked

articulately.

"Nerys, we have heard Ithel, now we must hear you," stated Merfyn simply.

"Why'd you corner Ithel?" asked Bleddyn, scratching his beard, then laying the hand back on his sword hilt.

I sighed heavily. How could I tell them anything without telling them everything? I trusted them. I trusted all of them with my life but with this? With who I was, what I really did? Not yet.

I made myself stand a little straighter, shoulders back.

"I overheard Ithel and Haul in the stables. I heard Ithel demand Haul tell him something, but he wouldn't. Ithel said to tell him or next time he wouldn't be safe. That's why I chose Ithel's men to ride south first, to get him away from Haul." I sheepishly looked down at my boots before remembering I was their lord. I pulled my neck up long and held my head up. "Then when... Haul died, I... I had to get away. Then we got here and I..."

"You confronted Ithel," Steffan said, voice completely steady, mouth slightly curved. He gave a quick look to Siorus who I saw grin.

"Yes." I felt myself grow calmer, as if the explanation for it all had made the situation easier. Then I remembered. "My father, just as he passed, he said one word to me." I drew my spine up tall and stared Ithel down with a hard gaze. "As he died in my arms he said 'Ithel'. Why?" I demanded.

All eyes darted to Ithel, curious and expectant. He did not hesitate.

"Neirin talked with me, in the days after the leader fought you. He told me of things that he had never told another. I will tell you them, Nerys, in time. Not now, I promised Neirin I would tell you and I keep my word, but not now."

My court seemed to accept that answer. Merfyn gave a solemn nod and Bleddyn looked almost bored by the simplicity of it. I was calm no longer. He was just avoiding the question with more of his good, kind, apparently trustworthy act. Fine then. I could accept that for now, but I would not forget it.

"So, Ithel, your word is that Dilwyn, a court member, killed Haul and the two stable hands, right?" Bleddyn asked him bluntly.

"Unfortunately, yes."

"Mmm, this is serious indeed," Merfyn said.

"Why would he do it? What could he possibly get from it?" Siorus asked, confused. Though, I noted, not disbelieving

Ithel.

"This." Ithel pulled out a crumpled piece of parchment from his leather jacket. My hands were already trembling as he held it up.

"No," I said, wishing I hadn't.

"You already know what it says, Nerys."

"No." I quickly stepped backwards, not wanting to be here.

"Nerys?"

"Nerys, what is it?" Siorus lunged round Steffan and was at my side. He held my hand and walked me back to the circle. I tried to push the emptiness in my mind away. Tried to fill it quickly lest that lone shadow got to it first. I did know what it said. It was the letter I had written to Haul before I had gone to the stone sanctuary. Before I had got the necklace of the vessel. I didn't take it from Ithel.

I closed my eyes to steady myself and opened them as I dropped Siorus's hand. The court should hear this.

"Forgive me for making you carry this burden. I never meant to let anyone else carry it with me or for me. I can change this. I know what to do and where to go. I will get it and I will change this. You are my family, Haul."

H. J. PITHERS

There was silence. I had just let all of them hear the affection and trust I had for Haul. My head began to ache.

Ithel broke that silence.

"Dilwyn has read this too. He knows whatever it is you went to get, he knows."

"No. Just no. Stop saying Dilwyn."

"Nerys, think about it."

"Think about what?" I asked with a rising voice.

"What Ithel is saying, it isn't completely-"

"Completely what, Bleddyn? Completely what?"

"You may not have noticed, Nerys, you weren't always around but Dilwyn... hadn't been himself lately," Steffan said as gently as he could, which was still matter-of-factly.

"What do you mean?" I asked through gritted teeth. This was Dilwyn they were talking about. Dilwyn. He wouldn't do this; why could they not see that?

Before Steffan had a chance to reply, Ithel spoke.

"I didn't get there in time. I couldn't save Haul, or the boys. I saw Dilwyn leave the stables, saw the bodies, the blood and I saw that letter. I know I shouldn't have taken it but as I read it, I knew no-one else could see it. Nerys, whatever it means,

Dilwyn knows." He took two large steps forward. "He knows."

The conviction in his eyes was so strong I had to break away. I turned to see Siorus give Steffan a knowing look. No. Bleddyn made to step towards me but I had had enough.

"So you all believe this, of Dilwyn? You all believe he killed Haul and the stable boys and fled." I stepped back further into the hall, out of the light.

This was... this was too much.

My breathing shallowed. I turned and ran to the nearest wall, head in my hands. I fought against the shadows, they danced across my mind, pushing themselves to go further into me. To force me to do their will.

"No," I said firmly to them.

"Nerys?"

"No," I said again.

Only this time, the shadows didn't obey. They forced me to remember that night.

"I saw him," I said taking my head out of my hands. "I saw him outside the stables after I... after I gave the letter to..." I couldn't, I couldn't say his name. Haul. He had died for me, trying to protect me. Just from the wrong person.

I turned around to see five worried faces, all looking at me like I was about to collapse. Truth is, I could have, the strength in my legs had gone. But their stupidly worried faces changed that.

"You all believe this, don't you? You all believe this of Dilwyn?"

The only answer I got were nods, some sharp, some soft. Dilwyn, my blood. He had killed… I could barely stomach the thought, so I pushed that aside too.

"I am sorry, Nerys, truly I am. I know he was close to you."

I heard Ithel's words through a shroud of shadows and pain. As he walked towards me, Siorus went to stop him but didn't. My eyes began to sting, forcing themselves to stay open. They had all accepted this. They all thought Dilwyn could do this, did do this. Why?

Ithel took hold of my shoulders, this time I didn't shake him off. I stared at the floor and tried to fight the tears that were stinging my eyes. Why did they all think this of my cousin? How could my blood kill my friend?

"Nerys?" Ithel said my name the way he always did, though this time it was different. This time it pulled on something inside me, I felt the blackness lift a little although my head still ached. I looked up to his face and wished I hadn't. His dark

THE SHADOWS ARE WAITING

eyes suddenly made my pain rush to the surface. It took all the strength I had to fight my tears. To remember the oath I had made. Every breath was a struggle, a fight within me but Ithel stayed with me. For how long I don't know, though I sensed the court leaving the hall and the candles dim.

As I came back to myself, I was in Ithel's arms, standing safe within them, the rest of the court had gone. How long had I been standing there, with Ithel just waiting for me to come back to the present?

"Nerys? How do you feel?" His voice was dry and thick. He pushed me back a step to look at me. I rubbed my hands over my face and quickly ran a hand down my plaited hair. I was fine. The shadows were no longer in my mind though I could sense their presence in my veins. That was fine, they weren't controlling me now, but they were still close.

"Fine. Thank you."

I surprised myself then. I took a deep breath and looked up to Ithel. Apparently, I now trusted him. As did my court.

Then it clicked.

I took a step back and span around, clapping my hands together. It all made sense now.

"The necklace."

"The necklace?" Ithel asked, coming round to face me.

Caution didn't stop me as I told Ithel. I didn't worry about anything at this point, only hearing my thoughts out loud.

"The necklace of the vessel. It connects us to the shadows, our ancestors, and the shadow gods. It's why the land has been slowing dying the last eight years."

"I heard the necklace was lost. Even in the Midlands, we thought it was lost, since your-"

"Since my mother died, yes." I took a steadying breath. My heart was racing, as was my mind. "The necklace of the vessel was lost, to the people. But it has never actually been lost."

CHAPTER 14

"What do you mean?" Ithel asked as he stood still.

I started pacing. How had I not seen this? I was jittery, anxious, relieved all at once. Ithel's presence no longer bothered me, what I had just worked out was so much more important. There was a tug, a prick somewhere in my mind that made me hesitate. I hadn't even told my father this, could I tell Ithel? Could I tell a man I barely trusted the secret I had hidden from everyone? I shook my head and crossed my arms, making myself think. If I was going to do this, become a leader to my people, I had to trust them. And I should start with the court. They trusted him. He was Gruffyd's son after all, and I trusted Gruffyd.

I unfolded my arms and I didn't worry as I told him, friendly, calm black shapes dancing and swaying with me.

"Ok, I'll go back, to where it started." I stopped pacing and faced him directly. The dim light making his eyes look even darker.

"Eight years ago my mother died. While we were on tour in the Midlands," I gestured my hand toward Ithel, who nodded. "Before anyone could realise, my father took my mother's necklace. We travelled back to the South, it was a miserable journey. Then, barely a day's ride from home, he walked off in the night. All the guard were asleep, as I was meant to be. But I saw him leave the camp and followed. Then I saw this large stone enclosure and heard the trickling of water. It was then I saw my father, it was so dark that night, like it used to be when the shadows could roam. He bent down and held the necklace with a cloth-wrapped hand as he put it into a chest. I hadn't even noticed him carrying one, that's how dark it was. He waded into the water, raised the chest above his head and prayed. I stayed there long enough to see him bury it, then I sprinted back as quickly and quietly as I could. I remember my heart pounding. I didn't understand it then, even now I don't know why he hid it." Then I said it, as quiet as a whisper. "I have been trying to make up for it ever since."

He stood in patient silence, listening to it all. I didn't look at him; I didn't want to see his face. I just hoped he was the right person to tell. It was too late for that now anyway.

"So why would Dilwyn take the necklace?" he finally asked.

"Because we are blood."

"But that doesn't-"

"Because of our grandfather," I said plainly. "Our grandfather was the vessel before my mother. It usually follows blood. He must believe he has a claim to it." I sighed a breath. "I hope for his sake he does."

"What do you mean?"

I turned away from Ithel, memories prickling my mind, making the shadows thicker.

"He cannot touch it. Not with his bare skin. If anyone but the vessel touches the necklace, they will die." I looked down at my palm. Straight across the knuckles was a thin, waxy scar. Ithel walked around to face me and I showed him my hand. "From when I touched it."

"But you didn't die?" he questioned, holding my hand up to his eyes.

"No. My mother said the shadow gods spared me." For what I don't know, I prayed they would spare Dilwyn too.

Ithel kept hold of my hand as he brought it between us.

"Then we go back. To the men of the rocks, the men of the North. We find Dilwyn, get the necklace back and end these men."

The passion in his eyes, in his strength, gripped me. All I could respond with was a nod. With that he left the hall. I froze on the spot. The emotion that suddenly swept through me was intense. Everything flowed through me, shadows, memories, sadness, relief. Then my legs did collapse. I slumped to the floor and forced myself to stay in control.

Pushing myself up on to all fours, I noticed the cold ground, the dim hall. I breathed as deeply as I could, filling the back of my lungs. I felt raw. Human. My throat clogged with feeling and my eyes ached in their sockets. I did not want to cry. If I had learnt anything over the years, it was discipline. I would not cry. However much I wanted to cry for my father, the loss I felt for him every day, I knew I would not shed a tear. Not yet.

I forced myself to stand and felt a new wave. Not of emotion, but of shadows. They whispered across my mind, comforting me, encouraging me. This was all moving so fast. I held my hands by my sides and held myself up straight. I would not fail. This was it. This was it, the end. I could sense it. I silently said my prayer to my gods, whispering the last part aloud.

"Give me the fight I need to live the life ahead. Through the years and the night, to keep my people well fed. From this land I will give, from this land I will die. For you, my gods, I will give, without fear or cry." I left the hall.

Outside, the night had begun to settle. A grey sky hung low with a small, cool breeze. More fires had been lit. As soon as I exited my house, my guard were behind me. I saw them and nodded, they were another thing I would have to get used to. I had barely made it to the stone well before Celyn and Mairwen found me. They both looked strange in trousers and tunics compared to the usual long linen dresses and aprons they wore. But they had been helping the healers and smiths prepare for the coming battle and trousers were more convenient.

"M'lady, you need food. Come." I didn't object as Mairwen walked ahead and Celyn took my arm. They walked me to the kitchens, which were bustling and hot and full of warm stews and small loaves of freshly baked bread. The smell alone made my stomach growl. Even though there were now more mouths to feed and less food, the cooks somehow still managed to keep the stews tasting like stews, rather than oaty water or fish-bone broth. I had had it once as a child, it had made me gag.

My maids both watched me eat the small bowl they gave me, gentle eyes inspecting my every chew. Once I was done they spoke.

"Nerys," Celyn started timidly, "we heard, we are so sorry. I can't imagine what you are going through."

The sincerity of her words warmed me. A new wave of feeling washed through me.

"Thank you Celyn, truly. But don't lie, you know how I feel, both of you. Now I know how you felt when you lost…" I couldn't finish my sentence. As I spoke the words, the meaning behind them hit me fully. She gave me a soft smile and squeezed my hand. I continued to hold it.

"We want to help. We want to do something to help you, Nerys. You don't deserve to lose anymore." Mairwen's blue eyes were intense. She meant what she said. How were they so generous, so loyal?

"Thank you." I reached for Mairwen's hand as well. "I can never thank you both enough for being this kind and patient with me. I… I need you both here. You have to be safe and survive, I need people back here that I fight for. I haven't got many people left now," I said, my words thinning, "I need you to stay here."

They were silent as they listened. Mairwen's expression harder than Celyn's. Celyn was fighting back her tears.

"Well then, tell us how we can help. I want to do something other than strip cloth and move herbs."

It was the first time I had heard some defiance from Mairwen. I knew it was always there. She might just be my maid but she had a stubborn streak in her that she constantly kept in check. If anyone else had heard her, she would have been scolded. I laughed.

"Very well. When I need something done, I will come to you."

* * *

Once the night had descended fully, I ordered a meeting with my court.

I waited for them on logs set by the stone well. The men of my guard stood at paces around the logs. I caught Aeddan's eye, he gave me a quick nod then averted his eyes. He too had a hard time believing the news of Dilwyn.

Most of the men stationed in the town were settling for the night, a few stood on watch by the gates. The mood was better, still tense and worried, but they were happier to be in a familiar place. Those who weren't from my father's lands seemed to be happy to see the town that acted as their protector.

I held my head in my hands as I waited. The last few weeks were a blur. So much had happened. So much travelling, emotions, death. I tried to block out the sounds around me. The sounds of the men I was putting through a restless journey of uncertain but coming battle. I prayed they would stay with me.

"Father, if you can hear me, if you made it to the shadows, help me. Please. Help me to lead as well as you did. Help me to protect our people." Tears caught in my eyes and I pushed them back. I needed to be strong. As always, my grief could wait.

My court arrived individually, all still armed with their swords and daggers.

Merfyn, Bleddyn, Siorus and Steffan took their seats routinely. Ithel remained standing. I indicated for him to take Dilwyn's log, he wouldn't be sitting there again. Ithel hesitated but did. Now, we were at court.

"As we all now know," I began, my voice stronger than I felt, "Dilwyn has fled. This by itself has... affected us all. But there is more." As I paused for breath I felt something dull in my chest, something dense like guilt. I steadied myself for what I was about to confess to. "For the last eight years, the necklace of the vessel has been lost, forcing us to be detached from the shadow gods, and us from them. This has been...." I didn't want to say it. My throat suddenly constricted. I couldn't say this, not about my father. I couldn't blame him to the people

THE SHADOWS ARE WAITING

who trusted him most. I couldn't speak ill of him. I missed him.

"The necklace has never been truly lost."

Then I told them. I told my court that the necklace had been in my possession, that I had lost it and that it was the thing in the letter I had gone to get, the thing Dilwyn knew of.

"So he has taken the necklace, stolen it?" asked Siorus. His usually light face was stern against the night.

"As well as murdered for it," Steffan added, a voice as hard as Siorus's face. They both seemed to take the news severely. They had every right to.

There was a strained quietness between the court. Each breath made me feel more and more like a foolish, arrogant child. How could I have not told them this before? Because of my father. It was that simple. He might have been distant and the reason all this had happened in the first place, but he was my father.

"What is it you intend to do with the necklace?" asked Merfyn.

"If we get it back," added Bleddyn bluntly.

"I would have it choose its' vessel. I would have us live as we did, with the shadow gods blessing us and the shadows communicating with us. With our land being rich and thriving again and the people happy, not half starved and desperate." I said those words to the night air, I said it to the shadows that hung invisible to us, to all who would hear its' whisper on the wind.

As I did, I felt a small pulse run through me. Not like the pulses the shadows gave me after killing. This one was slow, subtle. It made me think of my mother. It felt like her.

"Can you forgive me?" Those words surprised me, I hadn't even recognised them as they left my mouth. No one answered. I was about to ask again, with less strength.

"I can," came Steffan's reply. He faced me directly. "You know I can for this." It felt like an age ago. Steffan's parents had both been killed by a band of nomad's, the first of a series of attacks. That's when it had started for me, or when I finally noticed Gruffyd's words were true. That our land would die. "We must look to the future now."

"I can. You don't need to ask, Nerys. I'm all for better days." I smiled at Siorus, who winked at me, his face back to normal. I quickly breathed, they were the easy ones to convince.

I turned to Merfyn and Bleddyn. They both had been court members as long as I had been alive. I knew if Cledwyn was here, he would never forgive me.

"This is news far worse than any I have known. The past can never be changed." Merfyn kept his face solemn as he clasped his hands together. He said a silent prayer. My breath caught in my chest, was that his answer?

"The past is filled with decisions and memories we cannot alter. The present is where we make change and the future can be changed. If you are to change it for the better, then yes. I would like to hear my gods again."

Relief swept through me and I loosed my breath. Now Bleddyn. He took in the moment when all eyes were on him. His face was unreadable.

"This, this is not something I can overlook. This has caused us all pain." He fists clenched and his beard twitched with all the words he wanted to say. "I can forgive you, Nerys, if you make this right, only if you make this right. But I cannot forget it."

I nodded slowly, trying to understand fully. If I was going to trust my court, I had to let them speak freely.

"I understand, and thank you." Deep breath. I made to turn to Ithel when Bleddyn spoke again.

"Then we fight. We take back what is ours and we fight."

I closed my eyes in my own silent prayer. My heart felt lighter, apprehensive, but lighter. Then it thudded. Hands grabbed me off my log and span me around. My eyes burst open to see Siorus hold me tight in a hug. He put me down gently and returned to his log. I quickly laughed.

"There is another matter," stated Steffan. Eyes all on him now. "The men, they are tired. Many want to go back to their homes, especially those who work the land. Neirin held all their respect."

It was a moment before I realised his meaning. "So I don't have the men's respect?" I asked, trying not to take it personally.

"Not all of them." I was surprised at Merfyn's words. I knew, I knew not all of them would follow me instantly, I just didn't think it would be so soon. I tried not to feel hollow.

"What do you suggest then?"

"You have to prove that you respect them," Bleddyn offered as he leant his hands on his knees. "Show them."

Show them? I felt like shouting it to all of them then. I did respect my men. I had been killing darkened souls half my life so that they could all live a better one. I had darkened myself so that they could all go on living. But no, I still had to show *them* that I respected them. Deep breath. Listen, I told myself.

"There's been something I have been meaning to ask you," Steffan stood as he talked. He looked more serious than usual.

"My cousin, Delyth, wishes to have an audience with you. I... I do not wish her to ask but I believe that her solution will help us all." He came to stand his dominating figure in front of me. "Nerys, not all the men may respect you, but there are others you have inspired. If you agree, I will tell her you will hear her tomorrow."

"Yes, thank you."

I hid my surprise as Steffan bowed and left, Siorus following him. No one had ever bowed to me before. I didn't feel hollow anymore. Steffan's respect meant a great deal to me.

Merfyn and Bleddyn also left. Bleddyn gave me a tilted nod and Merfyn took my hand in his. Then I turned to Ithel, who was still sitting quietly on the log. He stood, gave me a swift look and left as well.

Now my court knew. Most of it. But they knew. I sat for a while longer, alone but with the guard still around me. I just wanted to ride Midnight to the edge of the land and be swift and silent in the night, as we used to. With no one relying on us. But those days were gone. I realised that with an ache. My days of impulse and freedom were gone. Now I had to fight to earn my people's respect and keep them safe, as my father had tried to do.

* * *

"Nerys, this is Delyth," said Steffan as I turned around, "who I spoke of yesterday."

The next morning, I waited in my hall. My sleep had been broken with recurring words and voices, whispers and shouts. I had to move on. I had to find a solution, hopefully, this would be it.

"Yes."

Steffan left and re-entered with Siorus and a woman.

A nod from Steffan and Delyth moved forward. Her hands were a little restless though her eyes were fixed on mine. This, after all, was the opportunity she had apparently bullied Steffan relentlessly into getting for her. Nothing else would have made him ask it of me. I let the quiet remain for one more breath.

"Speak."

"Ner- I mean, uh lord." She flinched as I waved a hand. I saw her intake breath and relax. Her skin was a pale dark like a coppery-brown hazel, her hair was darker still. Her eyes were Steffan's, though somewhat softer and brighter, with the same strength as her cousin's. She reminded me instantly of my mother, of her warmth, her gratefulness for life.

"I would fight with you. News of what you are doing has spread all around. Us women who aren't allowed to do anything other than weave and cook and follow what our fathers say have heard of you. You are the only woman in all these men around and you fight better than all of them. You fought the Northerners' leader and lived. I would fight with you."

Ha, I liked her. I kept my smile to myself, my face unmoving. Her hands quietened as her courage grew.

"I can fight. I have trained well, Steffan used to teach me. You need more men; I can be one of them. Please, let me, us, fight." Her eyes shifted shyly at those last words. So she wasn't just here for herself.

She was right though, we did need more men and sending those willing to fight was far better than having those who weren't. But could I? Could I send women out to their deaths? I stamped on the thought as soon as it sprang up. Yes. I sent men out, women would be no different. And women knew death, women bore death. There was no greater evil than giving life to a child that was already dead. I had seen my mother pull out the children of the dead from women before. We gave life and we gave death. We should be able to take it too.

I sighed deeply. I didn't know how the men who didn't respect me would react to this. Doubtless not well but I had to do something.

"How many are you?"

"Twenty. But we can get more." She sounded certain.

"You can?"

"Yes, lord. I can. We can get more women willing to follow you, to fight."

I would probably regret this.

"Steffan, Siorus, this be on your heads. Only those who can match both of you with blades, or arrows," I added with a slight darkness to my smile, "may fight. But none who are mothers. Or wish to be." I left them in the hall. I would not wish any child to be born without a mother.

* * *

I had got back to the boundary in just under three days. I was edgy. I was worried about moving the men and women, army rather, as they were calling themselves now. Army. I knew that I could ride fast and swift enough but moving an army, whatever size, would take its time.

I let the court prepare the men, and the hundred or so women who had joined us as I leaped at the chance to relieve the scouts up here. The court did not want me here, they were steadfast in their protests against my riding to the boundary again, no doubt thinking that I would ride off again. I couldn't really blame them for thinking that. So their compromise was that Ithel and a few of his men rode with me. I didn't like it, I didn't want them with me but they kept up. As soon as we arrived on the boundary, I sent the scouts back to the town, they would need to rest and be fresh.

Midnight and the other horses were grazing as I went over to the boundary ditch. Looking out at the dry grass, the brown trees, the sky. They were in the woods, the Northern men. Then it struck me, as sudden as lightning. Dilwyn was probably there too. Where else would he go with the necklace, if not to our enemies? A grunt left my throat. Traitor.

I heard the crunch of the grass behind me as he approached. A twinge of dread threatened to knot my stomach. I had hardly spoke to him since the town, barely even looked at him as we rode. He had offered to help Siorus and Steffan train the women but the court had sent him with me. Now Ithel stood beside me and watched the clearing. I had revealed myself to the son of our greatest ally, who was now my greatest threat. It was one thing to tell the court of the necklace, to admit to them that I knew where it was all these years. But to tell Ithel, to tell him I had been trying to make up for it all these years, was a risk. Even if he didn't understand what I had said, I had still said it.

And what if he realised and told the court? What if they knew that the one they had been searching for all these years, all the countless patrols they had been sent on to find him, was me? Would they accept me as their lord then? Would they even understand why I did it? There were too many threads of thought pulling my head apart. Focus.

Focus on the fight.

One fight I needed to have right now was with myself. I knew I would have to apologise. I looked forward to the days when I wouldn't have to say sorry to anyone. I glanced at Ithel, whose eyes were forward and his bow by his side. I focused back on the trees. I didn't want to see his face.

"I should apologise to you. I misjudged you." I paused. "The first time we were both here, when you rode south, I spoke out of anger. I thought the worst would happen if they knew. I still do."

His words came out plain, a little husky. "You need not apologise to me, Nerys. I came here with my own intentions.

I soon realised you had several complications of your own to deal with."

"Right, answers. You believe I can give you answers."

"I believe so," he replied, rather certain, "but for those I can wait."

"If you wish."

A comfortable silence progressed. I waited, sensing he had more to say.

"It is good, what you have done for the women. They have the right to fight for their land too."

"Yes, they do. How do you think they will do?" I was relieved so many had joined us, almost a hundred, but I doubted they would be ready. A few days intense training would not prepare them for the slaughter that would come.

"As well as they can." He paused just a little too long. "They have hope."

"The men don't?"

"The men," he made a sound, struggling to find the right words. "The men have to be there, to not carry Neririn and the shadow gods's displeasure. That is right, yes?" He turned to me with asking eyes.

"Yes, that is." As oath-sworn men, they had to avenge their lord's death as he fell in battle. They had to or the shadow gods would know they were oath-breakers and torment them and their shadows.

"The women, they want to be here, that will help." Yes, it would. "The only problem is weapons."

"What of them?" I had the thought that he was trying to avoid talking about what he really wanted to say.

"We need more. Not all the women will have one and few of the men are prepared to give them spares."

"Then they use what they have got, staves, knives. They'll have enough when they pick them off of the dead."

Another silence. His intake of breath was strong.

"You asked me before if I was the son of Gruffyd. What did you mean?" There it was. That knot of dread tightened, though I decided to pay no attention to it. It seemed I was to tell Ithel everything, however much I disliked sharing.

"Gruffyd, your father, has been a significant part of my life. Will always be a significant part of my life. Of my family's. He was there for us at our worst and it was he who led me to this path."

He turned to face me then. Genuine surprise on his face. I

continued to watch the trees. What I was about to say, he knew. But he did not know it all.

"When mother died, we had just left your lands for the South. We had stayed with Gruffyd for a week. I remember him as being kind and energetic, not at all like the other lords we had visited. You weren't there... I don't remember you being there."

There was a pause while he thought.

"Eight years... no. I was with Ledin, one of the court's sons," he explained with a quick wave of the hand. "We were being tutored on the coast."

I nodded as I resumed. "As we left we were ambushed. It was a clear day but cold. They surrounded us. My father defended us, the guards were at the camp, unaware of our attackers. Mother tried to defend me but she was no fighter. They got her from all sides. The shadows took her quickly, she was spared the pain. Gruffyd came and took me and my father in. A whole new moon we were there. My father was badly hurt."

I took several deep breaths. That was the part he knew.

"The same night Gruffyd spoke to me. Even though I was young, I will take his words with me to my death. 'Choose this path and the shadow gods will hear you. They will hear you and they will guide you, yet they will take what they wish, they are gods and they will not be trifled with. This path is dark for a reason, it will test you. You alone can do it child, but it will be you alone, for all your life, should you choose it.'"

I let the words fade into the wind.

"For a few years after that, life continued as normal. Gruffyd's riddles were just an old man's ramblings to me. Then Steffan's parents died, brutally and it all fell into place. They were found on a large patch of dead grass. All the grass around it was green. Gruffyd came down for the death day. It was then that he told me of the darkened souls path. Apparently he heard it from a travelling shaman long ago. A prophecy he called it." I stumbled over the word 'prophecy,' it was still unfamiliar to me. "Since then I have chosen my path." I found myself rubbing my scars. "That is why I want no one to know. It would only hurt them more. I must do this alone."

I was surprised at how easily the words came out. Like they were always just at the back of my tongue, waiting to be said. He turned to me and took my left arm, pushing up the tight sleeve. I didn't stop him, despite my stomach almost cramping. He traced the scar softly, as if absorbing as much of it as he could.

"You showed me this before. Why?"

Looking down at it brought a flash of black. Deep breath.
"This is the price I paid. The price that can be seen anyway.
These scars started my path and I will have them until my last
day. These scars are how I will... am bringing the shadows
back." He held my arm for a breath more then rolled back
down the sleeve. As Ithel let go, a prickling sensation ran
under my skin, right where he had touched it. I focused on
my breathing. There was silence between us until I sensed his
nod. Then his hands stiffened on his bow. My eyes narrowed.
Birds darted into the sky. No other movement came. I had an
idea.

We would go to them.

***

It took a while to get the camp moving again. Frustration
had set in now. Most of the men just wanted to be back with
their families and their farms but eventually they roused.
Eventually the court roused them to hear their new, untested,
untrusted lord. If I was even that.

Ithel and his men had stayed two days with me on the
boundary, watching, waiting. We rode back down to the town
as new scouts arrived to relieve us. And now I was home, faced
with a challenge like I had never known. I had to gain people's
trust.

The men gathered in the town, all eyes towards the stone well. As tired, expectant eyes stared at me I felt my chest tighten. I would need these men, women, to be strong, unbeatable, so I had to be strong. Right now. I was wearing all black, from my cloth-strip hair-tie to my thick boots and I climbed up on the well so that all could see me and the crowd became quiet. I thought of every speech I had ever heard my father say.

"Brothers, sisters, you have given your blood, your sweat, your lives to this earth. And this earth has not been what it once was. You may think the shadow gods abandoned us but they have not." As I made my voice strong and firm, I felt some of the men slipping, not wanting to listen to the fickleness of their distant gods. My jaw felt tight, like it wouldn't open again, but I had to say this and I would get their attention back. "They are with us still, they are with me and I will defend you. I will defend your land as you defend your brothers. These Northern beasts have threatened our lands and we have lost. But our lost are with us still. They are with the shadows and they will guide us as we fight." A slight murmuring ran through the crowd. I had to do better. "This battle was not yours to bear, it was mine, it *is* mine but I would ask you fight it with me. I need your help to keep our land. I need your help to spill these foul men's blood all over our land."

I jumped off the well, grabbed some earth in my hand and stepped back up. I held my hand high. "This is our land. It is within us all. And today it will know hell. Today we will fill hell with their screams and cries and their wasted souls." More murmuring, some shouts of agreement. I sprinkled the earth over my head in a quick prayer then made my voice cry out through the town. "I am Nerys, heir of Neirin, and all those who follow me will be more than men. They will be shadows. They will be the shadows of death, the bringers of blood. And these Northerners will see us. They will see our shadows and they will fear us. Because they will know. They will know that we have come for them."

Cries and yells sounded. My heart missed a beat with relief, though I realised the cries weren't loud enough to be coming from all the men. So, there will still some I needed to convince. Then they all quietened again as movement started somewhere at the left of the crowd. It carried on until Delyth was roughly in the middle of the Southerners, a small area around her separated her and the crowd she was standing in. The same expectant faces that were on me all now turned to her, as did mine. Somehow she kept all their attention. She knelt down to the ground and then stood and faced me. Her dark hair was back in a plait similar to how I wore mine.

"I will fight with you," she started, a commanding note resonating in her voice. "Who else will?" Then she turned and eyed all those around her, daring them to speak. My mouth curled slightly. I could learn from her. She came back round to face me. "I will fight with you, Nerys, heir of Neirin. I will fight for you and my family. I will be a shadow."

The slightly higher-pitched yells of women echoed through the crowd. I had them at least. Then a loud grunt sounded and the crowd soon followed. All of them screaming and chanting and yelling out "Shadow, shadow, shadow." Hairs stood up all over my arms and neck. I looked to where the grunt came from and smiled to see Siorus and Steffan, who both gave me innocent smiles. I loosed a breath and jumped off the well. Good.

CHAPTER 15

The guard had pushed the thick oak tables from the edge of the hall into the middle of it, in a large square. Parchments were scattered across each of the tables, along with quills, ink pots, candles, wooden tools used to represent numbers.

My court had invited some of the town's most respected workers and traders to this war meeting, including the blacksmith, the farmers and the head healers. This was supposed to be a council for war, to decide when to leave, what route to take, how much food each man and woman would need, what our tactics would be. It was chaos. I was leaning against the wall, one foot bent up, just watching. I much preferred doing this alone. No wonder it took so long to move an army, this many people couldn't even agree on who was speaking, let alone the important things. Several conversations were happening at once and I couldn't keep up.

Siorus was playfully mocking Bleddyn about what was the best fighting style, but Bleddyn was trying to convince the smith to melt whatever metal he had to make more swords and daggers. Merfyn was looking incredibly calm as the farmers ranted and shouted and pointed at him. I heard the odd word- "fields," "now," "sow," "you do it then." Steffan suddenly slammed his fists down on one of the tables, making the wooden tools on it jump up and the healers around him scuttle back. My guard had also decided to join in, breaking up groups that were getting too heated, shouting at Steffan to calm down, trying to correct Siorus on fighting styles even though he was mocking them and they didn't realise. Generally, they were all just making noise. This was such a waste of time. I wanted to be back to the fight by now, not waiting for men to calm down.

I waited a few more breaths, just watching how this was supposedly how things got done. My head was starting to pound, only if I thought about it. The shadows tried to make me think about it. How they needed blood, how I needed blood. I had to force myself to not think about it, even though I wanted to. A wave of grief hit me and I had to fight back the tears that threatened to leave my eyes. He just wasn't here.

The candles on the tables were burning brightly, slowly filling the hall with a smoky scent. Quietly, I walked over to the hall door, where two of my guard were stationed. They were both young men, just older than me. "Fetch them," I said to the nearest guard and he left. The other one nodded at me as I turned back to the hall. I didn't even know his name.

"Enough," I said, well shouted, but it wasn't that loudly. My court, guard and respected townspeople silenced themselves as I moved closer to the tables.

"What I need to know is how much food we have left, what route will be best to move our men and women, how many swords and daggers we have. Can you answer me those, or not?"

The hall was silent. I stared at each of the men in front of me, waiting and waiting. This was such a waste of time.

Finally, one of the grain farmers stepped forwards an inch. His shirt was loose and dirty and he fiddled with his hat as he spoke. "We, we don't have enough store for the winter if, if we have to feed all these people now." He slightly bowed his head as he stepped back.

I just nodded, waiting for another.

"And I can't just make metal appear from the air," started the smith. He was huge and broad and had small blisters all along his neck and chin. "No good iron, no steel, nothing worth trading." He emphasised each of his last words, showing his annoyance. I clenched my jaw, I needed solutions, not problems. I already knew all the problems.

"Anyone else?" I asked, throwing my arms wide. Silence again.

Merfyn spoke so softly, I almost missed his first words. "We must trust in our land. It is the land that will lead our way."

"What land? I know this land better than most," replied another farmer. He wasn't as forbearing as the grain farmer. "This land is giving up. Giving up," his arms threw themselves up and hung loosely at his sides. "Lead the way," he muttered under his breath.

"I am yet to hear anything helpful from you." I made my voice loud and deep, drowning out the mutters that had started. The door to the hall creaked open as my guard re-entered. "My lord." I turned to see him bow slightly and lead three women towards me.

Mairwen had chosen to wear tight leather trousers and a loose fitting cotton shirt, held tight to her by a leather belt, quite similar to mine, I mused. Celyn was back in a long linen dress, but she too had a leather belt tight around her waist. My maids nodded as they bowed slightly and turned to show me Delyth.

"Delyth is ready for you, m'lady," Mairwen said with a clear voice.

"Delyth," I gestured for her to stand next to me, facing the war council. She looked even darker with dark leather trousers, boots and jacket, a contrast to me as I was not wearing all-black for once.

I faced the council as I spoke to Steffan's cousin, ensuring they all heard me. "Tell me, how many women were fighting with these men a fortnight ago?"

"None, lord." Delyth followed my lead and looked forwards at the council.

"How many do we have now?"

"About 80, lord." She kept her eyes forwards.

I raised my hand towards her as I spoke. "That, that is a solution. That is what I want. I don't want to hear about any other hindrances we may face." I stood myself next to the tables, looking at the parchments. A small voice creeped louder in my head, repeating its' want for blood. I had to force myself to push it aside. That wouldn't help me now. "Tell me, how do we do this?" I asked to the hall, hoping these men, my men, would start thinking.

***

Another day passed and scouts brought more news. The

Northmen were making their way east, off the Ea and into the farmlands and meadows north of the town. It was a small relief that they were off the river, small. Yet I did not understand it, why would they move away from the water? I could curse the shadow gods all day, but that was not to be. I left my house, intending to go to Midnight and ride for as long as possible on this cold but clear day, when I bumped into Siorus. He literally came out of nowhere and stood himself in my path, ready for me to walk into him.

"Gaaw. What was that?" I asked as I pushed him playfully back.

"Just making sure you saw me," he said with an annoyingly happy smile. I mocked him and he kept smiling. "Come on." And he was off to the east gate. I sighed and followed him, longing after my ride.

Siorus whistled sharply and I turned to see why. As we walked past the stone communal buildings, Steffan stopped talking to some of the women who had recently joined us and bounded over in a few strides. The women giggled softly and watched after him.

"I'll be back later ladies," shouted Siorus after them, making me laugh.

"What are you doing? Come on" muttered Steffan as he sped up the pace. I laughed more and Siorus blew kisses to everyone we passed.

Out of the east gate we veered north to the guards' training area. And it was busy. Some of the guard, those that weren't following me, were training but most were stood to the sides, watching. The 80 or so women that had joined us after Delyth's entreaty were spread out, sparring, and some were off to the side, listening to Celyn. I could see dried leaves and jars and knew she was teaching them to make poultices and ointments. She noticed me and bowed her head slightly and I nodded back. It made me proud to see, to see all of them, ready and trying.

"Mairwen." shouted Siorus and my other maid walked proudly over to us with loose strands of hair sticking to her face and her sleeves rolled up high on her arms. As she approached, I wanted to laugh, she looked so unkempt, so different to how she usually looked.

"Yes, Siorus," Mairwen replied quizzically, as if a puppy had barked at her.

"Erm. Yes. Here."

Steffan shuffled towards me and whispered. "I think Siorus is intimidated by her. She is not afraid to speak her mind."

"Ha. No she is not."

I stepped forwards to save Siorus, patting him on the shoulder. As soon as Mairwen saw me she bowed and smiled. "M'lady, come. The women will be pleased to see you."

"Thank you, Mairwen," and I followed her. I quickly turned back to see Steffan laughing at Siorus as he shook himself free of whatever trance he had been in.

"Fill me in," I demanded as she led me through the groups and pairs sparring.

"Most of these women have come from Delyth's town, or the surrounding towns from the east of the land." Several nods and smiles came my way as we kept walking through the women. And one man. I knew him. I stared at him and back to Mairwen, she didn't seem to notice my confusion. I looked back at my duck-like friend, who had seen me. He gave me a very small shrug and bow and I shook my head in disbelief. What a small world. Mairwen continued. "Almost 20 came from the Ea villages and could have some useful ideas, if you would hear them."

"You think I should?" I asked her, following her implication.

"Yes, m'lady. They could help." She bowed slightly as a smile pulled her cheeks. I raised my eyebrows at her and laughed. The shadows felt so far from me in that moment.

Mairwen took a few steps forwards as I scanned around. These women were doing well, nothing like my trained guard, but well. A moment later my maid returned with Delyth, whose hair was barely kept back in her plait but her eyes were bright.

"Lord," she smiled and lowered her head. "What do you think?" she asked as she placed her hands on her hips.

"This is good. Tell me, what do these women think? Mairwen tells me they have ideas." I left it open so that Delyth would answer honestly, I had learned enough about her already to know she would.

Her eyes scanned around before she replied, taking a step closer to me. "They can help, lord. Most of us come from villages and towns that barely have anything left. Food is shared, to the young and old first. Clothes are reused, shared. Babies are put together in one cot to sleep for warmth. We have learnt to use whatever we can to get through each day." Mairwen slowly moved away and back to a group sparring. I watched her go, lost in thought. I wanted the shadows to help all of us, not just me but a flash of black crossed my mind and squashed that thought. The shadows were mine, they told me. I felt a brush against my arm and almost flinched to see

Delyth right next to me, also watching the groups. "We are ready. We need to do this," she said then turned to face me. "I think we need this as much as you do," she told me brightly, with a twitch of her mouth. I was confused, not knowing her meaning. She did smile then and called to a few of the women to come over to us.

As we waited for them, Aeddan walked into my view and bowed slowly. "Lord, scouts have returned. Bleddyn wishes to speak to you." He stood up straight with his arms behind him. I sighed. Bleddyn had been wanting to talk for days. I just wanted to ride.

"Thank you, Aeddan. Arrange a court for tonight." He bowed again and walked out of view. I could feel Delyth eyeing me and snapped myself back to the present. Two women stood in front of me, both dark but not like Delyth. Their hair was fair but their eyes and skin were as dark as a black poplar. A gentle breeze had picked up and sent a quick shiver across my back.

"Lord, this is Eirlys, from a farmstead north of the Ea." Eirlys gave me a quick wave and clasped her hands in front of her. "And this is Heledd, a child of two river towns."

"Mother's from a southern village, father was from the northern most one. He swam to the southern village most days, before they married," she explained and I nodded along.

"I hear you have ideas that could be of use to me." I looked between each of them, hoping this would help. I needed something that would as I was starting to accept that I couldn't do all of this by myself. Starting to.

Eirlys made to speak but Heledd got there first. "Oh, yes. We do, don't we?" She tapped Eirlys in the stomach who grimaced in response. "We always make nettle tea and soup in the winter when we have to save the grain and meat. Mother's town that is. But father's town does something similar with the stewed elder berries and we can always find nettles and berries." She leaned in closer and cupped her mouth with her hands. "Tastes *sour* but keeps you full when there's nothing else." She shrugged her shoulders and smiled, looking at Eirlys as if she was going to agree.

Eirlys slowly nodded as her eyes widened then added her piece. "My family make cloth from nettle fibres, usually we trade for it with the other villages on the Ea with clay goods."

"Oh, yes," butted in Heledd. "You make those really pretty pots with the spiralling." Eirlys nodded. "And the large jugs with the handles." Another nod. "Oh, and the wax melts that filled the whole hut with, well... they used to fill the hut with scents. I don't actually remember when we last had one." Heledd was lost in thought and I took my chance.

"Thank you both. These ideas *may* help but I need something that I can turn to war. We need more cloth strips for bandages, leather for armour and shields, food to feed all of these mouths now. If you can turn these ideas into solutions for these problems, then I will listen to you." I nodded sharply and left. I breathed out deeply and kept walking, aware Delyth was following me.

"Speak and do it quickly," I almost barked at her. I was struggling to hold in my anxiety about all of these lives in my care and just wanted to ride with Midnight through the trees in the black of night.

"Nothing," she started, keeping up with me. "You were quite something to see up close." I turned my head to her, unable to catch her tone. She smiled at me and carried on. "Steffan has spoken about you, in letters mainly. He always said you had this streak in you, something that could just turn, like a flash."

"Well, I-"

"I liked it," she said and stopped, letting me walk back to the town alone.

***

Dusk arrived and the night was cold, even with a small fire burning in the middle of the courts' logs. Bleddyn was rambling on about the men needing to get back to their homes, about the food running low, about 'some' of the men not comfortable fighting alongside women. I should have paid more attention, I should have, but I'd also heard enough. The same issues were being dragged up every day and we were no closer to solving them.

"Our scouts report the same," Merfyn was saying. "The Northmen are still to the north of the town, slowly heading back to the woods. How long they'll be content to travel is unclear. We have to be ready."

"Ready for what?" Siorus asked, knocking his rings together on his hands. "The men that can fight are getting restless, the injured need more rest and the women, don't get me wrong, are great but still weeks away from being ready to fight those..." he shivered, "things."

"Merfyn is right, we need to be ready for another attack." Steffan balled his hands into fists as he spoke. "They may be far enough away now but who knows when they could be on us again. And this time, we are not ready."

I tried to fill my lungs with air to stop from cursing the shadow gods. Why couldn't I just go and end them all now?

"We must act, lord. We must ensure they do not attack us

before we are ready," Bleddyn offered, which was the most useful thing he had said.

"That I agree with." I turned to Aeddan, he barely left me alone these days. "How many of the guard are fit?"

"Most lord. About 200." He faded back into the circle of guard around us, standing still again.

"We will need to make sure that the Northmen do what we want them to do, so they don't come to us when we can't face another battle. Not so soon, anyway. We have to go to them," I said, mostly to myself but the court heard my thoughts.

"I can sort that out," Siorus said with a mischievous grin.

"Keep it to yourself, by all means," toyed Steffan. Bleddyn and Merfyn did not look amused.

"Well, we need to keep them away from us," Siorus started, gesturing a hand to me, "and we need to make sure that they don't attack us any time soon." He stood up and started walking around the fire. I would have laughed at how unhurried he was, but my jaw kept clenching. Bleddyn matched my feeling.

"We're waiting," he reminded Siorus.

"Yes, yes," Siorus muttered, unphased by the interruption. "We slow them down, make them move where we want them to, which is obviously away from the towns, so out of the land."

"Yes?" Bleddyn longed for a straight answer from Siorus, we all did at this point.

"Well, it's simple."

I sighed loudly, as did Bleddyn and Merfyn placed his hands on his knees as if steadying himself.

"A series of quick, small battles. Skirmishes if you will." Siorus had stopped walking and was staring off into the cold night sky. "We attack at night, always at night. We take their food, their weapons, their horses. You know, burn things that they'll need. They had so many shields, we can burn all of those," he sounded wicked at that last sentence. I was pleased.

"Rob them of their stores to restock ours," Merfyn mused as he nodded.

I stood too quickly and my knees ached from the cold. "Done. Bleddyn you arrange a group to take, for three days' time. Siorus, yours goes in five. We rotate groups as often as we need to until we are sure they are weakened. And we are ready." The court rose and I left, eager to get back to my room. Midnight and I would be the first group and we would ride tonight.

Finally, I would get blood.

***

I was free. The cold was still in the air as Midnight and I rode north. The moonlight was waning but we kept riding. We would be the first group to rob these Northmen of their goods. And their blood. Definitely their blood.

I had needed this. It had been far too long since I had been free to just do what the shadows wanted me to. This is what I knew, what I was good at and what I wanted my life to be. Not the rank of lord, not when I had this.

I slowed Midnight to a trot as we neared a small farmstead at the edge of several fallows. They had been here. The Northmen. I cursed. Embers were still burning in the barn, most of the roof was crumpled on the ground. Patches of grass had been set aflame. A cart was burning, I could feel the heat from where I was. I took a small, smoky breath and charged Midnight on.

I would burn them.

Less than a league north-east I found them. The last group of men from this northern army of beasts. They were in the middle of another farmstead, two groups around fires that were large and wasteful. I could see the trees that they had felled and cut into logs next to the fires. There were so many logs. If they were only here for a night, they would waste over half those logs.

I slowly slid off Midnight and walked her to a low, prickly bush outside the farmstead. I stroked her one last time and stalked around the nearest barn, watching.

As I slipped through the barn and to the farmhouse, my gut wrenched with anger. The bodies of the people who lived here, my people, were strewn on the grass. A pile of limbs and blood. There were children there, laying cold. They would never get to know what our land was really like, what it could be.

I called the shadows to me then. I asked them to come to me and they rushed through my blood in an instant. They filled my head with black and that was it.

I ran out into the night, towards the fires and I was a shadow against the flame.

Before any of the beasts even saw me, I held the closest ones' neck in my arms and was squeezing, the shadows were pushing me on, making me squeeze more. His life left his body and I was on to the next one.

The joy I felt from feeling the pulses again was freeing. I lived in the night, with the pulses coursing through me and the shadows leading me. And they led me until each of the Northmen were still and their blood covered their cold bodies as they laid on the ground.

As I backed away from the slaughter, my knees buckled with another pulse. That had happened so quickly, the adrenaline, the shadows, the pulses. My body needed time to catch up.

I forced myself up again and slowly walked through the farmhouse, praying to the shadow gods as I did. I found a few blankets and placed them over the bodies of my people. Tomorrow I would tell my court that the Night-Rider, Blood-Pourer did this for us, that he was on our side of this fight. I would tell them to bring the wood, the hay and straw, the weapons from the dead and whatever else we could use, back to the town.

Slowly Midnight and I walked to the nearest brook and washed, refilling my waterskin. The ride back I was cold. The shadows had warmed me from within, yet I was still cold. The children laying on the ground, thinking of their faces, that made me shiver.

I was the one they called Village-Burner, I would burn them all.

***

I took my time brushing down Midnight, just like I used to do in these stables. She was happily grazing on the little fodder in her stable as she recovered from the ride. My mind kept wondering back to Haul, how he would chide me for disobeying my father or for being away for days at a time. My eyes started to well with tears but I pushed them back. It was hard being here and being reminded of him but I made myself stay. I had to feel this because this is what fuelled me. All the ones I had lost. The death. This was the only way I would finish this path.

Some time later I walked through the town in the dark, quiet hours before dawn and into my house. The maids had left the corridors half-lit and as I turned to my room, I saw a figure against the flames. Immediately my mind was black and I was ready to fight. Without thinking, I snuck up to the figure and had my hands around their throat, ready to squeeze.

"Wha-. It's... it's me," coughed the figure as I let go. It was just a little taller than me and slim.

"Delyth?" I took a quick step over to the large candle and held it up to see Delyth rubbing her throat, an odd look in her eyes.

"Delyth, I'm so sorry. I thought..."

"It's fine, fine," she waved her hand and slowly took the

firelight from me. "I shouldn't have been waiting in the dark." She put the candle back on its' stand and the flames flickered against both of our faces.

"Why were you waiting? Is everything ok with the women?" I asked quickly. I didn't want to think that something else had happened here whilst I had been slaking my cravings for the pulses and blood.

"Everything is fine," she said caringly, placing a hand on my arm.

"Ok, well is there enough food for now? Have Heledd and Eirlys come up with a solution yet?" I spoke fast, starting to feel a whirling in my stomach.

"Nerys, everything is fine." The way she said my name, it was soft, sweet. But it made me think of something, something that I couldn't place.

"Oh, well, is…" Before I could say another word she had moved so close to me that our eyes were locked and I could feel her breath on my lips. She moved my arm to her waist and slowly slid hers to my neck. I took a small breath, still looking into her eyes.

"Sh. Stop thinking," she whispered as her lips brushed my neck. I moved into her kiss and could feel her body against mine. I closed my eyes, trying to do as she said. Her lips were soft as they moved up to my jaw and I felt myself bring my other arm to her waist, pulling her closer.

"Better," she whispered as her lips stopped. I moved a hand to her back as she did the same to mine. My stomach was whirling with something like adrenaline but not. I pulled her closer and we stumbled back to the wall. A chuckle escaped her and I opened my eyes. "Much better," she breathed. I gently kissed her jaw and she breathed deeply. Her hand moved down to my thigh and I felt a rush. Then her lips were on mine and she was kissing me and I was kissing her back, slowly at first. Then both her hands were circling the small of my back and I was pulling her even closer. She was warm and soft and moving my lips swiftly as I tried to keep up with her. I was trying to not think but as she whispered my name again something shifted. My stomach ached and I gently pushed her away.

"I can't. I, I." I held my stomach as I felt the cold between us.

"What is it?" she asked.

"I... I don't know. Something..."

"It's ok, take your time." She moved back towards me, the flames dancing in her eyes and I wanted to kiss her again but did nothing as her lips briefly touched my jaw. And she faded into the dark corridor as she left my house. My stomach was aching with something. I think it was guilt.

CHAPTER 16

There were so many flashes, blue and white. So many shadows and wisps fading in and out. I could hear screams and cries and the slow, longing cry of someone in the distance. I just wanted to reach out to them, to help them. I tried to. I tried to search for them through the black fog. It was so dense and shifting.

The cry came from in front of me so I ran forwards. Then it came from behind. No, it was to my left. I ran through the fog but I could never find the source of the cry. Another flash of blue. A strip of white blinded my eyes.

"Your fear you fear…"

What was that? I span around where I stood. Someone had said that. There was someone else in the fog. I tried to shout out but my voice… my voice didn't come out. I screamed and there was silence. I held my hands around my throat. What was happening?

"You are the shadow…"

I span again and again. Fear was starting to sink in.

"Walks... the... shadow..."

No. No! I screamed as loud as my lungs could bare but there was no sound. The fog suddenly felt thick. It was pushing against me from everywhere, everywhere. I had to breathe. I had to keep breathing. But the fog, it was so thick, it was pushing against my skin, forcing itself on me. It was pushing me and moving me and it was slipping into me. I could feel the shadows slipping into me through my skin and my eyes and my ears. I could smell them through my nostrils and they smelt like blood and death. No. My head was being crushed from inside.

"No!"

I was awake. My heart was pounding and my night clothes were sticking to me from the sweat that covered my whole body.

"No," I whispered, catching my breath.

I flopped back to the bed and was asleep.

***

There was no sun in the sky that morning as the clouds were grey. And the clouds covered the sky from the horizon up. As I made my way to the kitchens, a low fog rolled through the town. The well almost looked haunted, like the fog was white shadows, clinging to the earth.

"Morning," I heard and turned to see Steffan and Delyth behind me, also heading towards the kitchens.

"Morning," I replied, with a small smile. The last five days had been a blur. The town felt like a rekindled flame, with a sense of purpose. It felt like the town again, busy even. Everyone had a task to do and I had made sure that I had stayed away from as many people as possible during that time, including Delyth.

"We can eat together," Steffan spoke as the three of us walked through the stone archway that led to the large, open kitchens. There was a small table in the nearest corner and Delyth and I sat as Steffan sourced food for us.

"Lord, Nerys, how are you?" Delyth asked me with bright eyes.

I cleared my mind as best I could before I replied. "Worried."

"And how do you feel?" she asked and I still couldn't gage her meaning. I looked down at my hands as I replied.

"I feel... tired. I'm just tired." I breathed before looking at her and she was looking at my hands.

"Don't worry so much," Delyth offered as she looked up at me. "It will sort itself out," a pause. "As will we."

"Thank you," I breathed and was saved by Steffan bringing a tray over. He had managed to get us a small bowl of thin, grey-looking porridge, slices of dry cheese and a small cup of the stewed elder berries Heledd had been cooking.

"It's actually not too bad," Steffan swore as he set the tray down and took the stool next to Delyth. One of the cooks brought over three cups of clear water and wooden spoons, then bowed to me as she went back to the wood fire.

"So," I began, taking a sip of water and dipping my spoon in the elder berry stew, "what else is there to do?" The stew wasn't horrible but nor was it easy to chew. It was a little sour, bitter, but once I had got used to the taste, it wasn't too bad. Steffan and Delyth had not copied my pick of the food.

"Honestly, I think we have finally made some progress." Steffan took a slice of cheese and carried on. "As you can see, the women have proven useful." Delyth gave a smug smile. "With a little nudge," he said as he nudged Delyth. I clearly missed something but waited for Steffan to continue. "They have been working harder, longer even, than most of the men. Even some of the guard." Delyth tutted and Steffan's eyebrows raised in response.

"Most of those men you call *guard*, are uneasy with the idea that our women work better than they do. Which they do," she said proudly, leaning closer to me. I chuckled then straightened my face.

"Can the guard accept the women as those they can trust?" I tried not to let them hear the concern in my voice. I needed my people to be together and stay together.

"I think they are starting to, lord." Steffan finished his cheese and moved on to the porridge. "The women have shown themselves to be hard-workers, willing and able to learn. They have many skills to teach us and the men are slowly learning to..." Steffan took his time chewing, searching for the right word.

"Realise," Delyth cut in. "They are starting to realise that their wives and sisters and daughters and mothers actually can do more than they can, and know more than they know and can be more than they ever thought." Again, she finished with a smug smile as she turned her shoulders to her cousin.

"I never said you couldn't do anything," exclaimed Steffan, as his cousin was boring down at him.

"So, we have found a way to, if not feed everyone, at least keep them going. What else?" My mind was starting to wander and it was filling with black shapes and voices. The shadows were growing hungry. And so was I. I had to push them aside, I had to stay focused on the present.

"The guard not on any work duty are helping the women, gathering berries, making nettle cloth, collecting more wood and fodder from anywhere they can. We are working, lord," Steffan finished, his brows looked tight. He believed what he was saying, I just didn't know if he believed it would really work in the end.

"Good," I said, more like a whisper actually. This had to work.

"And..." Delyth started. Steffan seemed to be irked with Delyth but took her opening.

"And, Bleddyn's group should be back by noon. We will know more then."

"Yes, we will."

***

A little after noon Bleddyn's group returned through the east gate. Their horses seemed tired and the men more so, two were taken to the healers as soon as they slid off their horses. Stable hands were quick to take the horses away and other guard helped with the packs from the saddles. They seemed heavy. Heavy was good.

I pushed through the crowd that had gathered and found Bleddyn quickly. His beard had flecks of dried blood in and his leather was dirty. I could feel something brewing from him, he was going to shout to the gods.

"Bleddyn, what happened?" I asked as calmly as I could.

"What happened? What happened?" Yep, this was going to be bad. I tried to stand taller and not let him tower over me but he stood heads above me anyway. "What happened was they knew we were coming." His voice was deep and loud, bringing silence to those around us. "What happened was they were waiting for us in the night and we had to fight our way out." He threw his arms towards the stone buildings. "Rhys and Ioan are good men, and those good men are now out of the fight because *you* put them in danger." He had started pointing his finger at me and I took it for now, but the shadows were stirring in me.

"I put them in danger? I did?" Several shadows were calling for his head, I almost laughed out loud at them. "As far as I can see, you all made it back." I sounded more accusing than I had wanted to, the shadows were trying to force themselves into my mind and I was keeping them at bay. For now.

"They spoke of the Night-Rider," Bleddyn blurted out, "even with their half words, they could shout 'Night-Rider'. I could sense those around us getting edgy. I really didn't want this to play out in front of anyone. I crossed my arms and tried to focus on the movement of my chest, in and out. Bleddyn took several steps in all directions and started shouting.

"The Night-Rider, of all things. This damned Night-Rider, your friend is he? He cursed us all when he helped the other night. When he slaughtered a whole group of those Northerners and put them on to us. This is his doing. And yours!"

"Enough!" I yelled. I took a few steps towards him and just breathed. He held my silence. Slowly I made my way through men and women and felt all eyes staring at me. I got to the first saddle-pack and opened it. I was right, it was heavy. I took hold of a large wooden shield that had one side covered in a thick hide and used two hands to hold it up to Bleddyn. "Was this the danger you meant?"

He huffed and mumbled something that I didn't care to hear and I moved to the other pack. As I did, movement stirred in the crowd and I heard him before I saw him. Ithel, and a few of his men, were now watching too. Slowly, I opened the other pack and found a grain bag. I could sing. I placed a hand inside, lifted it up and let the grain trickle out of my hand and back into the bag. I shook my head at Bleddyn, wishing he would say something else, anything. The shadows were wishing for it to.

"Nerys," warned Ithel quietly. I didn't need his warning however. I walked back over to Bleddyn and took a deep breath.

"Bleddyn, you have done well. Rest, and we will wait for Siorus' group to return." I made to turn to the packs but stopped. "And I will tell the Night-Rider of your kind words."

Some of my guard busied themselves with the packs and in a matter of moments, the crowd dispersed as if it was never there.

"Nerys," came Ithel's voice as he caught up with me. I sighed aloud and hushed the shadows to the back of my mind. What could it be now?

***

Sirous's group returned with less event than Bleddyn's. Three days after Bleddyn's group Siorus found me in the hall, looking over the parchments that were still out from the war council. I was trying to do something, anything that didn't make me think, but it was no use. Waves of emotion kept hitting me. I had to keep telling myself they just weren't here. My father, my cousin, my friend. They just weren't here. But I was and Midnight was and I had the shadows. They were with me, they wouldn't leave me.

"Lord," came Siorus's voice and it snapped me out of my daydream.

"Yes, Siorus." I turned to see him looking tired, and a little forlorn. I had not seen Siorus like this in years, since Steffan's parents had died. What else could we take?

"Tell me," was all I said. He filled his lungs with breath and the words that came out were harsh, his voice husky.

"We, we lost... We lost." He tried to say the names but couldn't. "We lost two guard. We're sending the bodies to their families." Siorus looked up at me quickly then fiddled with his belt. "A death day would, would be a nice, a nice gest-"

"Sh," I hushed as I held his hand. I felt my court member and friend take a deep breath and I let go. He stood up a little straighter and spoke clearly.

"Lord, we lost two on our skirmish but brought back water skins, a few flint daggers and a deer carcass that still has enough meat on to be stripped. I would ask that we have a death day, for the families of those we lost."

"Thank you, Siorus. Make sure your men are well and rested. The day after tomorrow at dusk, tell the families. They aren't able to be here for it, but they should know."

He bowed and left. My head and stomach felt heavy. Another

wave rushed through me and the shadows taunted me. They knew how to make me feel better, they were saying. That one shadow was urging me to feel better, to spill blood. It was so insistent, so angry. It wanted blood and it wanted to get it. It was so strong, it almost felt like it was clawing against my skull, shouting and screeching for blood. I couldn't take it. Any of it. It was clawing at my brain and skull and the screeching was growing louder and louder. I couldn't even hear my own voice in my head. It was hurting. It was hurting me. I fell to the floor and crawled into a ball. The shadow was still shouting and clawing and I couldn't control it. It was so angry. So vengeful. Why was it doing this to me?

**

Gathered around the well and filling the space between my house, the stone buildings and the Ea that ran through the town, were the men and women defending our land. My court had ensured as many of them were here as possible and they all shared the same look on their faces. A look that I did not like to see, as it meant I had failed.

The day was cold with a warm breeze. The sun was slowly lowering on a gloomy sky. A few fire-torches were already lit and dotted through the crowd. I took a small step forwards and stood as tall as I could.

"Today, we are here to honour death. Without death we cannot have life and only life comes from death." This was so hard. Without my mother, my father, my cousin, my uncle even. None of my family were here, none of them could see me or support me through this. My stomach was tightening. How could I be leading a death day with no shadow gods or vessel?

I bent down to the ground and tried to grab some earth in my hand. The ground was dry and hard. I barely scraped off enough to fill my palm. I could cry at how pathetic it felt, to hold my land in my hand. The land that used to be so full and rich and giving. And now, I was barely holding anything, just crumbling, dry earth.

"I don't know how this is supposed to go, but I think you need to say something else," whispered Ithel quickly into my ear. I hadn't stood up yet. Everyone was watching me and I was just staring at my hand.

A small breeze shook me from my thoughts and I stood back up. A few steps behind me were my court and guard, all standing patiently and Ithel, with a few of his Midlander men. Delyth and my maids were to my left, I glanced over and saw Mairwen and Celyn doing weird hand gestures for what I should be doing. This was just so not what a death day should be. The vessel should be here, connecting the shadow gods to us, letting our ancestors, the shadows, fill us with their warmth.

I felt Ithel's tall frame stand next to me and took the hint. I held my hand out to my people and continued.

"This land is our home and from it we are blessed. When we die, we return to it, completing the cycle of life and death." I held my hand high and sprinkled the dying earth over my head. Those in front of me bent down and sprinkled earth over the heads of those nearest to them. I noticed Ithel still stood tall, so I bent down to grab more earth. As I turned to him, his eyes were dark but they were also filling with something. I couldn't work out what, it wasn't how eyes usually fill with water when sad, this was something else. Something foggy.

"Ithel," I said quietly and he bent down so that I could raise my hand over his head. As I faced my people again, a wave of shadows blackened my mind. They wanted to be free, all of them. They just wanted to be free and home and with their families again. Their pain was so strong I could feel them in my stomach, pulling me down the ground.

"Lord," Bleddyn warned, his voice no longer patient. I pushed the shadows aside as best I could and decided they should hear this.

"Although our land has been fading and our gods have been away from us for too long," mumbles echoed through the crowd. "Our shadows are still close and they are with us. They will always be with us." More murmurs and mumbles. "This fight has been blackened by those that we have lost and we have all lost so many. I feel your pain and hurt and I share in it." A few people were shouting now but I understood why. So much had changed over the years and so many had lost hope. I took a deep breath and stepped forwards. The words that came out next were slow and heavy. "I share in your loss. Those we have lost in our fight with the Northern men will never really leave us, we will take them with us wherever we go and they will fight with us in the days ahead. They are with us still as they are shadows and the shadows never leave us."

Most of the crowd clapped or cheered. Most. Some still shouted at me, sending their anger towards me and what I was making them do. I took it, all of it. They hadn't asked for this.

I nodded my head and walked away, before any of my court or guard could block me. Aeddan was right next to me as I pushed through the guard but I growled at him and he stopped. I had managed to get to the east gate before hands were on me. But these hands didn't stop me, they carried me forwards until we were out of the town and by the north wall.

Ithel let go of me and Aeddan came a moment later, lungs panting hard as he stopped sprinting. The night was almost upon us and the moonlight was weak.

"What was that for?" I asked Ithel harshly. His eyes had gone back to normal and I felt another pull in my stomach, like the shadows weren't in pain anymore. He didn't say anything, just moved a hand towards Aeddan. My guard just lifted his hand before placing them both on his knees, still breathing hard.

"Aeddan has something to say to you, Nerys, if you'll listen."

"Very well," I turned back to Aeddan and he was just flapping his hands around, still recovering. I half laughed, half sighed.

"Some guard," I muttered and swear I heard Ithel chuckle. As soon as I turned back to face him though, his face was its usual calm.

"Aeddan heard something that he needs to share with you. It is serious and concerning." One more look at Aeddan and I gave up.

"You'll have to tell me, Ithel." Aeddan nodded and bent over again.

"As you wish," he replied and stood a little straighter. "When Aeddan arrived back with Bleddyn from the first skirmish, he found me and told me. He said he didn't want to go to another member of the court as he was worried about who knew." I should have remembered this, Ithel was good at dragging out a story and not getting to the point.

"Knew what?" I quickly cut in. The night was dark now and it was a struggle to see Ithel's expression.

"Who knew how much and for how long this had been going on for." Wow, I said to myself, Ithel was too good at being dull sometimes.

"Aeddan, please," I almost begged to my guard. Thankfully, he seemed to have recovered by now. Aeddan filled his lungs with air and stepped closer to us.

"Lord, I, I am ashamed that I have not told you sooner. What with what happened with," he didn't say his name, just waved his hands around but I knew he meant Dilwyn. I tried not to let the thought take hold, tried to keep his name as just a sound in the night. "It was just when we came back from the raid, you and Bleddyn seemed..." Aeddan struggled to find the right word. I helped him along.

"Loud?"

"Er, yes. Er, you two were...loud. And it wasn't the right time but I saw Ithel and well, I thought I could tell him because he isn't from here and he doesn't know the court that well and you two are ok now, right?"

"Right," I slowly agreed, glancing at Ithel briefly. I saw his head move slightly and took that as a nod.

"And so when I told Ithel, he told me I should tell you as soon as possible, but then you were always moving and busy and it was very hard keeping up with you and some days I was on work duty or wood gathering, so I wasn't with you. Which, looking at it, was probably on purpose, if Bleddyn suspected anything, I guess and then I-"

"Woah, Aeddan, slow down." The man could speak way too fast. "Go back to the part about Bleddyn." I crossed my arms as the night air turned cold and started moving from foot to foot.

"Well, when we had made camp the night before the skirmish, someone came to our fire and spoke to Bleddyn. He was gone a while and when he came back, all Bleddyn said was the man was a lost trader, looking for somewhere to stay the night." Aeddan ran his fingers through his hair. "I mean, we didn't think much of it, we were focused on the next day and Bleddyn led us, so we followed him, obviously." Aeddan's shoulders moved up and down and I heard him breath in deeply. Now I wanted him to talk faster so I could get warm.

"Here," Ithel said quietly and I felt him place a jacket around my shoulders.

"Erm, but won't you-"

"I'm from the Midlands, remember? Our winters get very cold." I wished I could see his face then, there was something in his voice that was light, comforting almost.

"But it's summer now." I wanted to give it back to him but I was cold. "Thank you," I quietly said and felt the warmth from his body through the jacket.

"So, the next morning we were moving closer the to the Northmen's camp and then, bam, the trader from the night before was in our path. Bleddyn pushed to the front and grabbed the trader. I mean, I was worried for the trader at this point, Bleddyn should not have grabbed a stranger seeking company, that goes against our fundamental oath. The rest of the guard carried on but I hung back because my mind was just not happy with it and I couldn't let it happen again, you know?"

"Aeddan, please, just say it," I begged.

"Oh, of course, lord." I felt him step closer towards me and he lowered his voice. "I overheard Bleddyn talking to the trader. He said 'it has to be done and soon, the people are starting to trust her.' Then the trader said 'well, whose fault is that? You

were supposed to make it hard for her.' Then Bleddyn growled
something and said 'you were the one who failed the first time,
that man you chose from the coast barely made any noise.'
Then they said something else and I heard 'my lord is growing
restless, he knows his man will be ready. You must do this,
or I will not be so forgiving.' Bleddyn took something from
his belt and gave it to the trader and then the trader started
walking away but he said 'do not fail me again, Bleddyn,
or you'll join her.' And that was it, lord. I do not know if
Bleddyn can be trusted right now." He coughed several times
before speaking again. "I do not like to say this, lord, it is not
something I ever thought I would do, but I cannot be quiet.
Dilwyn's... Dilwyn showed me that."

I took several breaths before replying to Aeddan. That was so
much to learn and hear and think about. My mind was racing
and I was trying to hold the shadows back, trying to keep my
thoughts separate and my own.

"Aeddan, I am grateful that you told me this. Ithel was right,
I had to know. Keep this to yourself now, and do your best to
act normally. If you chose to stay away from Bleddyn for now,
I will back that decision. Please, now rest and I'll find you
tomorrow." My mind was getting colder and darker.

I heard my guard let out a long sigh. "Thank you, lord, thank you." Then footsteps sounded and Aeddan was gone.

Ithel took my hand in the dark and I felt my mind clear, it was weird. Like his touch sent the shadows away, or at least, sent them back.

"What now?" he asked quietly.

"Will I ever have one quiet night?" I wanted to scream that to the shadow gods, to shout at them for this. The darkened path was trouble enough, without all these day-to-day people troubles getting in the way. Then it clicked, or rather, I remembered something I should not have forgot.

"No," I breathed. Ithel's hand held mine tighter. "I. I. This trader, this is not the first time I have heard of him. Damn."

CHAPTER 17

They came back frantic and screaming. Ten or so women ran
through the east gate and into the town a little before noon.
I was with the smith, still trying to convince him to make
anything he could from any material he had when the sounds
of pain echoed through the town.

I ran to the sounds, heart pounding. There really would not be
a quiet moment ever.

I found Siorus and Steffan already there, holding on to women
as they were crumbling to the floor. One I recognised, she
was the only one still standing so I went to her. Eirlys's knees
were dirty and she had twigs sticking out of her hair. In one
hand she was gripping a bunch of twigs so tightly her skin had
turned white over her knuckles.

"Eirlys, tell me what happened?" I asked gently.

Her dark eyes snapped to mine as if she was shook out of a
daydream.

"Lord!" She took a filling breath. "Lord, sorry."

"It's fine, Eirlys, tell me."

"They attacked us, those Northern...." Eirlys made a sound in her throat as she shivered and I agreed, those men were hard to describe. I placed a hand on her shoulder briefly and she rolled her shoulders back. "We were collecting more wood, lord, from the village not six leagues north of here. We left at dawn, as we were walking, and, and." She looked at me square in the eyes and hers were filled with fear and disappointment. "We hadn't even filled our baskets with wood before-"

"Before they ran at us and attacked us with knives and spears and they growled. So loud were their growls. And their teeth, gods above their teeth were awful." Heledd had bounded over and her eyes were wide with horror as she rattled on. Her hair was matted and her skin wet with sweat.

"Thank you, Heledd," I said as patiently as I could, but I wanted to talk to Eirlys. Only Eirlys. At just the right moment Delyth appeared and was by my side.

"Come, Heledd, let's go to the kitchens," she said gently. "We can get you some nettle tea." Delyth glanced at me as she led Heledd towards the kitchens and I gave her a small smile. Siorus and Steffan were also leading the other women to the kitchens.

"Oh, I do love nettle tea," Heledd mused as she walked with Delyth. I breathed easier.

"Eirlys, do you remember how many there were?"

"Maybe five or six, lord. Sorry, lord," Eirlys looked down and started brushing dirt off her clothes.

"For what?"

"We, we didn't even bring back wood, and our baskets, our baskets…"

"We can recover the baskets, and the wood easily. Don't worry about that." I tried to sound calm but I didn't feel it. The Northmen were bold to come so close to us and we were still struggling to make enough weapons for everyone to have one each.

"And we were," she definitely hiccoughed but it sounded so strange. I tried to keep my face blank but my eyebrows raised themselves. Eirlys pressed her lips together before she continued. "We've been training so hard, to fight these… and we ran away from five." And there it was, the shock. It hit her now and instantly, Eirlys was crying and wiping her eyes with her dirty shirt.

"Go, Eirlys, go to the kitchens, ok?"

"Mmm," was all I got from her and she slowly made her way to the stone buildings.

Steffan was ready beside me as soon as she was gone.

"We can't have this, lord," he stated.

"No, we cannot." The guard had taken whatever wood the women had managed to bring back and now I saw Bleddyn and Merfyn standing, waiting for me to speak to them. Deep breath. How I would love the shadows to take over my mind now. To rage at Bleddyn. But I kept my calm and my mind my own. I had sworn to Ithel that I would not do anything, well, anything that I wanted to do.

**

My room was dark as I puffed out the candles my maids had lit for me. Sitting on my bed, I fought back tears that were trying to fall. Everything was starting to build in me, pain, anxiety, grief and not just my own. The shadows were so sad, in such pain. They longed to be free, to see their families and their land again. They could sense it too, the end was near. It must be soon. I rubbed my scars, it must be soon.

I stood myself up onto weary legs and slowly walked out of my house. Sleep was alluding me. Normally, this would have been when I hunted, the time when I would come alive and feel the warmth of the pulses. But now, now I had to talk to my court. Again. I did so much talking these days, I missed being alone, with only Midnight and the shadows. My jaw was aching.

Standing around the logs of the court were them, Bleddyn, Merfyn, Siorus and Steffan. Ithel was there as well, as was Aeddan and my guard. Bleddyn's hound was laying by his master's log and I thought he looked a little thinner.

The night was dark and the fire in the middle of my men was small, an attempt to save the wood. I wanted this to be over already.

As soon as I was by my log, I gestured for my court to sit and for Ithel to take Dilwyn's place again. He did, but was the last to sit.

"Well," I started, my voice snappy.

"We must do something, strike back," offered Siorus eagerly.

"Yes," was all I replied.

"We should start the move up to the boundary soon," Steffan said, looking straight at the fire.

"They must not see us as weak. They cannot be allowed to have the last strike." I looked at Bleddyn as he spoke, trying to see something, anything, that would hint at what he had done.

"Then we do both," Merfyn recommended. "We pack up and start moving north and set off one group for a final skirmish. But this time, we must be quick and unseen. We cannot lose any more lives needlessly." I could hear the sadness in Merfyn's voice and bit my tongue. I knew Merfyn meant well.

"Have it done," I ordered as I stood. My court rose after me and left with silent bows.

"Ithel, wait." He hadn't moved from his spot anyway. I walked away from the logs and slowly made towards my house. He walked next to me and I shivered quickly.

"I'd like you to do something for me." After all, I did trust him now. I turned to face him and held my hands in front of me. How far I'd come from trying to kill him the last time we were both standing here. "I've sent for Brynmor to meet you here tomorrow morning." I'd finally learnt the name of my duck-like friend. Ithel nodded and waited for me patiently. "Find out who the trader is, as Brynmor has seen this man as well. And find him, we need answers and we need them fast."

He dipped his head and started to move but I spoke again. "And Ithel," I looked at my hands, not sure why I suddenly felt my stomach flutter.

"Yes, Nerys?" His voice was so calm and gentle. It irked me at how calm and soothing it sounded to me.

"You must do this quietly, no one but you and Brynmor can know." I looked back up at him and his eyes were intense.

"I'll do this as best I can." He took my hand and squeezed it, walking away and leaving me in the dark. My hand felt colder after his warm touch.

***

The next day was a blur. Men and women were busy with packing up. Sacks were being filled with fodder, carts loaded with wood and weapons, although, only the men were loading the carts, I observed. Still being protective over their weapons. Saddle packs were being loaded with bedding, cups and pans, the cooks were shouting at anyone who would listen to not eat anything lest they want their fingers chopped off. I walked passed the cook as she shouted again and raised my eyebrows, she just shrugged and mumbled that she wouldn't really do it.

The day was clear but for a few grey clouds, it seemed like summer might actually be upon us, even if it was two new moons late. I found Midnight in the stables and brushed her down. I missed this. Just me and her and nothing else. But everything else that had happened was because of me. All because of me. I growled to myself. No, this was all because of the damned shadow gods feeling blighted. This was no use. I had to stop brushing down Midnight, I was growing angry and the shadows loved it when I was angry. Deep breaths. I had become quite good at calming myself down with my breath over the year.

"Lord," came a gentle voice and I shook myself out of my head.

Delyth's head peered around Midnight and she slowly came into view. Her hands were dirty with green and mud but her hair was neatly pulled back.

"What is it, Delyth?"

"I wanted to show you more of the progress the women have made, before we have to pack it all up." She took a step towards me and held out her hand. I hugged Midnight's neck tightly and took Delyth's hand. She smiled quickly and led me out of the stables. As we crossed the south bridge, she folded my arm through hers. I went to say something but the words got stuck in my throat. I tried again.

"Delyth, I have something to ask you."

"Of course, what is it?" We both carried on facing the way we were walking and I nodded back to those we passed who greeted me.

"I'd like you to stay here, after the battle and everything. I haven't really had a proper... female friend before." She let me get everything out as we kept walking. "I have my maids, of course and they are like family but I've never had a friend by choice."

"You'd like us to be friends?" she asked slowly.

"I would. It's just, I've been surrounded by men for so long, I don't really know what it's like anymore." I took a small breath and tried not to look at her face. We had just got to the east gate and she let go of my arm. As we faced each other, her face was unreadable. I hoped I hadn't said the wrong thing.

Delyth looked around and as if by fate, the only people around us were men. She chuckled sweetly, a sound that made me smile.

"No, I don't suppose you do." She tilted her head as she looked at me. "Of course, Nerys, I'd like that." I let out a breath I didn't know I held and she squeezed my hand quickly.

"But, you have to plait my hair whenever I ask and wear dresses with me whenever we feel silly. Oh, and you have to-"

"Who's the lord here?" I asked, giggling. We walked round the back of the stone buildings and into the kitchens.

"Well, isn't that what girls do?" she asked, eyelashes blinking at me.

"Ha, that's what some girls do. Not us."

"And that's why I like you." She quickly pecked my cheek and took a spoon out of the nearest pot of elder berry stew. I nodded at the cooks and women around me as I stood myself next to Delyth.

"I meant-"

"Nerys," her tone was serious but also light. "I like you as a person and a friend," she then turned the spoon to me, "try this." I did try it, it didn't seem as bitter as the last time I had had it. "Try to respect me, as I respect you." That put me in my place. Maybe this was what it was like having a friend by choice and not because your parents were friends.

Delyth took me round the kitchens, the healing rooms and outside by the well. The women had made bandage strips from nettle fibres, clay cups and pots to use for food and water when we made camp. She showed me the leather belts and boddices they had made after begging for leather scraps from the tanners and saddlers by the smith. She also showed a wooden catapult on wheels that would throw small stones into the air, but they only showed me that with a leather belt, not an actual stone.

I felt less worried after that. The coming fight would still be brutal and I wouldn't even let myself think at how many we might lose. But at least the women had done something. They had used their time to build a catapult, all some of the men had done was hide their swords and spears.

***

At dawn four days later, we were off. I had not heard any news from Ithel and Brynmor, which I prayed wasn't bad news. Every day since we began to pack up had felt so long, people really could move so slowly when they dreaded what they would find at the end. I just wanted to be there, and now, I just wanted this over with.

The court led the men and women out of the east gate and north to the boundary. I hung back, just looking at the empty town. It was so sad to see that I felt a wave of sorrow clench my gut. "I'm so sorry, father," I breathed to the air as I turned Midnight around and followed the back of the army. I hoped I knew what I was doing. I prayed over and over to the shadow gods, asking for their forgiveness. I prayed to the shadows, asking them to make me strong, fast, fearless. I had felt myself drift lately. My mind was distracted with the thoughts of people and feelings and looking after all these lives. I had lost so much time to being lord rather than killing for the shadow gods. I could have been so much closer to the end by now, I could have done it by now, made all of this end. And the irony of it all, I wasn't even the lord yet, not properly. I was still just an heir acting as lord. What would my father say?

CHAPTER 18

I left my tent just as the sun rose on a grey day. I had missed
this too. Just being able to see the sun rise, washing away
all of the past days with it. We had made camp south of the
boundary line and my court had set to work getting everyone
and everything unpacked and ready. Merfyn had led the final
skirmish and was expected back before noon. He had to be
back soon and all of them had to be unhurt, I could not take
any more bad news.

I span on the spot. Ruckus sounded from the north of the
camp and I saw Bleddyn run passed me. Nope, he was not
getting there first. I ran through the camp, dodging pots and
pans and shields and fires. I hadn't plaited my hair yet so it
was blowing all over my face.

As soon as I got to the source of the ruckus, I felt a sense of
relief and confusion. Merfyn was back, with all his men and,
I counted quickly, more. I moved round to the side of the
horses and saw two young boys being helped down from a new

chestnut horse. They were skinny and grubby and in need of a good wash, as was the horse.

"Merfyn?" I asked a little worriedly. We did not need any more mouths to feed. I watched Bleddyn stroke the chestnut horse and slowly move to the sack that had come back with it. He was a problem but the two young boys were more important right now.

"Lord, forgive me." My court member bowed to me then quickly gave instructions to his men and the guard who had arrived. "I could not leave them." I saw the pain in his eyes and nodded gently. He was a good man and this was a good thing to do.

"There is no need. I trust you will see that they are washed and fed." Merfyn smiled with his mouth and eyes and knelt by the two boys, who were huddling together.

"Bleddyn," I called and didn't wait for his reply. "Tell the cooks that Merfyn will need three big bowls for supper tonight, to be served in his tent. No questions asked." Bleddyn stared at me, then the boys and back at me. He stood in front of me and I could see his mind working, trying to find something quick to say.

"Aeddan," I also called, knowing Aeddan was behind me. He

dashed forwards.

"Yes, lord?"

"Help Bleddyn carry the bowls to Merfyn's tent later, when the cooks are ready."

"Of course, lord," Aeddan replied and stayed with Bleddyn as I turned and left.

I didn't even make it back to my tent before my knees gave way beneath me. My mind blackened and the shadows were screaming. I could see the dry grass and mud so close to my face but couldn't move. I couldn't make any part of my body move. The shadows were crying at me, screaming at me and all I could do was listen. Distant shouts and voices sounded around me and I was aware that hands were on my body but the feeling didn't make it to my mind. The hands held me up and moved me to my tent. I felt like I was floating through the air, my body was doing one thing and my mind another. All of my body was numb with black and shadows. And my arms. I started scratching at them. They were burning. I had to stop them burning.

"So hot!" I heard a cry through the shadows. "Too hot!" I had to make it stop, I had to stop the burning. I frantically fiddled on my belt for anything. Something. The happiness I felt when I held a dagger in my hand. That would do it, that would make it stop burning.

"No, lord. No!"

As soon as I put the blade to my skin, a coldness washed over me. It cooled me from head to toe in one swift breath. The shadows were gone.

***

I awoke to see Mairwen and Celyn either side of my bed. Celyn held a small bowl of water and cloth in her hand, Mairwen held what I hoped wasn't one of the cooks' pans.

I pushed myself up on to my elbows and looked from maid to maid.

"Er, what is going on?"

"How are you feeling, lady?" Celyn asked softly, dipping the cloth in the bowl. "Any burning?" she dabbed the cloth on my forehead. I tried to net her away but she was actually annoyingly persistent. I gave in and let her dab me.

"And Mairwen, do you really need a pan?" I questioned.

"It's just in case, lady." Her tone was sceptical. I just stared at her and she squinted her eyes back at me. I laughed out loud at the bizarreness of this start to the morning and got myself out of bed. Celyn was muttering her protests and Mairwen followed me with her pan.

"Do you not remember anything, lady?" she asked.

"Like what?" I asked as I saw a large bucket and a dark stain on the hide rug, but there was a lighter patch in the middle of it.

My tent flap opened and Aeddan stuck his head in.

"Forgive me, lord. Ithel has returned." His eyes shyly went to the ground as I too looked down and saw I was in a small night gown.

"Mairwen," I almost barked and she ran to the drawers. "Send him to me, Aeddan." My guard mumbled his response and left. A very bizarre start.

Just as I had changed and Mairwen and Celyn filled me in as they plaited my hair, Ithel's head came through my tent. He stood himself next to the door flap and waited with his hands behind his back. Mairwen and Celyn quickly bowed and left.

I took a step closer to Ithel and then to the drawer top. I lit a small candle and turned back to him. Still he waited.

"Where is Brynmor?" I wondered as I looked properly at his face. His eyes were sunken and his chin stubbly.

"He took the horses to the stable yard and then was going to find Delyth, to get back to work." He nodded so I felt I should nod and then he gestured for the chairs I had by a small desk that I apparently needed in my tent. He stayed where he was until I had sat. As he joined me, he pulled out a crumpled piece of parchment from an inner pocket on his leather jacket. It looked like the same jacket he had put round my shoulders… I shook my head quickly before I carried on.

"Well?"

He placed the parchment on the table and covered it with a hand. I noticed the knuckles were bruised and a little red.

"We found him, Nerys-"

"You did? Where? When?" Ithel held up a hand to calm me and slid his other one closer to me on the table.

"Brynmor told me that you saw him during your banishment."

"Yes?" I almost growled out slowly.

"He also told me that he didn't tell you everything because he was scared, terrified even, of you then."

"What? I wasn't-" Another hand. Ithel let go of the parchment and looked deep into my eyes.

"Don't read this yet, let me finish first." He waited for me to respond so I just nodded. Again, I forgot how slow Ithel was at passing on news. "We headed straight for the western boundary of your lands, and there he told me everything. Brynmor was earnest in his words, he really didn't mean to keep it from you. He didn't know he could trust you then." I was doing my best to stay patient and yet, those eyes that were looking at me felt so full of life. His voice was dull but those eyes, I could look at them and not be bored. I looked down at the parchment, that was better.

"He took me to the small farmstead where he had first met the trader. This man used to trade wool to all of the west coast but since sheep had been getting thinner and were being slaughtered, he had to give that up and find a new trade. Brynmor said he had invited him to the tavern in the next town that night and he met with him. The trader spoke of another lord to the west who did not believe in the shadow gods. This lord did not believe that the shadows gods had left, that any of the this was their fault. He was stubborn on his point that it was Neirin, your father, who had done this and only him. The trader took work with this lord as a messenger, as he already knew most of the land." I stood up and poured two glasses of watered down milk for Ithel and I. This was going to take a while. He took a small sip and continued.

"We had planned to go further west and head up to this other lord but fate cut in, it would seem." Ithel's tone had lightened at those words and he pointed to the parchment. "We found the trader. We stayed overnight in a barn that an elderly couple kindly offered. They told us that another traveller had stayed not two nights before. That he said he was heading back east, to meet a friend at a river village, the one with all the reeds." He shrugged his shoulders and pulled a face, guess he didn't like reeds. "We rode as fast as we could and came to this reed village. We asked the elder and they told us that a man had left them at dusk the day before. We followed his tracks and the next day, he had made a small fire." Ithel's face turned sour at whatever he was thinking.

"I'm afraid I did not complete this task as best I could, Nerys. I am ashamed to say that I let anger cloud my mind." His voice was so blank of any feeling, it was a stark contrast to his face that had furrowed in on itself.

"What do you mean, Ithel?" I made to place a hand on his but he pulled them away before I could reach. He lifted up both hands then slowly let me hold them. All of the knuckles were red and bruised, just as I had seen. But I had not seen the scratches and flecks of dirt and blood under his fingernails.

"Bleddyn will not be able to meet with him anymore." Ithel took back his hands and downed his glass. He nodded to the parchment and I read it.

**

Rage. I stormed out of my tent, followed quickly by Ithel. I heard nothing that he said to me as I thundered across the camp. Rage was all I saw, all I heard. Small fires were dotted around the camp as the day was grey enough to be dusk.

As I made my way through the camp, I heard more voices join behind me but kept going. The shadows came as soon as I called to them, dancing through my mind with glee. Where was he?

I saw his hound before I saw him. I could hear people behind me trying to shout at me but they would not get through my rage and shadows. Bleddyn was sharpening a blade with other men on small logs around him but that did not matter. Who heard this did not matter. All that mattered was that I was rage and Bleddyn was over.

The men saw me and stood abruptly. Bleddyn took a moment to look at me and what I could only guess were the rest of the court behind me.

"You will stand at your lord," I deeply commanded.

"What is it that has rattled you so, lord?" he sneered as he stood, keeping his blade in his hand. I felt a hand on my shoulder and a whisper in my hear. Ithel's voice calmed the shadows and I did not like it. My mind seemed to be clearing, and my rage fading.

"You will face a court trial for your actions and you will be removed from your position at court." I spoke clearly and deeply, staring coldly into his eyes. He never so much as blinked while I spoke. Out of the corner of my eye, I saw Ithel nod at Steffan and Siorus and a head of blond hair.

"Aeddan," and he stood next to me. "Place a guard of four on this man at all times. He is to be tied hand and foot and watched day and night. No one is to speak to him and he is not to speak. He cannot eat unless he is given food and cannot shit unless he is told to." Aeddan nodded and pointed to four guard who had heard me. Instantly, Bleddyn was tied up and being marched to the other side of the camp.

Before I turned to face my court, Ithel spoke for me.

"Nerys has her reasons and you will all learn them tonight." I nodded approvingly at Ithel. That sounded rather like me.

***

Our progress was slow. I was glad of it this time. I needed the men and women to be quiet if we had any chance of getting through the woods unseen. And that catapult. The women were stubborn to bring it and I prayed it would make it in one piece. I travelled at the front of our army, leading on Midnight quietly. Pangs of emotions, memories tried to force themselves on me as I rode through this wood but I pushed them away. I replaced them with the urge to feel the pulses, I hadn't felt them in so long. I needed to feel them again. I knew it was close. A few more pulses and the shadow gods would have received their required souls, they would feel listened to, they would feel useful again.

I wouldn't, couldn't deny them that.

As I led Midnight through the woods, my company got smaller and smaller. My court and Ithel would each lead a troop of men and women into the beast's camp from the east. I kept heading north-west, to cross the stream. The first group to break off would be led by Merfyn. His loyalty never wavered and he wanted the gods back as much as I did. I would need that now since his men would have to wait the longest.

As dusk approached I was over the stream. Just me and Midnight. We would be riding alone, how it used to be. The woods were quiet now. Now it was dark and I was in its heart. What little life still lived here showed no signs, I didn't even hear a bird tweet or a branch break. Soon, these woods would be alive. Alive with the screams and cries of dying men.

Once I was happy with my position, I started the league south. The moon was high in the sky yet its' light was waning.

Adrenaline, mixed with the shadows who never left me now, coursed through my veins. I knew where my prey was, and I would hunt each and every one of them down. They would see me, the Night-Rider, fully covered in black, and they would know death.

The stillness of the woods started to fade. Faint voices, crunches, clangs reached my ears. So did the smells. Of smoke and sweat and burnt, rotting meat. Pleasant. Then fires came into view. I was close. Then came the makeshift tents, boys scrubbing boots, sharpening swords, more fires surrounded by cold, hungry men.

I rode Midnight straight through their camp. Her warm body gave me strength as my heart slightly faltered. I remembered the cage.

The first few Northern men to see me did nothing. They armed themselves with axes but did nothing. Smart. I continued my path confidently and they followed. Probably out of curiosity but also so I had nowhere to run. Equally smart, even if it did mean their own deaths. As more men noticed me, they in turn joined and followed. It was almost as if I was leading them by the time I reached the middle of their encampment. Although, what they shouted at me along the way was crude. I smiled though, this was their end.

I stopped Midnight as hundreds of the Northerners surrounded us. If I was alone, I would have broken down and cried and let fear take hold of me. But I wasn't. I had Midnight and I had the shadows. I always had the shadows now. And I had to end them all. I gently stroked my friend, making sure she was calm.

Then he came out of the darkness. Their leader, Gwrtheryn. Wrapped in his cloak of grey. He parted his men with ease and he strode in to the circle they had formed around me. A circle of shouting, angry, hungry men whose souls were what I needed. Dark and cold and far away from the shadow gods. Gwrtheryn looked rougher than last time I saw him, his beard messy. And he looked pleased. He had come to gloat.

"My little leaf, a surprise." He held out his arms wide. "You come back to me. I am glad."

I willed the shadows to me instantly, all of them. Just in case.

"As am I," I struggled to say over the catcalls and jeers.

"Now I can have you and there is no little lord to stop me." He turned to get the cheers from his men. "Because your little lord of a father is dead." Uproar.

I focused on the shadows, told them to show me the way. He began to circle me. I kept my gaze forward, tightening my grip on Midnight's reins. Seeing only the shadows in my mind.

"Your land has given my men fight. They like to fight, but they want more." Sniggers echoed. "I have not had the challenge I wanted. I have not fought this Night-Rider. Maybe he does not exist." At that point I wanted to shout out 'Really?'. I was head-to-toe covered in all black, what I wore on my hunts, I had already fought his weak-thing of a 'best warrior' and still he did not believe me. "Maybe he is a coward. I do not like cowards."

"Must we go through this again? Last time it cost you your best fighter, apparently," I offhandedly waved my left arm towards him.

His laugh seemed to bounce off the trees. It was cold, grim.

"You say you are him, this Night-Rider. You are not. No. Only man could be so cruel. Only man can kill so many and enjoy it. You are no man."

"True, but I'll enjoy killing you."

In less than a heartbeat he was by Midnight's side, looking straight into my eyes. I didn't have far to look down, he was up to my shoulder.

"You, you are brave. It is shame you are not a man." He leaned forwards just a little too far for me to back away. "I would kill you with glory. Now," he shrugged his large shoulders as he stepped back, "now, I will just kill you. Then forget it."

"Oh, I doubt that."

I went to unsheathe my sword when movement caught my eye. I didn't believe it, not completely. Not until I saw him here, with my own eyes. Not until he was right in front of me.

Dilwyn walked into the middle of the circle, less easily than Gwrtheryn did, with a smug smile on his face. He wore the same cloak as the rest of them, grey and thick. My stomach lurched and Midnight's reins dug deeper into my palms. It was strange to see his face like that. Twisted.

"You know each other, no?" asked Gwrtheryn. I ignored his question as I stared at my cousin, he was different. He stood taller, his chest puffed out, his arms held strong. He wasn't Dilwyn, not as I knew him.

"Hello cousin." His voice seeped with satisfaction.

CHAPTER 19

My mind was black with cold rage. How could he? The shadows started dancing within me, they could sense a fight was coming. Not yet. I willed them aside for this. This was my fight.

"Dilwyn, I'm glad you're not dead. Now I can kill you myself." I had meant to ask him to stop this, to realise what he was doing, but I saw him smile again and didn't care.

"Nerys, what would Neirin say if he heard you? We're blood, you should-"

"One word about my father and I'll rip your traitorous tongue out of your mouth." My voice was venom.

His eyes betrayed his fear as my dagger was at his throat. I had jumped off Midnight and leapt at Dilwyn in one quick breath, drawing my dagger as I did. Then I saw it. A flash of silver against the fires. Under his cloak and around his tight-necked shirt was it, the necklace. I blinked my relief that it hadn't touched his skin as I traced my dagger along it. He flashed a wicked smile but I did nothing. I looked into his blue eyes and did nothing. I stepped backwards towards Midnight and replaced my dagger, taking my sword out.

I turned to Gwrtheryn. "Strange company you keep. I'll kill him first, if you don't mind." I barely heard his laugh over Dilwyn's spiteful words.

"I am the vessel now. You can't kill me. You won't kill me."

"You aren't the vessel Dilwyn, you know this," I said pleadingly.

"I am. I hold the necklace. I am the vessel. I hold the power of the gods."

"You have no such thing."

"I am the vessel," he bellowed.

I took a step closer to my cousin, aware that Gwrtheryn was allowing us to have it out in front of him. I had to get him to understand.

"Dilwyn, you have not been chosen. Think what *your* father would-"

"No. My father was weak." His hands balled into fists. The camp was strangely quiet, save for Dilwyn and I. "He had no power. He stood next to power his whole life and did nothing."

The more my cousin spoke, the more venom his words had. He started punching the air around him. "He could have taken it. He could have taken it from your mother, from his father. I am not so weak."

"No." I threw my hands up. "No. You're a greedy coward. And I will kill you, slowly, for this betrayal." One breath and I changed my tone. "Please, Dilwyn."

"You will-"

"Enough," interrupted Gwrtheryn. He was amused. I was annoyed I'd let so much emotion, so much knowledge, show. "You will fight and then we will know who holds the power." It sounded simple enough.

"Agreed," Dilwyn said as he drew his sword. I had waited long enough.

"Agreed."

I mounted Midnight and squeezed my legs against her hard. She neighed loudly, wildly, in response. That was the signal. Sure enough, the ground began to tremble. An army was coming. My army. I smiled as I raised my sword.

"You will die cousin, you will die at my sword and I will watch as your soul is taken by the shadows to hell."

Dilwyn barred his teeth in an ugly growl. That's when I

brought the shadows back to me. That's when I opened myself up to them and they flowed in eagerly.

The circle around me began to move. The trees were creaking with movement. Then, all from my right, horses poured out of the darkening woods. Horses, men, women, swords, spears, axes. Everything burst into the North's men camp half a league long. Screams and grunts, clashes and bangs resounded. Adrenaline hit me and I charged.

The Northmen were chaotic. Without their ranks, their order, they were just men. Strong, fearless, but just individual men. They hadn't expected us to attack them. I sliced down at one who poured red from his throat and immediately stabbed back at another. Midnight lunged to the left as one stupid man pulled on her reins. I swung my sword across his forearms, enjoying his screams. Before he could catch a breath, I span my legs over the saddle and rammed them into his chest. One more stab finished the job. I was on foot now. I pushed Midnight away and knew she would get to the trees.

Elation, that's what I felt. I could feel the pulses boiling my blood, urging me on. I would follow them. The echoes of the fight warmed me. The din was louder here, surrounded by the trees. With little space for the men to move in, the fight was compacted. I didn't mind. It only made finding Dilwyn easier.

I slammed my boot into a roaring beast and span him as I made for Dilwyn. He was out of the fight, standing with the leader. Watching. Oh, I would give them something to watch.

My mind was not my own as the shadows controlled my sword. I sliced and stabbed, slashed and cut. Blood lay on the ground behind me as I made my path. Blood, sweat, probably some guts and other men's body fluids, were sputtered over me but I saw none of that. The shadows showed me where Dilwyn was, my prey, and that is where I went.

As if the shadows had suddenly appeared before me, I was facing my cousin. Dilwyn stood in front of me, a mixture of disgust, fear and arrogance on his sunken face. The disgust I figured was probably from how I looked. But that only made me pleased. He had seen just what I could do.

I was not to have my fight, however. The coward span and sprinted into the safety of the battle as a stumbling man fell into my sword. Fine. I would get him later. I was enjoying feeling the pulses again, feeling free of all thought other than what the shadows were making me think. They were pulling every inch of my mind and I let them.

Thunder sounded the clearing. It was loud enough to stop everyone who heard it. And they all did. The catapult. Merfyn's group of men and women were pushing it further out of the trees and grappling to lift another rock onto it. The first rock to fall had squashed I don't know how many Northerners. They were just a pile of fur and guts.

They saw their brothers dead and screamed. The Northern men suddenly rallied together, charging for the catapult. No, I could not let that happen. I kicked out hard at a body, rammed my sword through and ran on. I heard Merfyn's yells and sprinted. I sliced into a shoulder and stamped a leg and kept running. I had to get there.

The shadows were with me, every step, every breath. And I was with them. They pulled me left as two men grappled at throats. I fell forwards over a body as the shadows forced me to miss a swinging axe. I could still hear Merfyn shouting and I heard the thuds and slams of wood on wood. The Northmen were already there.

My black mare neighed loudly and ran for the catapult, parting the Northern men, pushing them away from my people. Midnight neighed again and I sprinted for her as she stomped through the battle. With one grab of her bridle, I swung a leg up and was on the saddle, yelling as she neighed. Merfyn's group gathered behind us as an arrowhead. The catapult was still standing, a rock ready to throw.

"LOOSE," I yelled and watched it fly through the clearing and squash bodies. "WE ARE SHADOWS!"

Then we charged. We charged as one shadow back into the battle and Midnight neighed loud and ferociously. Too loudly though, as all those around us turned to face her and the battle went oddly still. This was madness. In one breath, the whole clearing was quiet, no more ringing or shouting or cries of pain. No more spluttering of blood or desperate pleas.

Night was approaching. The shadows screamed within me to feel the earth. I jumped of Midnight and slapped her. She trotted back to the trees and this weird quiet gave the men rest. Slowly my people were moving behind me, as the Northern beasts moved to the other side. I paced up and down, daring them to move but none did. My jaw tightened, waiting for them to do something. Why were they waiting? No. The shadows didn't care for questions, only action.

As I continued back and forth, I scanned my eyes for Gwrtheryn. Even though this was a welcome respite, it was worrying what it meant.

"Fight me." My head swivelled to find the disembodied voice. "Fight me."

There. There he walked out of his men, parting them as easily as the last time. His mis-matched eyes shone eerily bright against the flickering fires that were still alight.

"Fight me!"

"Gladly."

The silence seemed to grow louder. Grey, thick, silence. The air felt thicker, like a heavy fog was rolling in, but my vision was still clear. There was no one else in that wood. There was only me and him.

He pulled out a sword from behind his back. It wasn't the one he had used before. This one was the size of his huge arm and he had to use both hands just to keep it off the ground. And still, it looked unruly. An unruly sword wielded by the most ferocious man I had ever seen. This was going to be brutal.

I could feel the edges of the wood getting closer. The sides of my skull being crushed, as if the shadows were pushing it in from the inside. The men were moving in from both sides, eager to see the fight. I held my gaze on him. There was only me and him. Me and Gwrtheryn.

Well, me, him and the shadows.

The Northern men's leader shrugged off his cloak and his men roared. I stood still. Waiting. Waiting for the shadows to show me the way.

"Your men fight well. But you have women to fight. Women

should not fight. Women should make us warm!" More roars and jeers. "Now I will have you. Now, you and me, little leaf, and no-one is to stop it!" I couldn't make out his face this far away, but his words I heard. Everyone heard. That was his point. This was a fight to the death, and no one was to stop it. I turned to my men and nodded slowly, agreeing. If they didn't respect me now, they had better respect me after this.

"No-one is to step forward. No-one is to interfere with this fight. It is one-on-one. To the death." I said the words boldly, as loudly as I could, searching for Ithel, any one from the court. They were the ones who would try to stop me. I saw Delyth's eyes on me. She gave a strong nod back. This was why she was here, why they were all here. Whatever happened, this was why we were here.

I turned back to my opponent and caught a flash of teeth. Very well.

Without warning my eyes turned black. I thought I was blind. I couldn't see anything, not the fires or the trees. Black. I tried to stay calm but I needed my vision. I needed to see. I breathed deeply. I could still hear, so I focused on that but my heart was pumping panic through me. I had to see. How else would I defeat that sword?

I heard a thud and grunt and thought I'd moved out the way. I hadn't. I turned into a boot that slammed me to the floor then stamped on my head. I was spinning. With the little thought I had I swung my sword low. It hit bone. Still spinning, I yanked it back and swung again. I heard a laugh which stopped abruptly. I had hit flesh. But then a foot drove into my stomach, forcing the wind out of me. I doubled to the ground, coughing. Still my eyes saw black.

Where the hell were the damned shadows? They couldn't have left me now. They couldn't...

I managed to push myself straight up, hand on my sword. I calmed my breathing to hear his. I couldn't. I heard yells and taunts and the bashing of shields. But I didn't hear his breathing.

Then a thud. I slashed my sword instinctively and it hit metal. Again and it hit nothing. I was alert now, straining to hear. Where was he? The damn shadows.

"Nerys. Nerys!" Ithel's voice.

I couldn't even work out where Ithel was. He shouted again and I turned. I turned into a fist. A warm ooze ran down my face as I fell to the ground.

Darkness.

***

Screams and shouts faded away. The battle sounds came suddenly close, a raucous sound then faded. I faded in and out of the darkness.

Darkness was my home and that was where I went.

My head was a blur. Images kept rushing against my eyelids. Shadows that I couldn't touch, memories that I couldn't place. A blurry face swam past me, making me feel warm, but it faded as quickly as it came. Whispers and murmurs and shades and wisps.

Then fire, screams, blood. Death. I heard shouts and cries and Midnight neighing nearby. Fantasies of those nights, the times I had hunted, burned, killed, blinked against the blackness. I saw all their faces. Heard all their screams. I heard my screams.

I was with them. I was with the shadows, in their realm. I felt them all, warm against my skin. It comforted me, that gentle warmth. I felt them reaching to warm all of me, taking me with them. Then a new heat, like a tickling of fire. I felt them reaching for me. I could see them, just at the edge of my vision. They were there, we would be a family again, together. I felt their presence and all was done.

I was at peace.

Or was I?

Something was on my face. It was hot and wet and thoroughly annoying. Why couldn't it leave me alone?

I pushed it away, wanting to be back with the shadows. It didn't stop. It nudged me harder, all over my head and neck. I pushed it again and again. I wanted to be *alone*.

It didn't stop. The darn thing pushed me and breathed on me to the point where I'd had enough. I sat up and opened my eyes.

There was nothing. Just black. What was this?

It pushed me again. I felt a familiar warmth from it. A strong, constant warmth. How could I have been so stupid?

My oldest friend nudged me again and neighed. I sprang up and wrapped my arms around Midnight's neck. No wonder I couldn't see anything. She stayed with me a moment longer and then galloped to the trees. I followed her with my eyes until she was gone and I saw what surrounded me.

I was back. I was back in the land of the living.

And the dying.

* * *

I bent down to pick up my strewn sword, wincing from the

bruise lining my stomach, when I noticed the gasps. The sharp intakes of breaths that were rolling around the wood. I saw the nightmare before me. Night hung proper in the cleared woods and fires and fire-torches were dotted around and sprawled out as chaotically as the two sides must have been. The Northern men were now stretched out across their wooded camp, no longer along the edge of it, shouting and jeering and insulting the Southerners. Some were even throwing wood and makeshift chairs as far as they could towards them. They were still there, my men and women, hovering on the western side. I barely made out the catapult in the crowd. Gwrtheryn was in between, no doubt taunting my army into a slaughter. Well, there would be one, I thought as I stepped forward.

As soon as I gazed upon their leader, that was it. His men growled as they moved back to their trees, forming a semi-circle. Again, I would face Gwrtheryn. This time I would not fail. I stalked over to him slowly, focusing on nothing but him. This was why I was here; this was why I was among the living.

To end him.

I slowed my walking as I got closer and felt an ancient surge through my two scars, my heart and blood. The shadows. The damn fickle shadows were with me, in me, were me.

They would do this with me. I didn't need the sun to see, the shadows were my sun now and they let me see.

I stood in front of him and I was calm. I was black with calm. A killing calm. I didn't need to see or hear or think or do. The shadows would do that for me. They were me. And I was them.

He raised his sword with both hands fast, the air sighed in response. It was a fearsome blade, just not to me, for I was no longer just human.

I raised my sword and stood my ground. I would let him come to me. He bellowed as he saw me unmoving, thinking I was scared to approach. Then he ran. He pounded the ground with his feet as he ran at me. Still I did not move, keeping my grip relaxed on my hilt. Two more breaths. One.

The thrust of his sword was low but I parried it easily. Moving quickly, I stepped to the side and drove my blade where he was least covered, into his stomach. It came out slow. He grimaced but kept on his feet. Good. I instantly stepped back and let my sword swing high. Before I could process the hit I was dodging to the right and stabbing with the hilt, right at his temple. He grabbed his head with one hand and wildly swung the huge sword with the other. Not good for him.

He lost his grip on his unruly sword and it made directly for me. The shadows got there first. My hand grabbed the hilt, following its path, and swung it back. It sliced through its' owners' stomach, blood gushing out. Without another breath, my sword thrust all the way through his neck, one side to the other. His eyes were wide and bright with their colours. Blood spewed from his mouth and throat. Tiny hairs stood up all along my neck. Not from the blood but from the strength, the power of the shadows.

Then a flash of memory. *"It will be your fear you fear then."* Those words left me as instantly as they had come. Because the shadows urged me on. Next they had me slice my sword that was still in the leader's neck. I obeyed. My arm sliced forward and back and it was done. Gwrtheryn, the supreme king's, head rolled to the floor as his body lay in a puddle of his own blood. I was satisfied. The shadows, however, were now deeply hungry.

Their leader might be dead but there were still hundreds of darkened souls I could send to the shadow gods. I would send as many as they wanted.

The shadows throbbed and danced through me as another pulse arrived. It was the strongest one yet, which I liked. Both of my forearms throbbed and pulsed so intensely that I thought they would burst. I felt like my heart was fully made of shadows, like they were replacing all the blood in me with black shadows. It had to be so close now. That thought didn't stay long. Blood. That was what I wanted.

I took my time cleaning my sword on the grass, mainly to let my forearms calm. Not one man moved. The growls of the Northern beasts turned in to animal howls as they charged as one, no need other than to kill for their dead, 'supreme' leader.

Good.

I barely saw any of my men and women through the slaughter. I barely saw anything except the nearest beast to slice. Those who were near me were unlucky. Their blood was the first to spill. I had to drop my sword and use my fists as my arms were almost shaking but I was swift as a shadow, fluid as water. Whatever the shadows showed me, I did. Gladly.

Then it stopped.

The last pulse didn't come.

My muscles were throbbing with adrenaline, exertion. My mind was black with wisps and shades. But still it didn't come. Why? I demanded to them. Where was that dreaded pulse?

I span round, looking for the next kill. Anyone. Anything. I needed to kill something. I needed that pulse. Now. I ran to my sword and held it high.

Slowly the wisps began to fade. No. I held my sword to my head, praying desperately to the shadows and the gods. I needed them to come back, I could feel them slipping away. My blood was cooling slowly down. No. Why were they leaving me?

My head throbbed. Even with my sword cool against it, it still throbbed. And pounded and span and felt like It would burst any moment. Why were they doing this?

The pain suddenly broke. My head felt ready to burn like a fire. I fell to my knees, not knowing anything else other than pain and fear. My breathing was shallow. My arms felt instantly cool and my forearms were shaking again. I looked down at them and would have screamed had I not been in shock. My scars were black and out of them... Out of them the shadows were leaving me. Black shapes swept out of my arms and I tried to push them back in with both hands but it wasn't working. They were leaving me. I felt my eyes water and a salty tear sting as it passed a scratch on my face and still the shadows were leaving me. I tried to push my sword against a scar, forcing the shadows to stay but they swirled out of my arms. The battle had long since left me. I didn't care about it. All I wanted was the shadows and they were leaving me. No.

Not now. Not now I had done it.

But they did. My mind cleared, it was mine and mine alone. My muscles ached from the fight they had performed. I could feel all the cuts and bruises, all the stings and aches. I was myself again and I didn't like it. I just wanted to cry.

I sat down on the cold ground, taking in what I was abandoned to. The woods, the faint dawn approaching. The fog that had started to roll in, layering the ground above with a muffled silence. My dwindled, but apparently alive, army were scattered across the destroyed camp. A few held men at dagger point. Most looked at me through the faint light horrified, afraid, awed. I guess I never did know what I looked like when I killed. Then I saw two figures bound towards me. I instinctively held my sword out as one bounced lithely and the other ran strong.

I relaxed. It was Siorus and Steffan. They were bloody, panting, a thick slash mark was all along Steffan's forearm, but they were standing. Steffan gave a quick jerk of the head and I turned to see the last of the Northern men bolting to the north. Dirty cowards. A part of me wanted to hunt them down. To find each and every one of them and break them, bone by bone, limb by limb. Another part didn't care. That part was empty, hollow, exhausted. It was that part I followed now.

Slowly I stood. Every fibre of me was stiff and aching and felt stubborn. Nothing wanted to move. I turned to my men and women, those who were still alive. They were cautiously gathering together, separate from me. None spoke. None bent to pick up swords or other valuables from the dead. They just stood, waiting. I breathed in the quiet. The welcome silence that hung in the air like the fog. It was the most refreshing sound I had heard in a long time. It matched the silence that filled my own mind.

Then it was broken.

Muffled shouts echoed through the trees and into the wooded clearing. Out of my scattered army came the guard. Their silver swords all dulled with blood. They walked towards me slowly, carefully, most of their faces were disgusted, scared. Aeddan was among them, blinking with every breath. Then I saw why, they were hiding something in the middle of them. As they split apart, the fresh sunlight shone faintly on us.

And there he was.

Merfyn and Drystan held my traitorous cousin by his wrist and shoulders. He wriggled and struggled pointlessly. Against one of them, he had no chance, against both my court and guard, he was seriously outmatched. I laughed emptily in his face.

They brought Dilwyn before me and he stopped struggling. Now that we were here, I didn't know what to do. Half my life I had dedicated to this moment, to finally appeasing the shadow gods. Now I had done it. The last pulse that didn't come had bitterly told me that, the shadows leaving through my scars had told me that, even if I didn't want to accept it. I had fulfilled their required souls. My path was complete.

I looked into Dilwyn's eyes. I don't know what I was looking for. Something familiar, something that would make all of this forgotten. I didn't see that. I just saw a coward.

A cough brought my attention up. Aeddan had stepped forward. His eyes were pale and his face was grim. Covered in blood and sweat, with a slash across his cheek. He looked at me beseechingly. I responded with a blank nod. Dilwyn had betrayed all of us, not just me.

Aeddan took purposeful steps to face his former friend. The tension that built between them was intense. Dilwyn barred his teeth in a grin and Aeddan snapped. He stepped his hips into an angry blow that split Dilwyn's lip, he spat out a tooth as if impressed. Aeddan pulled back his arm and punched again. Dilwyn's neck twisted unnaturally as he was held still by his captors. He did nothing, just taking the blows. Aeddan's hand was red. He made to punch again but Steffan stood in and pulled him away.

Now it was my turn. My cousin spat out more blood as I stood in front of him. I crouched down to his eye level, tracing my sword point along the necklace, surprised and grateful that it still hung round his clothed throat.

I breathed quietly before I spoke, aware my throat was dry. "The necklace of the vessel does not belong to you. Place a hand on your coat and remove it from your neck. Then drop it on the floor." I moved my sword down to his stomach so that he would be able to move his arm as Merfyn released a wrist. Nothing. Another breath. Another breath and I faltered.

"Why, Dilwyn? Why would you do this?" I asked in a breath, resting my knees on the ground.

He moved his mouth slowly into an ugly smirk. "You will never understand, Nerys. You have always resented power. You still do."

"Because it's peoples' lives!" I practically screeched. Dilwyn's face softened to the one I knew.

"No." Then it hardened. Darkened. "It's our lives, Nerys! We could have done it. But if you weren't going to do it with me, I would do it anyway. I *did* do it anyway. I did it for you, Nerys. All of this. Don't you see?"

"See what, Dilwyn? See what?"

"This!" He yelled as he grabbed my sword to the necklace. "I had to help you, Nerys. I knew you were doing something and I had to help. I had to have the power to help. We were supposed to do this together. We still can, Nerys. We can still be together. We're all we have left; this will keep us together." The pleading in his voice made me feel nauseous. I pushed myself back to move away from him. From the change in him. Or rather, the him I was only just seeing.

"No. No, Dil." I stood up quickly and hurriedly took two steps back. "No." I had to say the word out loud to stop myself from listening to him. Then I took a deep, filling breath and closed my eyes. It didn't matter now. Only the necklace mattered. Yes, only the necklace mattered. I opened my eyes as I moved my sword back to my cousin's stomach.

"Cover your hand and remove the necklace." My voice was firm, if hoarse. Still the weasel of a boy did nothing. I inched closer. I watched his eyes dart between his two captors, still trying to find a way out. His loose arm flinched before recovering down. I gripped my sword tighter and dug it an inch more into his gut. Then it happened.

Before I could blink he did it. Dilwyn grabbed the necklace with his bare hand and pressed the chain against his throat. Merfyn tried to grabbed his arm but fell awkwardly, yelling in pain. It was too late.

The necklace of the vessel had been touched.

CHAPTER 20

Thunder instantly roared. The dawn sky blackened as lightning screamed down, sending flashes of white across the landscape. The fog thickened, covering the ground and everything up to the sky in a misty white. Rain the size of small stones fell to the earth, bruising all those it fell on. The ground shook. This was the doing of the shadow gods. Cledwyn would have yelled that to me as he ran for cover, just like the last time we had a storm.

This was not good.

I yelled to take cover, barely audible over the angry, wild nature. Most of the men and women ran into the trees, some stared in disbelief. I didn't blame them but we had to do something. Quickly. Before we all died.

"Nerys?" came a shout from in front of me.

"I've got him," I yelled as loudly as I could.

Another flash of lightning burst across the sky, giving us a breath of light. Within that moment I lunged forward to Dilwyn. My court were ushering some of the closest women into the trees, but Ithel had appeared and also ran at Dilwyn. Then the darkness resumed.

I flailed my arms around, trying to grab my cousin. I managed to grip something but slipped straight off. Then another grab. That one pulled me into their chest and I didn't object. Whoever it was, they were breathing just as heavily as I was.

Another roar deafened the land. It was coupled with a single bright fork of lightning that landed straight in the clearing. It blinded me. I dug my eye's into the chest that held me then slowly peeled away. I opened my eyes to Dilwyn and a sight I had never seen.

I thought my eyes cheated me, that it was a trick of the shadows. Even with the rain splashing down and the fog hanging in the air, I could see everything, the wisps were stark against the white fog. I watched in shock as Dilwyn was struck by the lightning. Then his eyes went foggy, his face sickeningly pale as black and blue sparks crackled around him. The necklace glowed fiercely. A gust of wind burst through the woods, knocking the breath out of me. I held on to my protector's chest.

"Shush, it's ok. It'll be ok."

I finally looked up and saw Ithel. His face was not as calm as his words. Another clap of thunder made me look back to Dilwyn. He rose off the ground, the necklace dragging him up by the neck. The shadows were dancing around the necklace as they lifted it up higher and higher to the blackened sky. I could only watch, stunned into silence.

He fell.

The black wisps disappeared and the necklace hung limp for a breath, the two of them were floating in the air for what felt like an age. Suddenly, my cousin crumpled to the wet earth and immediately the rain stopped. The wind ceased yet the lightning continued to ripple through the sky.

I didn't move. Ithel didn't move. My whole body was numb and heavy. I could barely process what had happened. Yet I did move. Slowly I peeled myself away from Ithel and walked towards the body. The body. My heart faltered as I saw it close, saw Dilwyn close. The quiet that reigned over us was almost a presence in itself. No one dared break it.

I crouched down next to Dilwyn, he had landed disjointedly. I took my time putting his limbs, cold, dead, limbs back into place. He was a traitor, he had died a traitor, yet he had been like my brother for so long.

Standing up, I felt the air crackle again. Lightning pierced down, bringing with it the shadows. They danced everywhere. In the woods, in my eyes. Wisps and shapes and voices, whispers, cold shivers, warm touches. They were with us. And they were here to choose the vessel.

I tried to look around at Ithel but it was useless. So many shadows were here, they felt both like home and chaos. They had been trapped for so long and now they were free. And probably angry. But this was it, this was why I had done everything. All of it. The shadows were free, they were with us again.

I heard screams and shouts from the people around me as the shadows moved through the air, brushing against anyone and anything they passed. Some shadows felt happy, peaceful. Others felt rushed, earnest. A few seemed to be wicked, I almost thought I recognised one that brushed up against my arm and along my neck, sending a cold shiver all the way down my spine. It felt like that one shadow in my mind that was always urging me, to spill more blood.

I span around, trying to find anyone else through the shaodwfog who was seeing this too. I took a few steps and saw someone fade through the greying fog. Brynmor. I almost let a chuckle sound, he was alive. He walked closer to me and stared at me when we were only a few feet apart. I saw a deep gash down one arm and he had a limp but his face was beaming. He held up his hands to the sky and shadows twirled around his arms. I did chuckle then.

But it was short-lived.

Out of the dark, a faint blue glowed. Brighter and brighter. I could see it, sense it. It was moving, humming, like a small blue flame . The shadowflame came closer and closer, forcing my eyes to squint against its light. Even from a distance I could feel the warmth it radiated, the familiar warmth the shadows gave. It comforted me.

Then it vanished.

The blue was gone and the shadows with it. Dawn rose and the light was clear.

The vessel had been chosen.

Looking upon my surroundings in the new light brought both pain and comfort. There were so many bodies, so much blood staining the grass. So much death. The smell that lingered in the air was both horrid and calm. The smell of decay and burnt grass and burning flesh, mixed with an earthy, warm smell from the rain.

There was also life. I had done it. I had given the people their lives back. Back from the slow, unnecessary death they would have had before. And the vessel... the vessel had been chosen. I was pleased. Relieved actually. I felt a warmth within me, even from my scars. And something else I had not known. I think it was hope.

I didn't have long to think about anything else as Merfyn uncharacteristically ran to me and pulled me into his arms.

"It's' over, Nerys. It is done. We are free." I didn't catch the tone of his voice, somewhere between relief and concern. "Meet the new vessel." He took me by the shoulders, then opened me to where the majority of the remaining army were. I thought he was showing them me, that he was showing the people me, the new vessel. After all, it should have been me. My mother was the vessel and my grandfather before her. That's when I did it, what I should have done before.

I put a hand around my neck and felt it. The necklace. There was a necklace around my neck, but the stone pendant was familiar and the cotton was damp. This wasn't the necklace of the vessel, this was my father's old one. I was not... how could I not be?

The vessel had been chosen. I knew that, I had felt that. Yet it was not me. It was not me. Who else could it be? Dilwyn was dead, the shadow gods had killed him.

I traced my eyes back to Merfyn, trying to gleam some understanding from him. His face was deep, tired, blood was still spattered all over him, despite the downpour. But he gave me no answers. He merely pointed. I followed his arm and my gaze fell on another sight that I had never seen.

The new vessel.

The necklace around his neck pulsed blue. His eyes were grey and black at the same time and a faint shadowglow hung around his figure.

Ithel rose in the air the same as Dilwyn had, lifted up by blue and black shadows. Yet the shadow gods did not drop him to the ground like he was useless. He was placed down gently, feet soft against the wet earth. When the necklace became dull once more and the shadowglow faded, I knew. I knew it was never meant to be me. I was never meant to be the vessel.

I don't know how long we stayed there. How long all the people stayed where they were and just looked at Ithel, remembering the sights they had just seen. I never wanted it to end.

The sun was warm on my skin and clothes; the birds were singing a sweet song from the trees. I almost welled up from the sounds. Birds were singing. It was a new day. Then Ithel walked over to me. My feet were firmly rooted and I felt hundreds of eyes watching me as the new vessel moved closer. The anticipation was almost as thick as the fog that had hung in the air moments before. His eyes were still a shadowy grey, like the fog was now in his mind. I did nothing. I let him and the shadows speak.

"The shadow gods are pleased. You have brought their people back to them. They have chosen to reward you, The Shadow That Walks The Earth." The new vessel took my hand and I flinched it back, but it was still in his hand. As soon as his skin had touched mine, I had felt the shadows crack. Not how I knew them though, this time they were both hot and cold, crackling like a fire and icy as water. My hand felt like it had been scolded by iron and dunked in the sea at the same time. I looked up into his eyes and saw Ithel. The shadows were gone, replaced by the dark eyes I knew.

The eyes that were now the vessel.

* * *

It was strange how one day could change the lives of so many, yet it had. Hopefully for years and years to come. After a week of clearing the dead and sending them to the shadows, the 'feasting' had lasted for three days. There wasn't much food to be had but there was laughter and hope. After the mourning came the celebrating. The whole of the town was high on joy and ale, and specially brewed mead that had appeared out of the kitchens as though it had been there all along.

The news of the new vessel had travelled all over the South and hundreds more had journeyed from the surrounding towns and villages and farmsteads to join the feasting. People from so many parts of the South that I didn't even know of all the names of the places some said. Thankfully, all those who had to leave their homes before the battle had returned safely. So many had come who wanted to see this new age with their own eyes.

But this could wait no longer.

Ithel had sent two of his own men back to the Midlands moments after he had been chosen. Gruffyd had ridden down quickly soon after, since there was no longer any challenge from the North men. Other lords from the Midlands rode as well. As did the other three minor lords in the South, all who had chosen not to fight with us. They were all here for my father. For today was a day of death, and of life. Of ends and beginnings.

Even with a clear, blue sky, and birdsong drifting on the wind, the town managed to mourn. My court members, Merfyn, Siorus and Steffan had all made it through the battle alive.

Merfyn had to use a wood staff to stand up with and Steffan's left arm was held in a cloth sling but otherwise, they were unhurt. They started from the south gate, carrying the salted, wrapped body of my father in a thick, wooden box through the crowds of Southerners. All through the town to the eastern gate.

As they passed, children threw dried leaves and petals at my father, mimicking the cycle of life. Then he was carried out to the grass beyond. To his grave. I followed behind, carrying his grey battle hide all the way. Behind me were Mairwen and Celyn, letting more dried leaves and petals fall from woven baskets behind them. As my court laid the body of my father in the ground, the people who wished laid treasured items that they could spare with him. Leather belts, jewellery, pots, daggers. Their possessions for their fallen lord.

Then the humming began. I was standing high on the ditch, with my court, guard and maids around me. Ithel was there too, but standing to the side with his father and the other Midlanders. The other Southern lords were to the other side of the grave, looking out on our people. I looked at each of them slowly, trying to work out which one of them knew the trader. I shook my head, now was not the time.

As the throng of people outside the town bowed their heads to their lord, Merfyn led the song. Gentle at first, soft and calm, then it rose till all around people were humming their lament to the wind. I was the last to lay my gifts to my father. The dried flower of brown and white, my mother's favourite. The one I had given to my father over a year ago, the one he had saved. I took my time and prayed. One single tear rolled down my cheek and I did not brush it away. I stepped back from the grave and joined the song. It was sad, deep, sorrowful and it was the most beautiful sound I had ever heard. I hoped my father could hear it too.

Once the humming reached a natural end, I stood with the court. The guard had given each of them bows and a single arrow and Siorus handed me one as I came next to him. As one, we lit our arrows from Mairwen's flame as she walked below us with a fire-torch and aimed. The arrows were swift and silent, leaving a smoky arc against the sky. My father was alight instantly. Then more arrows rained down from all around. Warriors paying tribute to their lord.

And that was that. My father was at rest with the shadows, as was my mother. Now I could rest. Well, maybe one day.

***

By the ancient stone well, my people heard my oath.

As I stood in black trousers, a delicately sleeved cropped bodice and a thick, heavy, beaded cloak, I watched the people packed into the town, as well as the Midlanders and the other Southern lords. They were a crowd of faces and a sea of colour.

With no elder of the court, Merfyn led the ceremony. I held the necklace around my neck, my father's necklace.

"Nerys, heir of Neirin, lord of the South. Step forwards."

I did and stood opposite Merfyn, circled by the guard. Their mail shone as brightly as their swords, glistening from the light rays of the midday sun.

"You will be a lord, and they will all call you lord," Merfyn whispered to me as he stepped in front of me. I simply nodded, unsure of his meaning. He gave me nothing else and turned to the crowd. "In the presence of the people, the court and the vessel, Nerys, daughter of Neirin will make her oath."

He stepped back beside me and gestured Ithel forwards. He almost glided through the guard, wrapped in a thin, grey cloak that sent a quick shiver down my spine. It was the colour of the fog in his eyes when the shadows had come. There was silence as Ithel stopped beside me, also facing the people. His necklace glowed a faint blue.

"Kneel," Merfyn said. I crouched down and placed my knees

on the ground. Two pairs of feet appeared in the corners of my eyes and I felt earth land on my head and sprinkle down. Siorus and Steffan went back to their places in the circle of the guard.

"You will provide for the earth..." Merfyn led.

I spoke to my people from the ground, taking some in my hand. "I will provide for the earth as I provide for the land. I swear to protect the land and all those who depend on it."

"One knee." I lifted one knee up. "Open your hand."

This time, the vessel spoke. "You will honour the shadow gods..."

"I will honour the shadow gods and the shadows. My people will hear the shadow gods as they guide us and the shadows will live among us, as messengers of the shadow gods. I will honour and protect the vessel as the vessel is the shadow gods on earth." Ithel took a small dagger from under his cloak and slowly cut the back of his hand. The blood dripped into the earth I held.

"Stand."

I stood before my people, listening to their breathing. I'm sure I heard a baby wailing.

"I will serve..."

"I will serve my people with honour and respect. I will provide them with land and food and safety, in return for their oaths, their swords and welcome at their hearths." Ithel held my free hand and sliced the back of it, dripping the blood into the earth I still held. With the dagger I dug a small hole and mixed the earth and blood together, packing it flat. After a quick breath, I stood tall and proud, the shadows nowhere near my mind or blood.

"I, Nerys, lord of the South, ask that you all hear my oath."

They cheered. I had done it. I was lord now and I had not told any of them that my father had made me his heir again. I had done this on my own.

For years to come I will remember that ceremony and those cheers. And for years to come I will swear I heard shouts for my head.

My breath grew deeper as I listened to the cheers, waiting to move. I prayed to the shadows gods, that if this was my life now, I would be good at it, that they would keep my people safe.

***

The celebrating continued. I was happy, all the South deserved this, yet I just wanted to get away. I wasn't used to being constantly on show, passed round from hand to hand, forced to smile and talk and be touched like a talisman. Surrounded by so many people and laughter and freedom. I was still waiting for the next thing to happen. The next person to kill or the next time to ride. I tried to relax, to enjoy the day like they all did but I couldn't. Not really. In a group of women I saw Delyth. She was wearing a tight bodice and flowing trousers. I hadn't properly spoken to her since the battle. She noticed me a gave a small smile. Before I had even stepped forwards, I heard a shout.

"Lord, lord," cried a familiar voice. I turned to see Aeddan and Drystan, his brown hair kept tight to his face in plaits, and a fresh black-eye. Both were breathing heavily.

"What is it?"

"Lord," breathed Drystan dryly.

"It's Bleddyn, lord. He's escaped," Aeddan finished with a sorry kind of smile.

"What?!" They both just stared on at me. A few people around us had stopped and looked on but that did not matter. "What are you waiting for? Find him. Now!"

Neither of them managed to get a word out as they dashed away. This could not be happening. He could not get away.

He still had to be court trialled. I tried to will the shadows to me but they didn't come. I tried again and nothing. Of course they weren't going to come to me. I had finished the darkened path, this, the town, was the whole point. I stamped on the ground, balling my hands into fists.

"Nerys." I heard Delyth call me but could not face her now. Not like this.

I practically sprinted to the stables before knocking in to someone on the bridge. I bent down quickly to pick up the parchment I had scattered out of his hands. As I stood, I saw his eyes. I knew those eyes. Not well, but I knew them.

"S-sorry, Elis."

"Not at all, lord," he said formally. The thin, calm man took the parchment from my hands and looked at it for a few breaths. I wanted to get away from this town, from this stuffy, infectious celebrating and the thought that Bleddyn was gone, but something in Elis's eyes held me still.

"As you know, Nerys, I served your father as his personal messenger for several years."

"22, I believe." I knew Elis to be an exact man, so for him to not say those exact years intrigued me. And also worried me.

"Yes. Now my service has come to an end. I resign from my

position once this letter has been delivered." His voice was so steady, so formal, I didn't quite know how to respond. I nodded my head, hoping that would do. Honestly, I hadn't even thought about Elis, or what he would do now.

He held out the letter to me. I didn't understand.

"This letter is for you," he had to explain, "the last one your father wrote. It comes with this message: 'The words written on this parchment are words I wish never to say. But in case I cannot say them to you, trust in them here. And trust in yourself, Nerys. You are my only regret and my greatest achievement.' Your father was a good man, a good lord. I pray you will be too." With that he put the letter into my hands and left me dazed, standing on the bridge. If there was ever a time I wanted the shadows, it was then. But they were still gone, leaving my blood cold and so was my father, leaving my heart empty.

I took Midnight and rode to the edge of the town's lands as quickly as I could, far enough away to clear my head. Although there were still parties of people dancing and drinking out here.

I took my time wandering at the landscape around me, imagining how it would change. That calmed me, distracted me from the letter burning a hole in my belt pouch. From the anger that was still trying to burst. Then I realised there was still something else nagging at the back of my mind. I knew it wasn't the shadows. I hadn't felt them since they had chosen the vessel. It was something Ithel had said. "The Shadow That Walks The Earth." It sounded so familiar, yet, I knew I had never heard it before.

"This wouldn't mean you're tired of the celebrations already?"

I turned and saw the bow before I saw the man. I was glad for the distraction. Ithel walked his horse next to Midnight and gazed out at the land as well.

"This is your time now. Your land now. How do you plan on using it?"

"It's yours as well," I said quietly.

Then I met his eyes and smiled. He took my hand, well, a finger, and I felt my anger fade. Turning back to the land, I knew. I was lord now. I would protect my people. Anyone who threatened them, harmed them or moved against them, I would find. I would find them and hunt them. And they would know.

They would know that I, Shadow-Hunter, Village-Burner, Night-Rider, had come for them.

ACKNOWLEDGEMENT

Firstly, this has been a long time coming. I would never have thought that I would self-publish a book, let alone think about a series. To all the people out there with worlds in your head, write them down and get them out there.

Thank you to my mother and father who have always been supportive of whatever I do, and to my sister and brother-in-law.
To Paul Klein, for being the first reader of this book. You'll read my books and I'll be in your films.
To my boyfriend, Max, for making this world fit onto a cover.

To all the readers, thank you in advance. Learning from your feedback is key to me.

Printed in Great Britain
by Amazon

10289087R00253